Linda M James is a writer of novels, non-fiction books and screenplays. She has also published many short stories and poems.

She has been commissioned to write three screenplays for a Young Legends series: *Young Ivanhoe, Young Helen of Troy* and *Young Jesus Christ.*

Her latest novel is a contemporary psychological thriller called *The Day Of The Swans*; she is now working on the screenplay.

Linda also runs writing workshops in Tunbridge Wells where she now lives after living abroad for ten years.

Before becoming a writer, Linda was a model, a singer and an English Lecturer.

Her website is <u>www.writingunderwater.co.uk</u>

Also by the same author

The Invisible Piper
ISBN: 978184386 508 7 (Vanguard Press)

How to Write Great Screenplays (How To Books)
ISBN: 9781845283070

Tempting The Stars

Linda M James

Tempting The Stars

Vanguard Press

VANGUARD PAPERBACK

© Copyright 2009
Linda M James

The right of Linda M James to be identified as author of
this work has been asserted by her in accordance with the
Copyright, Designs and Patents Act 1988.

A CIP catalogue record for this title is
available from the British Library.

ISBN 978 184386 509 4

*Vanguard Press is an imprint of
Pegasus Elliot MacKenzie Publishers Ltd.*
www.pegasuspublishers.com

First Published in 2009

**Vanguard Press
Sheraton House Castle Park
Cambridge England**

Printed & Bound in Great Britain

Dedication

To Kas, Luka and Elishka
With my love

Acknowledgements

I would like to thank members of **The Guinea Pig Club** to whom I'm indebted for their memories of the time they spent in the Queen Victoria Hospital, East Grinstead, under the expert care of plastic surgeon Archie McIndoe. They have honoured me by inviting me to a number of their reunions in the past.

My particular thanks to the effervescent Bill Foxley who not only made me laugh, but taught me how it is possible to overcome great trauma with humour and charm.

I would also like to thank Bob Marchant, the curator at the Queen Victoria Hospital Museum, for showing me all the interesting exhibits there and telling me about their history.

The poem **Do Not Stand At My Grave And Weep** is attributed to Mary Elizabeth Frye (1905 – 2004).

Last, but certainly not least, my friend Sarah Dawson for being an eagle-eyed proof-reader.

'Not everything that is faced can be changed, but nothing can be changed until it is faced.'

James Baldwin

Chapter 1

Rob lay on his bed in Ward Three, his eyes closed, his back to the world. He was living in a menagerie of noise: radios, trolleys, typing, voices laughing, arguing, screaming. No silence, ever. In the twenty-bedded ward were the remnants of young men, burnt, in many cases, beyond recognition. They were trying to sing now to the strains of *Shine on Victory Moon* blaring through the loudspeakers. Their ragged voices drilled a hole in Rob's head.

The ENSA programme was on again. The singing faded as the ruminative voice of the comedian Rob Wilton wafted around the ward.

The day war broke out, my missus said to me, 'What are you going to do about it?' I joined the Home Guards. She looked at my uniform and said 'What are you supposed to be?' 'Supposed to be?' I said. 'I'm a home guard.' 'Home Guard?' she said. 'What are you supposed to do?' 'I'm supposed to stop Hitler's army landing.' 'What you?' she said. 'No,' I said. 'There's seven of us on guard behind The Dog and Pullet.'

Those who could, shook with laughter. But not Rob.

'Reminds you of Dogberry in *Much Ado About Nothing*, doesn't he?' Owen Parry, a twenty-year-old Welshman from Swansea, called over to Rob. He'd been burned in a Whitley bomber, nicknamed 'The Flying Coffin'. Half his face and most of his hands had been burned away. The only programme he listened to now was ENSA; the rest of the time he read. After fifteen operations he could, at last, hold a book, and read constantly, completely oblivious to the cacophony of sounds swirling around him and the pain in his eyes. Rob didn't reply. But Owen Parry was used to this. Rob never replied.

Rob had had four operations in six months: two on his hands, two on his face. His hands were still claw-like but they were easier to look at without the black tannic acid which had coated them when he'd arrived. He turned over carefully to look at Owen Parry in the next bed; he was lost in another book. How could he be so positive with a face like that? Watery lidless eyes stared out of a patchwork face full of stringy keloid scars.

But then the whole ward was full of scars.

Every day Rob passed men with grafts; long tubular flaps attached to faces and cheeks: 'elephant men' with trunks hanging down in front of ravaged faces. It was like some scene out of *The Phantom Of The Opera,* Rob thought, except here, all the characters were wearing grotesque masks.

The ward smelt of an incongruous fusion of odours: flowers, burned flesh, and salt water, made all the more pungent by the steamy atmosphere which was conducive to the rapid healing of skin grafts. A cross between a scented sauna and an abattoir, Rob mused, almost smiling.

The most mutilated men of the war were in a number of little brown wooden army huts, hidden at the back of the Queen Victoria Hospital in East Grinstead. However, in two months, the huts had been transformed by one man: Archie McIndoe, a

18

New Zealander, nicknamed the 'Maestro' by the young burnt patients who worshipped him, and the 'Boss' by his staff who were in awe of him. Archie McIndoe was a consultant plastic surgeon of exceptional ability, but he also realised that the minds of many of his patients were more burnt than their faces. He understood the value of having attractive nurses; all nurses had had to send in photographs of themselves as well as an application letter before being appointed.

'Time for the saline bath, Rob.'

Mary Flynn, a pretty sandy-haired Scots nurse, stood at the end of his bed, smiling at him encouragingly, but Rob didn't respond. He just manoeuvred himself slowly into a sitting position, eased his feet to the floor and shuffled down the ward. Out of the corner of his eye, Rob saw the huddled form of 'Hoke', the American in the bed opposite his. Hoke and his crew had parachuted out of their plane and landed in the North Sea, but he was the only one to have survived. He'd floated around for days before being rescued and his depression was as deep as Rob's.

Rob headed towards the Saline Bath Unit: his only relief in the long, rowdy day. The 'Unit' was an elaborate name for a screened area of the ward in which there was a white enamel bath with claw legs. Various taps had been installed with protruding long hoses which poured saline into the heated bath and every half hour the staff checked that the salinity of the water remained constant.

Rob eased himself into the warm water, remembering his first baptism. After the initial agony, there came a flood of unexpected pleasure as the soothing saline caressed his raw flesh. It was the most comforting feeling he had experienced after being burned. The fact that the saline washing over his head was irrigating and cleaning his burns was an irrelevance. It was the caressing pleasure he coveted. He floated on a sea of ether, blocking out the noises around him. As he relaxed his head back into the water, the sun sparked off the chromium taps and he closed his eyes. There was Kate on the beach, the night of his first leave home, crunching along the shingled shore, throwing pebbles into the sea. He screwed up his eyes trying to remember how black her hair had looked in the moonlight; how dark her eyes. How beautiful she had been at seventeen. A hundred years ago. If only he'd savoured that moment instead of staring at the stars. He'd told her to look up at the galaxies spread out above them; told her about cosmic forces that were incomprehensible to mere mortals. What utter drivel. If only he had listened to Kate he might never have enlisted. And now he'd be able to look at his face.

He dreaded his parents coming to see him again, imagining their haunted faces as they drove through the gates of the hospital, past the long rectangular red-brick buildings towards him, imagining their conversation: 'Don't leave me alone with him,' he could hear his mother say. 'What can we talk about?' Rob didn't want to see their faces riven with excruciating helplessness; he didn't want to see the pain in his mother's eyes or his father's kindly, but now rapidly ageing face creased by concern; he didn't want to see their pity as they looked into his unrecognisable face.

He tensed as he heard his father talking to Owen Parry outside the bath unit.

'Hello, Owen. Where's Rob?'

'Soaking up the saline, Dr Adams. My turn next.'

'Is he any better this week?' Rob's mother asked Owen.

Rob held his breath. Didn't they know he could hear every word?

There was a long silence. Rob imagined the gestures Owen would use to say no.

'I see,' his mother said in a quiet voice.

He knew he'd have to get out of the bath; knew he'd have to see them. But did he have the courage to face their appalling pity? Suddenly Nurse Flynn was beside him, helping him out of the saline water; helping him dress. God, how he hated his dependency on people! She tied his maroon dressing gown around his waist and said, 'All ready, Rob?'

Rob nodded and she pulled back the unit curtain. There were his parents, waiting for him by his bed. He took some deep breaths to prepare himself and shuffled down the ward; his over-long dressing gown hanging loosely over his emaciated frame; his clawed hands dangling awkwardly down the sides of his body.

'Out at last, Robert,' shouted navigator, Bill Foxley; a man who refused to allow the severe damage to his hands and eyes to destroy his effervescent personality. 'We thought you'd drowned.'

Rob ignored him and shuffled past the central long table with its blaze of flowers. There was his mother, desperately trying to fix a smile on her face. Facing the Germans was far easier than this walk, Rob thought.

His father moved forward to meet him, a tentative smile on his face. He stopped a few inches in front of him.

21

'Hello, Rob. You're walking better.' Instinctively he went to shake Rob's hand before stopping abruptly.

'Am I, Dad?' Rob muttered, shuffling past him towards his bed. He knew his father would shrink at his words, but he couldn't stop himself; he couldn't cope with parents *and* depression.

His mother waited until Rob came near her before looking up into his large, dark brown eyes, a mirror of her own. He knew what she was thinking: *how is it possible to endure so much pain?* He had always known what she was thinking, even as a small boy.

'Hello, Mum.'

As his mother opened her mouth to speak, Rob saw the words wedge in her mouth. Why do we have to endure this ritual every week? Rob wanted to shout. It was an agony for them all.

Rob lowered himself carefully onto the bed, resisting the hovering hands of his parents. Pain shot through his body at each movement.

They sat down on either side of him as if to block out the world.

'Do you know what happened last week, Rob?' his father said, keeping his tone light. 'We were walking along the promenade with Charlie – oh, he sends his love – and a German parachutist landed on the beach. He walked right up to the barbed wire, stared at the crowd of people and gave the Nazi salute. You can imagine what Charlie said to him.' He paused, waiting for some reaction from Rob.

I can't give him what he wants, Rob thought. He wants his son back and he doesn't exist any more. I can't go through the motions of this charade any more. I don't care what Charlie said.

'You know who he reminded us of...' his mother said in a voice so unlike her own, '...your pen friend, Axel. He had the same green eyes.'

Rob turned his head slightly towards her. He had stayed many times with Axel's family in Bollerson, near the Lüneburger Heide before the war. They'd had long tramps across fields which Panzer divisions had since decimated and had many visits to the Schutzen Platz to fire guns which Axel might now be pointing at British soldiers.

His father gave him a small smile. 'He looked like a poster for the Nazis with his black leather jackboots and tight trousers. He had a flying eagle on his jacket. Here.' His father pointed to his left breast. 'Oh, and the jacket was greeny-grey.'

'No... they're always blue,' Rob said quietly.

His parents glanced at each other briefly. They think I'm interested, Rob thought. It was almost laughable.

'Well, *his* was greeny-grey,' his father said in an appalling imitation of humour.

Rob closed his eyes, the one part of his face that was still unscathed, and missed the silent look of pain between husband and wife.

'We're tiring him,' he heard his mother say.

'We'll go to see Mr McIndoe, Rob, then pop in to see you before we go.' His father's voice was frail. Rob wanted to press his hands into his eyes to stop the pain of remembering how vigorous his father had been before his accident.

'All right, Dad,' Rob said, making a monumental effort to sound normal. He heard their chairs scrape back on the stone floor and their worry pressed down on him like a weight.

'Right, then. Off we go, then,' his father said in the same jovial manner.

Rob opened his eyes and watched his parents walk away from him; noticing how his father's back bowed; noticing how the sun made a halo of his mother's white hair as it slanted through the oblong windows of the ward. It had only taken one crash and two weeks to transform her once beautiful brown hair.

Talking was torture, yet Rob remembered talking to his parents about a kaleidoscopic range of subjects before the war. Now, everything was too trivial for speech.

He drifted off into a deep sleep in which he was making love to Kate in a beautiful park where the birds were singing and they were happy. He pushed the memory away; he couldn't see her again, not when he looked like this.

There were voices somewhere far away.

'Your son's grafts are taking well. I'm very pleased with the last operation on his face. As you know, Dr Adams, speedy epithelialisation of wounds due to trauma or burns is largely determined by the situation and extent of the skin loss and the degree of involvement of deeper structures.'

The clipped colonial tones penetrated Rob's dream.

Rob opened his eyes slightly and saw the unmistakeable figure of Archie McIndoe standing by the next bed talking with his parents. He wore a pin-striped double-breasted suit and had a red carnation in his lapel. His black horn-rimmed glasses glinted in the sunlight as he turned his head towards Rob's mother.

'Fortunately, Robert's skin heals quickly. I know his face looks raw at the moment but that will fade in a few months – I can assure you.'

'So why isn't he improving?' Rob heard his mother say in an urgent tone.

McIndoe's body tightened. He didn't like to be questioned.

'My wife is certainly not implying your surgery isn't improving Rob physically, Mr McIndoe, but mentally... we ...' His father's voice trailed away.

Rob could feel the anguish in his father's voice. He closed his eyes. *Please go away and leave me alone* he wanted to shout at the top of his voice.

'I'm not going to lie to you,' Archie McIndoe was saying. 'I wouldn't insult your intelligence. At the moment Robert seems to be – how shall I put it – working *against* his recovery.'

'*Against*? But that's not possible!' His mother sounded horrified.

Was he working against his recovery? Rob opened his eyes to look at McIndoe. He had taken off his glasses and was cleaning them with a cloth. He only did this to give himself time to think, Rob had learnt.

'Rob must want to recover, surely?' his mother continued.

'The impact of disfiguring injuries upon the young adult mentality is usually severe, Mrs Adams. I'm sure Dr Adams has, unfortunately, seen this happen all too often in the last war.'

His father nodded briefly.

'All these young men were strong and healthy when they enlisted – that's why the RAF wanted them. They hadn't thought about illness or injury, nor to its possible future effects. In most cases, mentally, they are totally unprepared for the blow. When they come here many young men are *deeply* depressed and pessimistic.

'But look at Owen Parry – he's far more injured than Rob.'

'Owen has a goal to follow. Robert hasn't. I can't pretend that his depression isn't a problem because it is. I've tried to convince him that he *can* be of use to the world again, but I've failed. He believes that his life as a fighter pilot is at an end; that no woman will look at him without revulsion, and at best, he will remain an object for well-meant, but misguided pity for the rest of his life.'

That's exactly what I feel, Rob thought. As if my life has ended.

He heard his mother groan as if she was in terrible pain and he felt as if someone had stabbed him through his heart. Is that what he was doing to her?

'He has to find a reason to continue living,' McIndoe said.

But how? How? How? Rob wanted to scream.

Chapter 2

Kate and Bridget stood in their smart dark blue uniforms outside the long drive of Cardiff Castle in the gathering gloom of early evening. They had travelled in a corridor train for eight hours from Paddington station, then via an RAF truck to the castle. Through the slight drizzle they could see a solitary white barrage balloon shimmering above the Keep in the distance.

'Why on earth did I listen to you?' Kate moaned. 'Let's accept a commission, you said – we'll get a better posting, you said. Think of the adventure. Adventure! What do we know about balloons? Nothing. So where do they post us? A balloon unit in the middle of Wales!' Twenty-year-old Kate swept back a lock of dark chestnut hair. She was tired and irritable after their long journey. But Bridget, her indomitable Irish friend from Connemara, knew that her irritation wouldn't last long. They had become firm friends since they'd first joined the WAAFs and met at a dismal camp in Wolverhampton over eighteen months ago.

'Ach, it won't be too bad, Kate. I've always wanted to live in a castle. Now best foot forward, Section Officer Brazier – scheduled to meet Squadron Officer Virtue at 1700 hours.' Bridget spoke in upper-class tones.

For the second time that day, the girls exploded with laughter at the sound of their new Commanding Officer's name.

From the stony outpost of the Castle Keep they heard the voices of soldiers, and walked rapidly towards them. The eerie sound of the balloon's whine and creak wafted in the wind above them as they drew closer.

'Holy Mary. Have we to put up with that creaking every night now?'

'I hope not,' Kate said, shivering as the shadow of the enormous balloon fell over them, enveloping them in darkness.

Squadron Officer Virtue sat behind an oak desk with Kate and Bridget standing at attention before her. Both were struck by her beauty: glossy hair, the colour of lemon grass, swung over gentian blue eyes. Everything about her was elegant; her uniform, obviously made to measure, fitted like a silk glove. Her large wooden room smelled of lavender and wood-smoke from a crackling tortoise stove. Constable prints hung around its walls and chintz-covered chairs partially covered the colourful Welsh rugs which adorned the floor. They looked longingly at the steam wafting up from a cup on the Squadron Officer's desk. Ovaltine. Kate could recognise the smell of her favourite drink even through the aroma of lavender and wood-smoke.

'At ease, ladies. Welcome to Wales,' She smiled up at them, her remarkable, blue eyes crinkling. 'There's a story I want to tell you. Twenty-one centuries ago, an angry column of women marched into the Roman Forum and demanded the revocation of a law prohibiting them from wearing golden bangles and bright gowns.'

Kate and Bridget glanced at each other. What sort of officer was this?

'In the uproar that followed, the dour Senator Cato the Elder sat perfectly still and silent. When the hubbub died down, he rose and looked solemnly at his fellows before giving them a warning: "From the moment women become your equals, they will become your masters." Remember that, ladies.' They waited for her to continue. 'We'll dispense with formalities this evening. You've obviously had a long journey and must be hungry.'

'Yes, Ma'am.'

The Squadron Officer rang a small silver bell on her desk. 'I'll get Corporal Mellows to take you to the cookhouse. I've asked them to leave some hot food for you. Then she'll show you your quarters in the stables.'

Bridget frowned at Kate just as a diminutive corporal marched into the room, her frizzy red hair fighting to be free of her cap. She saluted smartly. The Squadron Officer stood and saluted back in one fluid movement.

Bridget and Kate held themselves rigid in an effort to restrain explosive laughter; Corporal Mellows was at least a foot shorter than the six-foot Squadron Officer Virtue. The girls, fixing their eyes on the ground, followed the flaming hair of Corporal Mellows out of the room.

*

They discovered in the ensuing days that there were eight balloon sites dotted in and around Cardiff Castle, all positioned some distance apart, covering Cardiff like a colossal shroud.·

The men were responsible for the maintenance of balloons and winches, the WAAF officers responsible for the girl operators. Each day Kate and Bridget had to inspect the sites under their control and report back to the statuesque Squadron Officer who, they discovered, managed to look elegant whether she was climbing into a jeep or riding a horse, which she did often. Then their other duties were disclosed. All the girl operators had to be super-fit to cope with the vagaries of rogue balloons. Kate and Bridget were assigned to instruct them in P.E. Corporal Mellows informed them that P.E. in the balloon units consisted of a series of rhythmic and strenuous exercises performed outdoors in all weathers at 700 hours every morning.

'What I know about P.E. wouldn't cover a bed bug,' Bridget said. 'I've no coordination at all.'

Kate had discovered this fact, along with every WAAF in the Officer Cadet Unit. Bridget created chaos each day by trying to march in opposition to everyone else, leaving bruised bodies and a trail of despairing Drill-Sergeants in her wake. Kate, to her surprise, had enjoyed both drilling and getting fit.

After reading her glowing Officer's Training Report, Squadron Officer Virtue decided to put Kate in charge, not only of training the women operators on site, but the men in the grounds of the castle too. She studied Kate from the confines of a nearby window as she put the men through a series of strenuous exercises which she timed perfectly.

Kate sensed she was being watched.

'How about some more *chest* expansion exercises, Section Officer?' Private Moore, a puny man who hated P.E. leered at her suggestively. Blood flooded into Kate's face as the men's laughter rolled round the parade ground.

'Since you're so interested in expanding your chest, Private Moore,' Kate shouted, 'you can do an hour's extra exercise tomorrow morning. 600 hours.'

Private Moore's leer transformed into shocked horror. This time the laughter was welcome.

'That's all for today, gentlemen …Take over, Sergeant Worth.'

She saluted smartly before marching off in her black and white P.E. kit, aware many eyes were trying to penetrate her shorts. She glanced up at the window and was elated to see Squadron Officer Virtue giving her the victory sign.

The north-east wind sliced into Bridget's thighs as she stood on a square of concrete outside the balloon hangar. The operators, all hefty girls capable of pulling the cumbersome balloons out of wayward positions, stood facing her – their faces, arms and legs marbled with blue.

'Right,' Bridget shouted into the wind, her pale blue eyes lost behind strands of curly auburn hair. 'Let's try the arms spreading and lifting in time with your legs again… one-two-one and two-one-two and one…'

The girls desperately tried to coordinate their movements to the random rhythm of Bridget's voice. Bridget, in an effort to get warm, joined in and all coordination disappeared under a confused jumble of arms and legs as they tried mirroring the wild flailing of her limbs.

One by one the girls stopped exercising and came to an embarrassed halt. They waited for guidance from Agnes, their corporal, an eighteen-year-old girl from Doncaster with legs that looked as if they'd been transplanted from two oaks.

'Excuse me, Ma'am,' Agnes spoke with a firm I'll-brook-no-nonsense-from-you voice. 'I think it would be better if me and the girls just followed your instructions without you joining in – if you follow my meaning.' The girls stared at Bridget whose face was now an undignified mixture of mottled blue and red.

'*Exactly* what I was going to say, Corporal,' Bridget said heartily, attempting a small laugh.

*

She threw her P.E. kit across Kate's room in the stables which had been converted into officers' quarters. Kate was lying on her comfortable bed, engrossed in the letters page of *Woman* magazine.

'I never want to see that bloody – begging your pardon, Holy Mary – P.E. kit again. It was awful. Imagine me taking rhythmic exercises, Kate. Dear God.'

Bridget collapsed into a chair, waiting for sympathy.

'Did you hear what I said?'

Kate looked over the top of the magazine. 'Listen to this: "I am very indignant. My daughter of eighteen wrote to you asking the facts about sex, marriage and babies; and a letter and a booklet came to the house which I burned immediately. I think young people should be protected from people who take away their innocence this way".'

'She sounds like me Grandma. She didn't even want me Ma to know where babies came from – even after she'd had eight.'

Kate laughed, but suddenly became serious. 'But she shouldn't have done that, should she?'

'Who?'

'The mother in the letter. She had no right... Oh ...' Something else in the letters page had caught Kate's attention.

Bridget sighed.

'What do you think about this then?' Kate continued. '"Me and my girl have been keeping company for four years now. I expect to be sent abroad very shortly and I look forward to the day when I shall come home and we shall be able to marry. What worries me – I cannot bring myself to discuss it with her – is the fact she is going to join one of the services soon. She will be meeting all kinds of men and perhaps getting in with the wrong kinds of girls. How can I be sure she will be true?"'

Bridget took off her utilitarian black service shoes and stretched out her legs. 'He can't, can he? Not with a war going on *and* she'll be mixing with types like us now, won't she?'

'Be serious. You don't agree with these people, do you?'

'No, but if this war hadn't started I wouldn't have left home. I would have married a 'Mara boy, had lots of babies and never discovered a different life. Everything's changed for women, but I don't know if it's for the better, Kate.'

'You've met me.'

'Ah, you know what I mean, then?' Bridget grinned and Kate threw her pillow at her head, narrowly missing a bowl of pink carnations which someone had placed in her room.

'I'm not saying that war's a good thing, Bridge, but look what women are doing now – riveting, welding, making bullets –'

'Holy Mary, who wants to do that?'

'That's not the point. Before the war they weren't thought *capable* of doing such work. Now they're ploughing fields, fighting fires, running government departments –'

'Having babies, cooking, washing, cleaning, ironing,' interrupted Bridget, knowing how to annoy her friend.

Kate flushed with anger. 'Yes – and that too! That's what's so important. We can do anything now.'

'We can't work down mines.'

'Do you *want* to?' Kate retorted.

'Ah – I thought that wasn't the point.'

'You really are the most irritating person I've ever met, Bridget Reilly.'

'I thought you said Rob was.'

Kate's face drained of colour.

'Oh, Katie darlin', I'm sorry,' Bridget said, jumping up to push the magazine away. 'Me Ma always said she'd cut me tongue out one day. Forgive me?' She put her arms around her friend and squeezed. 'Come on – let's go to the Mess for a drink. What do you say?'

*

There was a relaxed feeling in the Mess that Kate really liked. She felt at home there. As they walked in she saw Squadron Officer Virtue towering over one of the new RAF Officers, Sam Littlewood, to whom she had been introduced earlier that day. His round, unfinished face looked as if it was still waiting for some memorable features. He gave Kate a tentative wave from the other side of the Mess. Squadron Officer Virtue motioned them over. They had almost reached her when the telephone rang. One of the bar stewards answered it and called for Kate.

'Who wants you at this time of night?' Bridget said.

Kate sighed as she walked over to the phone. It had been a long day.

Ten minutes later she was travelling at high speed in an RAF lorry to the docks in Tiger Bay to investigate a report that two of her girls were inviting sailors into their hut. Bertha and Beryl were 'at it' this very moment the corporal of the site had told Kate on the phone, and the other girls were complaining.

It was cold and blustery when Kate and two RAF police officers arrived at the lonely site on the edge of the Bay. The three of them listened outside the hut for tell-tale sounds of passion. They didn't have long to wait. An unforgettable moan came from the room. Kate was glad that the men couldn't see her colour as she waited miserably in the shadows while they crept silently into the hut. Suddenly Blitzkrieg commenced as the police jumped the sailors. They retaliated by hitting everything their hands and feet came into contact with. After what seemed like hours, the police emerged looking bloody, but triumphant, with two battered sailors in tow. Kate took a deep breath before entering the hut to find Bertha and Beryl crying hysterically on their beds. They had been told what would happen to them if they were caught in *flagrante delicto*: dishonourable dismissal from the services.

After dealing with the hysterical girls, Kate climbed wearily into the RAF lorry to return to Cardiff Castle when an irate woman from a house opposite the site ran out shouting at Kate.

'You're an officer – what are you going to do about the French letters, then?'

'French letters? What French letters?' Kate had no idea what the woman was talking about. She saw the heads of the two young policemen jerking up and down. Were they *laughing*?

'The French letters what them soldiers are putting on sticks and waving about outside the windows near the balloon site where everyone can see them. What you goin' to do about them, eh? It's a disgrace to decent people. I don't want my kids seeing nothin' like that! I ain't seen nothin' like it in all the years I lived here. You're an officer – what you goin' to do about it, eh?'

It took all of Kate's diplomacy to calm the woman down. She explained that she'd ring the Army Officer in charge of men's billets immediately and find out who the culprits were.

Half an hour later, Kate was pacing up and down her room wondering how to broach the subject of French letters with an army officer when she had no idea what they were. She knew from the woman's anger that they were not designed to be hung on sticks outside windows for all to see, but how could *letters* make her angry? Kate was confused and embarrassed; not only by the woman's anger, but by the policemen's scarcely concealed hilarity at the situation. The only option she had was

36

to bluff it out. Her stomach felt full of electric eels as she asked to speak to the Duty Officer at the Tiger Bay site.

'Hello, Duty – '

Kate cut him off abruptly. 'This is Section Officer Brazier from Headquarters. I've just returned from the Tiger Bay site and was absolutely appalled to see that your men had hung French letters out of the barrack windows. There have been numerous complaints from the public and what about my girls? What would their parents think? If they are not removed immediately, I shall be reporting the matter to your Commanding Officer.'

Kate slammed the phone down and sat on her bed, shaking with relief. There – she'd done it, without even knowing what French letters were.

Chapter 3

Go! Go! Go!'

He's climbing steeply above one of the 109s and suddenly hoar-frost covers his windscreen. No forward vision. He rubs a small section of screen. Where the hell's the 109? He weaves and scans. Weaves and scans. Difficult to breathe. He breaks away and dives. 15,000 feet. 10,000 feet – He can see! No Messerschmitt on his tail. He's above the sea. It's misty. Jesus Christ! Tracers! Streaming past the cockpit! Large, black swastikas fill the screen. A Dornier 200 feet away! Climb! Climb! Climb! Bloody sweat everywhere! There he is – bank to the left. Hit the firing button! Bullseye! One Dornier down and screaming into the sea.

Relax. Only a second. A shape coming out of the sun – a Messerschmitt! – orange tracers streaming. A violent thump-thump-thump! Cannon shell. No elevator-control! Spiralling. Spiralling. Out of control. Climbing. Blackness. A red-laced mist. Flames. Tearing at the hood release. Stuck! Flames eating his fingers. He screams, clawing at the hood release. At last it slams back. He hits the release pin. Holds his head back from the flames. Tumbles through sky and sea. A chromium ring. Burning fingers hold and pull. He screams as a white silk canopy billows above him. He smells his flesh and sways crazily in space. Shaking. Shaking. Shaking.

Rob was woken from his nightmare by the fevered cries from the opposite bed and his fingers crabbed with tension. No one had slept well for over a week. Holebrook Mahn's legs were the problem. 'Hoke' was a pilot who'd had to bale out over the North Sea. He'd developed immersion frostbite after being in the water for days. Gangrene oozed insidious decay around the ward invading every breath. None of Hoke's grafts would take. Gradually, the whole ward watched his legs turn black and gangrenous.

Standing at the bottom of Hoke's bed were McIndoe and Jill Mullins, his top theatre sister: a tall, slender Irish woman with titian hair and intelligent eyes. She looked like the film star Gertrude Lawrence. They were whispering furiously to each other as they watched Hoke toss and turn with fever. Rob strained to catch their words.

'I'm a *surgeon* – not a bloody butcher …'

The desperate anger in McIndoe's voice constricted Rob's breathing.

Jill Mullins whispered urgently to him as they marched out of the ward. For once, McIndoe didn't speak to any of his patients.

Soon the whole ward was awake: listening to the squeak of trolley wheels as the orderlies pushed it towards Hoke's bed. Everyone watched as they manoeuvred him onto it and wheeled him towards the operating theatre. They didn't need to be told what was going to happen. Someone switched on a gramophone and music flooded the room.

Two hours later, Hoke, heavily anaesthetised, was wheeled back to the ward: three foot shorter.

*

In the following weeks, Rob watched Hoke's depression overtake his own as the memory of his time at sea deepened the shadows in his grey eyes. His long, silent periods affected Rob profoundly. At last, he walked over to speak to Owen Parry.

'We *must* do something for him, Owen.'

This was Rob's first demonstration of any interest in another human being. Owen knew it was a landmark. He carried on reading *Brave New World.*

'Oh, he's no worse than a lot of others, Rob. I wouldn't worry if I were you.'

'*What*?' Rob exploded. 'He's got no legs for Christ's sake!'

'Well, old Tom over there's lost his nose. Alan, the use of his hands and Peter, one eye. But they seem to be coping, don't they?'

'That's a bloody callous attitude to take, I must say.'

At last Owen looked up from his book.

'But better than lying in bed for six months, saying bugger all to anyone and wallowing in self-pity though, isn't it, Rob?'

Rob stomped off down the ward, forgetting, in his anger, to shuffle.

*

Archie McIndoe was exhausted: exhausted by surgery; exhausted by committees. It was the day of the Welfare Committee. So far, the meeting had been a series of complaints about his patients and his wards. They didn't like the *laissez-*

faire atmosphere; the men's language; their drinking or their carousing about East Grinstead. Indeed, some of those with young daughters were fearful of their honour in view of his patients' wildness. McIndoe sat slumped in a leather chair, fingering his glasses as they aired their grievances.

He stared out of the window at Matron's prize dahlias after the last complainant sat down. Someone coughed nervously. McIndoe stood up, shaking with repressed anger.

'I have several things to say, some of which you are not going to like. The Queen Victoria Hospital no longer simply serves the local community. Primarily, this hospital is to be used for the physical and mental rebuilding of airmen injured in the course of their duty. I had hoped, for some time, you would realise that from now on, this hospital will become less and less a civic organisation as the Services send in their casualties. But you have disappointed me.' McIndoe fixed the committee with a ferocious glare through his horn-rimmed glasses.

'Some of you object to pilots and aircrew having alcohol in their wards. Normally I might perhaps agree with you, but in this matter you overlook two points. First these men are not sick or badly injured. Their bodies may be broken temporarily, but their youthful spirits are still with them. Secondly, normal hospital discipline is all very well for a patient who is admitted for a few days or a few weeks, but it has to be relaxed when a man is to be treated for several years.'

There was silence after he had finished. An elderly lady stood up shakily. 'I expect we deserved that rebuke ... perhaps we didn't think it out too well. But if only, Mr McIndoe, you would take us into your confidence about what you plan to do, it may be in our power to help, rather than hinder.'

Archie McIndoe smiled at the elderly woman before saying, 'Thank you. May I suggest the next time you go visiting the wards, think of these boys as human beings. Think of them as if they were your own sons and remember that you're not doing *them* a favour by visiting them. They're doing *you* a favour by speaking to you.'

The chastened committee stood up and were about to leave when McIndoe spoke again.

'One more thing. A man who has lost his nose and is in process of getting a new one may not exactly resemble Clark Gable, although I hear he too has had plastic surgery. In fact, this man may look more like a pterodactyl until a plastic surgeon treats him. I want you ladies to spread the word around the town that these men must not be made to feel uncomfortable. I don't want people going around and feeling sorry for them. I want shopkeepers, publicans, customers at the four-ale bar to be normal with them and not gape at them as if they've come out of a freak museum. Will you do that?'

The committee, desperate to get away from the powerful pull of McIndoe's eyes, hastily agreed.

Over the next weeks, East Grinstead witnessed some strange and wondrous sights: men with patchwork faces, half-formed noses which had been 'borrowed' from foreheads, with crippled hands or pedicle grafts crawling from shoulder to face, drank and played darts in the pubs, ate and sang in the restaurants.

But Rob didn't join the men in their excursions around the town. He lay in his bed and stared at the ceiling for hours. Jill Mullins, the theatre sister, walked through the ward every day just to see if Rob had left with the others. After a number of weeks, she knew he never would, so she decided to do something.

She sat at the end of his bed and stared at the mask of his face. 'Rob, I've got something I'd like you to read. One of the Canadian boys wrote it. He was a flyer too.'

Rob didn't respond in any way, so she lay the poem down on his bed and walked away. Rob was immobile for several minutes. Why should he be interested in what a Canadian pilot had written? But at last curiosity overcame his inertia. He reached over the white expanse, pushed the paper up the bed with his clawed hand and read:

Oh! I have slipped the surly bonds of earth
And danced the skies on laughter-silvered wings;
Sunward I've climbed, and joined the tumbling mirth
Of sun-split clouds – and done a hundred things
You have not dreamed of – wheeled and soared and swung
High in the sunlit silence. Hov'ring there,
I've chased the shouting wind alone, and flung
My eager craft through footless halls of air.
Up, up the long delirious, burning blue,
I've topped those windswept heights with easy grace
Where never lark and or even eagle flew-
And while with silent lifting mind I've trod

The high untrespassed sanctity of space,

Put out my hand and touched the face of God.

The paper floated onto the floor as Rob fell back onto his pillow. He'd been there! In the sky tumbling through sun-split clouds. He'd been there! What sort of woman would want to torture him like this? He started to shake. No one but Jill Mullins heard the sobs tear out of Rob's body as the other men who remained in the ward lay in a drug-induced sleep. All the pain of Rob's loss was encapsulated in his lament and the sound made Jill weep. No one came to help him because she knew that Rob needed to mourn his lost life; his lost face. When the sobbing ceased, Jill sat beside him and told him about John Gillespie Magee, Jr, the man who wrote the poem. 'He was twenty-one and he died yesterday, but what a celebration he made of his life.' She paused before asking: 'Was it really like that when you were flying?'

She could see herself reflected in Rob's brown eyes as he nodded.

'Then I envy you.'

'Envy me!' His voice was shrill with disbelief.

'If you experienced half of what John Magee experienced, you've lived far more than most people ever will. Isn't that something to celebrate?'

Chapter 4

The day the leave list was pinned on the notice board the WAAFs went wild; everyone pushing and shoving, everyone hoping to see their name highlighted. Bridget managed to elbow her way through the throng until s he was standing in front of the board. She let out a whoop of excitement as she saw her name and Kate's pinned there.

'We've got it, Kate – three days' leave! Imagine what we can do!'

They hugged each other before walking back to the stables. It was then that Bridget deflated. She suddenly realised that *she* didn't know what to do. There wasn't enough time for her to go to Ireland to visit her family. She sat down on Kate's bed.

'I know where you're spending your leave, Bridget. You're coming home with me,' Kate told her. 'Start packing.'

'Oh, surely to God your Ma won't want me in the house.'

'*I* want you in the house and I'm sure my mother will too.'

*

Bridget and Kate had arrived after travelling for ten hours through crowded stations and overflowing trains. They were greeted politely by Kate's mother and ecstatically by Rose,

Kate's thirteen-year-old sister. Hilda had managed to give the illusion of a kiss to Kate. Bridget contrasted her own reunion with her family last year; she had felt cherished.

They were all sitting in the dining room on hard chairs, having just finished the best meal Bridget had ever tasted during the war: succulent braised beef and dumplings. Yet there was no warmth in the room. She remembered the two primroses seen through murky train windows, spreading spring onto a lawn. Colour had been washed out of this room.

'That was grand, Mrs Brazier,' Bridget said. 'Kate told me you were a wonderful cook.'

'Did she?' Hilda looked surprised. 'I can't remember the last time I had a compliment from her.'

A furrow appeared between Kate's eyes. 'I've *always* told you how good your cooking is, Mum.' There were years of pain in her voice.

'You know exactly what I mean,' her mother snapped.

'Does *your* family argue all the time, Bridget?' Rose stared intently at the auburn-haired young woman opposite her.

Bridget wanted to shout: Kate's the best friend I've ever had – why don't you appreciate her?

'No,' she said curtly. 'Have you had a lot of bombing here, Mrs Brazier? It's been terrible in Cardiff, hasn't it, Kate? They keep bombing the docks.'

Hilda looked momentarily startled by the turn in the conversation. 'Oh, yes. The tip and run raiders are the worst. The German bombers tip their loads over Hastings and then fly like the clappers towards the coast away from our Spitfires.

46

Hundreds of high explosive bombs have been dropped. They come over regular as clockwork. Eleven a.m. every morning and not a pea-shooter to fire at them.' She turned to Kate. 'You ought to see the town now … you won't recognise parts of it, especially where the Plaza cinema used to be.'

'*Used* to be?'

'Rose – go and make us a nice cup of tea, there's a good girl.' Hilda wasn't going to talk about the carnage she had seen with her thirteen-year-old daughter in the room.

Rose glowered at her mother. During the last year the sharp angles of her body had been transformed into unwanted curves. They disgusted Rose. She didn't like *any* of the changes that were happening to her body. She didn't feel 'Rose' any more.

'I know why you're sending me out. I'm not a child, you know. I'm nearly a woman!'

She stomped out of the room, slamming the door behind her.

Hilda sighed heavily.

'She always like that?' Bridget asked.

'Yes,' Hilda said. 'Puberty, I expect. Kate knows all about that. She had *terrible* spots.'

There was a small silence as Kate looked at her mother.

Bridget could almost taste the tension in the room. Her relationship with her own mother was loving and uncomplicated. She couldn't understand this relationship at all.

'What happened to the cinema, Mrs Brazier?'

'The cinema?' Hilda dragged herself into the past. 'I was walking along Robertson Street last September when I heard this gigantic explosion. I ran around the corner – I'll never forget it.' Hilda paused, holding the table with tightly clenched fists. 'There were bodies everywhere outside the cinema and not only bodies … but … bits of bodies too. And fire and smoke and … a boy.' Hilda shuddered, remembering all too vividly the sight of the fourteen-year-old, spread-eagled on the pavement, covered with a thick layer of grey dust and oozing blood from every orifice.

'Must have been awful,' Kate said, knowing what a shock it would have been for her mother. She hated the sight of blood.

They waited for Hilda to continue but she just sat in the small room, unnervingly immobile, staring at pictures in her head.

After long seconds she shattered the silence. 'Worst for the relatives though … I'd better help Rose or the cups will be broken.'

She bustled out of the room leaving the two girls staring at each other.

'Has it always been like this between you?' Bridget asked.

'Like what?'

'Oh, come on, Kate.'

Kate took a deep breath. 'Yes.'

'Why? What happened?'

'I don't know. I just think she hates me.'

'Don't be silly. How can your own Ma hate you?'

'I don't know,' Kate said abruptly before her eyes filled with tears. Bridget reached over the table and held Kate's hand. 'I sometimes thought my mother only wanted sons when I was a child. That's why she hated me. She always worshipped Colin. Then Rose came ...'

Bridget felt the trembling in Kate's fingers and smiled at her. If time had to stand still, Kate thought, it should be at that moment.

Their intimacy was shattered by a loud knocking at the front door. Kate withdrew from Bridget, hastily drying her eyes. 'No one calls this late.'

They heard a male voice and Hilda shouting with excitement: 'Colin! Oh my giddyaunt!'

Kate looked at Bridget, knowing exactly what she was thinking.

*

They were all crowded into the small, but warm scullery after Colin's arrival. The house glowed: everyone hugging and kissing. Colin embraced his mother and sisters with breath-constricting bear hugs before turning his attention to Bridget. The moment he looked into her smiling blue eyes he wished he'd paid more attention to his English teacher. *Give a woman a love sonnet and she's yours for ever*, the teacher had said. If only he knew what one was, he would give her hundreds.

'You're too thin,' Hilda said, smiling up at her son and ruffling his carrot-coloured hair. She was not the same woman who had stood at the door two hours earlier and greeted Kate with little warmth. Now her grey face was flooded with colour; she was almost girlish as she studied Colin in his RAF uniform.

She hadn't seemed to notice that Kate was half a stone lighter since joining the WAAFs. Hilda was charged with adrenaline, whisking round the room to make him a wartime feast. 'If only you'd arrived an hour ago. I cooked us braised beef and dumplings, didn't I, girls?'

'It was grand, Mrs Brazier.' Bridget smiled again at Colin, enjoying the effect she was having on him.

'Oh no!' Hilda suddenly wailed. 'There's no bed. Rose is in your old room and Bridget's staying.' Hilda stood by the stove, looking distraught.

'I'm sure there's somewhere I can stay round here, Mrs Brazier … Don't worry.'

'You can't go, Bridget,' Kate said quickly. 'There won't be any rooms anywhere.' She looked up at her brother. 'Why didn't you tell Mum you were coming, you chump. I did.'

Fluctuating emotions fought over Hilda's face.

'Meant to be a surprise,' Colin said. 'Sorry – not my best idea. Look, Mum, I can sleep on a chair in the dining room. Not to worry.'

'You certainly won't!' Hilda folded her arms across her broad breasts, prepared to do battle with anyone who thought her son could sleep on a chair in his own home.

'*I'll* sleep on the chair, Mum. I can sleep anywhere. You know that.' Rose was desperate to get some attention. She had been ignored since her siblings had arrived.

'Don't be silly, Rose. Nobody's sleeping on a chair.' Hilda dismissed the idea without even looking at her daughter.

'Well, I thought it was very nice of me.' Rose kicked at a chair with her hated school shoes.

'It was, Dumbo. I can't believe you'd sleep on a chair for your big brother.' Colin threw an arm around his younger sister's shoulder.

'Not for you. For Mum,' Rose said, smiling up at Colin.

Hilda placed an enormous tray of braised beef and dumplings, which she had been saving for tomorrow's supper, in front of her son. 'I'll think of something. Now sit down, son, and eat.' She watched with satisfaction as Colin ate every morsel with obvious relish. If only he didn't have to go back to the war, she thought. Hilda watched German planes every day flying over the coast, engaging in dogfights with Spitfire pilots. What if one of them …

'Mum, that was amazing,' Colin said, loosening the top button of his trousers. 'I bet the King and Queen don't eat any better than that.' Hilda could think of no higher accolade; her face glowed, all thought of the Hun evaporating.

'Look, what about this as an idea?' Colin continued. 'I'll go to Rob's house and ask if I can stay there. They've got masses of room. What do you think?' He looked at Kate. 'How *is* Rob, by the way? Haven't had time to visit him yet.'

Kate twisted in her chair – the memory of her last visit to the RAF hospital too fresh in her mind. She hadn't been prepared for a monster with a face swollen to twice its normal size staring at her with Rob's eyes. Her face flushed.

'I don't know,' she said quietly. 'I haven't seen him since he moved to East Grinstead.'

'Tell you what – why don't we all go and see him?'

'*Yeah!* Let's go tomorrow, Mum!' Rose shouted. She had never seen anyone who had burns all over his face before.

'Don't use slang, Rose, I've told you before. No one's going to hospital tomorrow and that's final. Now off to bed, young lady. It's way past your bed time.'

'I always miss everything. And where's Colin going to sleep?'

'Don't worry about me. Give us a kiss and don't whine.' Colin was looking at Bridget. 'Very unattractive trait in a young lady, wouldn't you agree, Bridget?'

'I surely would.' Bridget smiled at him, revealing small, perfectly white teeth.

Electricity sparked between them.

'Well, I'm not a young lady, am I? I'm only a little girl,' Rose said, sarcastically.

'Night, Rose.' Kate leaned over to kiss her sister before Colin threw Rose into the air as he used to when she was little. She squealed with delight.

'Night-night, Dumbo. Sleep tight. Don't let the bed bugs bite.'

Rose's face shone as he set her down again. She bounced out of the room before calling to her mother.

'Five minutes, Mum.'

Colin relaxed back into his chair as they heard her progress across the floorboards above them. 'She's exhausting, isn't she?'

'Being a thirteen-year-old girl is difficult.' Bridget stared at him coldly.

'I always said it must be awful being a girl, didn't I, Mum?' Then he grinned wickedly and the women burst out laughing. It stopped abruptly as they heard a knock on the door.

'I can't believe it,' Hilda said 'We never have visitors and tonight it's like the sea-front on a bank holiday.' She heard Mary in the hall talking to Rose and called out, 'Come in, Mary.'

'I'm sorry to call so late, Hilda. I just wanted to talk about…' Mary stopped short when she saw Colin and the girls. She couldn't possibly air her worries about Rob in front of them. 'Oh, hello Colin… Kate… I'll come back another time.'

'You will not, Mary. You'll celebrate with us. Colin's home.' Mary looked at Kate. 'And Kate, of course, with her friend Bridget,' Hilda added quickly. 'Sit down and I'll get my elderflower wine.'

Mary stood awkwardly by the door. The changes in her face shocked Kate. She had always been an attractive woman with the sort of classical features seen on a Greek statue and a direct look in her large brown eyes which some people found disconcerting. Now the directness had disappeared; her gaze darted round the room as if not knowing where to settle and the flesh over her cheekbones was so taut, it revealed the skeleton beneath. Pain was reducing her.

'No, I won't stop, Hilda. You'll have lots to talk about with a houseful.'

'To be honest it's a bit *too* full, Mrs Adams,' Colin said. 'Mum didn't expect me home, you see. No room at the inn.'

It took Mary a few minutes to understand him. She always had difficulty remembering the difference between Hilda's home and hers.

'Oh I *see*. Look, would one of you like to stay with us? We've got lots of spare bedrooms.'

'No, we couldn't impose on you, Mary,' Hilda said, hoping she could.

'Well, I hope I can,' Colin smiled at Mary, trying to conceal his shock at her appearance.

'No, *you* can't go, son,' Hilda almost shouted. 'You've only just come. Kate can go.'

Mary's picture of the Braziers' family harmony punctured in an instant. She was horrified to see tears in Kate's eyes.

'*Mum!*' For the first time in his life Colin was angry with his mother.

'I'd loved to have Kate stay.' Mary spoke in a rush. 'And her friend Bridget – if she'd like to come.'

Bridget's expression hardened. 'Where Kate goes, I go. Mrs Brazier – in Ireland we appreciate our daughters as well as our sons. I'll go and pack.'

The temperature was arctic.

*

An hour later, the temperature was almost tropical in the Adams' large, elegant drawing room, full of oak antique furniture. All over the house the girls had seen Charlie's hand-made cardboard rings around the light switches in the shape of faces. The knob of the switches formed the nose. He had written *PLEASE SWITCH ME OFF* round the edge.

'Very particular is our Charlie,' John said. 'We have labelled buckets in the kitchen, arranged in military lines.'

They were drinking a second bottle of Chambertin-Clos de Bèze, which John insisted on opening to toast their guests. The girls were now grateful that Kate's home was so small. The conversation, somewhat to Kate's bewilderment, had turned to the incident with the French letters. She spoke as if she had been dealing with them all her life. Mary obviously found the story amusing. John looked as if he'd just eaten a pickle.

He stood with his back to a roaring fire. 'Really, Kate. I don't think you should be joking.'

'Oh don't be so stuffy, John. You can't cosset the younger generation any more. This is 1941. I'm sure these girls know a great deal more about life and sex than ever we did at their age. You can't have a government telling women to get out of the kitchen to work in factories, offices or the services where they'll be meeting hordes of men and then expect them to be shrinking violets. I've always believed that we do women an injustice by shrouding sex in so much secrecy.'

Kate and Bridget were astonished. Neither of their mothers would have even mentioned the word 'sex' in front of them, let alone indulged in an argument about it with their husbands.

John turned to the girls. 'As you see, ladies, my wife is nothing if not forthright in her views.'

'Well, women have achieved very little by living in the shadows of men.'

'Ah, so it's women's liberation again, is it? You want women to have more power than men, do you? Where's the justice in that, Mary?'

Mary's face coloured. 'Oh don't be ridiculous, John, that's not what I want at all. That's a spurious argument and you know it. I want women to have power over *themselves*, not men.'

Kate jumped up excitedly. 'That's Mary Wollstonecraft's argument, isn't it? Having control over your own life. You've read her book too?'

Mary turned with pleasure towards Kate whose face was as flushed as her own. 'Of course I have. An amazing woman.' Mary realised, with a shock, that Kate was only a few years younger than her own daughters would have been if they had lived. If they hadn't died of diphtheria as babies. She wondered if her girls would have glowed with the agitation of Wollstonecraft's ideas like Kate.

'But Mary Wollstonecraft was mainly concerned about equal educational rights for women, Kate. I'm equally concerned that they have the power to do what they want with their own bodies.'

'Ah, but my dear,' said John, looking at his wife innocently, 'you know that women exist for the propagation of the species.'

Kate and Bridget hissed through their teeth.

'Don't take any notice of him girls,' Mary said. 'He says things like that merely to annoy me.' It was obvious to everyone in the room that he'd succeeded.

'All right. What about the upsurge of VD within the last year, Mary? How does that equate with your view?' In spite of the girls' presence, John couldn't resist using this weapon to support his belief in the erosion of moral sexual values.

The girls were delighted. Sex *and* VD in one night.

'That's because everything to do with sex is shrouded in secrecy,' Mary retaliated. 'What were you telling me only last week? That people with VD are only obliged to submit to treatment if they are informed upon by two infected patients. That's outrageous. What of the others? What about the large number of innocent women infected by their husbands and boyfriends who might contract the disease through no fault of their own? Indeed, some women might unwittingly transmit VD to their children, but it will remain untreated because no informer will be forthcoming! It's a national scandal, John, and one which the nation and Government must face up to. Edith Summerskill is right – we need compulsory notification of the disease – then it can be treated promptly and women will not be made to suffer its consequences.'

The girls burst into spontaneous applause. John held his hands up in mock surrender.

'All right. All right, Mary. I concede the argument, my dear. Once again your rhetoric has convinced me of the error of my ideas.'

'Nonsense. You know you haven't changed an opinion in years.' Suddenly Mary and John smiled at each other across the room. Kate and Bridget experienced the same feelings of isolation that Rob had had a year ago when looking at his parents' rapport. But now, John and Mary looked ten years older.

The door creaked open and there stood Charlie, trembling from cold and fear.

'Was that a *good* argument then? You're not really cross?'

'No, Charlie.' Mary smiled at him and he bounded across the room into her arms.

'Of course it was good, Charlie,' John said, dryly. 'Your Auntie Mary won, as usual.'

Charlie grinned with relief and smiled at Kate. 'That's all right then.' He turned to look at Bridget whose face was flushed with the unaccustomed Burgundy.

'This is Bridget, Charlie. Kate's friend.'

'Hello. You're not as pretty as Kate.'

'Charlie!'

'But you *are* pretty.'

'Well, when I want to get the truth out of someone, Mrs Adams, I'll come to Charlie.' Bridget grinned at Charlie. He grinned back at her, safe in the confines of Mary's arms.

'Uncle John … can I ask you a question?'

John was slouched in an armchair, perfectly relaxed from the warmth of the room and the fire of the wine. Nothing could disturb his composure. He closed his eyes. 'Yes?'

'What's VD?'

Their seventeenth-century grandfather clock chimed eleven times in the silence.

John opened one eye to look at Mary accusingly. 'Well, your Auntie Mary wants everything out in the open, Charlie. I'll leave her to explain. Good night, dear. Night, Charlie. Don't forget to turn off all the lights. Come on girls, I'll show you your rooms. '

He kissed his startled wife on the cheek, then ushered the girls out of the lounge. Charlie warmed his hands in front of the fire, waiting for a clear explanation to a question which could make him half a crown. The boys in his class had bet him he couldn't find out what VD was by Friday. Today was Thursday. He would stand waiting all night if necessary. Mary looked down into his determined face and knew she had been hoisted by her own petard.

Chapter 5

Two weeks after Jill Mullins had spoken to him in the ward, Rob allowed himself to be coerced into travelling to East Grinstead with her. As they walked into a small, fussy teashop Rob found his throat felt as chalky as it was on his sorties. They sat in a dark corner, but each time the bell jingled to announce another tea-drinker, Rob had to endure the surreptitious shock of people who didn't want their heroes looking like cicatrised bacon. He cradled a small white teacup in his clawed fingers concealing the immense pain this simple action created. Jill smiled, but didn't comment on this small triumph. She saw the sudden anger flare in Rob's eyes, the only part of his face which could still register emotion, and leaned towards him. 'Don't expect too much from people, Rob.'

'I don't expect anything,' he cradled his cup down to his saucer again before adding, 'but what I'm getting is revulsion. Is this what I'm going to get for the rest of my life?'

'I know how you feel. I've been working with burns patients for –'

'How the hell do you know what I feel!' The anger in Rob's voice jerked people's heads in his direction, before they suddenly found something fascinating to look at on their plates.

'People don't feel revulsion when they look at you. They feel attraction.'

'So you believe beauty is all on the surface?'

'That's just semantics. If I said that beauty comes from deep within a person, that wouldn't stop people finding me repulsive, would it?'

Rob watched Jill drinking the weak tea and knew McIndoe had asked her to help with his recovery.

'I've helped many disfigured young men, Rob. Let me help you?'

'How?' Rob asked her abruptly.

'Not everyone thinks you're repulsive, Rob. That's just your perception,' she said stridently.

Why was she speaking so loudly? Rob thought. Everyone had turned in their direction. He felt anger accelerate through his body.

'Then why is there such a large space around us?' Rob emphasised his point with a sweeping gesture which he instantly regretted as pain surged through his fingers. 'Have you noticed how everyone is squashed at the other end of the café?'

The sun played on Jill's hair, changing it from russet to titian-red as she revolved her head to stare at the other people. Every face in the café was angled away from them: almost as if everyone had developed a strange condition which constricted the movement of their heads.

'Because they fear difference. Some people will always react like that, Rob. You have to ...' Jill trailed away. The pain in Rob's eyes was suddenly unbearable. She leaned towards him urgently. 'Listen to me. Patients who have a good reason for their scars recover far quicker than those who are accidentally burnt. Did you know that?'

All the conversation in the café had stopped. People were listening.

Rob made a dismissive noise before answering. 'You mean that there's more prestige in being burned in a plane than being burned in a kitchen?'

'Yes. You've done something you should be proud of, Rob.'

'Getting burned, you mean?'

Rob didn't notice the look of guilt on the faces of the diners in the café.

Jill didn't react to Rob's sarcasm. 'No, you've fought for your country. You should feel pride.'

'It's difficult to feel pride when you look like a gargoyle.'

'Then have another operation. Archie McIndoe can work miracles.'

The silence in the room was startling. Everyone waited for Rob's answer. It didn't come.

His whole body tensed as he stared out at the bottled windows, vividly remembering the excruciating pain of his last operation. They had grafted a large section of skin from his leg to his face. He didn't think he could bear that much pain again.

'Talk to the other men, Rob. They want to help you. We all do,' Jill said.

Rob didn't notice a small elderly lady hobble towards him, the inflammation of osteomyelitis in every movement. He was startled when she touched his arm.

'My grandson was in the Navy, young man. He lost his life on the Hood a few years ago and I mourn him every day. Don't lose your life just because a few petty people are shocked by your appearance. You had the courage to fight. I'm sure you have the courage to undergo another operation.'

Her tissue-paper skin crumpled as she smiled at him. Rob tried moving the muscles of his face into the semblance of a smile, but he wasn't seeing the old lady; he was looking into the anguish on his parents' faces the last time they had visited him.

*

It took Rob another week before he started communicating with the motley collection of patients in the ward, and in two weeks, they became as necessary to him as breathing.

In an alcove near the entrance of the ward lay Squadron Leader Tom Gleave. At thirty-two, he was deemed the father of the ward. Gleave had parachuted out of his burning plane and landed on the ground to find his skin draped down his leg from the top of his thigh to above his ankle, like outsize plus fours. His face had swollen by the second and the fire had consumed his nose until he was left with two tiny holes near his eyes. Initially, he felt no pain.

Three beds away from him was Geoffrey Page, a twenty-two-year-old Hurricane pilot with similar injuries to Rob's. Gleave and Page remained cheerful and uncomplaining throughout every gruelling operation and reduced their injuries to 'singes'.

'You ready?' Geoff was standing at the end of Rob's bed. His slim frame covered with a dark blue dressing gown in stark contrast to the angry mottled snakes on his face; he had just had his tenth operation to reconstruct it.

'Yes,' Rob said as he moved off the bed and threw on his dressing gown. He'd seen five operations now and was looking forward to this one. Initially, he'd been horrified, but now he was fascinated by McIndoe's techniques which he explained in great detail to his admiring observers.

McIndoe wanted his patients to observe his operations because his surgical monologues were having a remarkable effect on his patients: the more they became involved in each other's progress, the more their recovery accelerated.

As Rob and Geoff walked into the large white operating theatre, the sun slanted through the enormous window which ran across one wall and part of the ceiling, blinding Rob for a moment. In the centre of the room was the familiar operating table, mounted on two heavy ball-bearing wheels at one end and a rotary ball-bearing castor at the other. The table was so perfectly balanced that it was easily moved by one orderly, although it weighed a quarter of a ton. At the head of the operating table sat the ebullient figure of anaesthetist, John Hunter, nicknamed *Falstaff,* because of his fondness for food and alcohol. He was leaning over Tom Gleave, listening intently to the sounds of his steady breathing. One of the orderlies drew the heavy green curtains across the window and another switched on the intense, white KBB shadowless operating light above the table, throwing the room into brilliant starkness.

'Good-morning, gentlemen.' McIndoe, an incongruous figure in green operating gown and skullcap, white apron and rubber boots, stood by a chromium trolley on which sparkled the sterile scalpels he would use for the operation. Jill Mullins, his theatre sister, stood close by his side, similarly dressed.

'As you know from previous operations, if you cut a piece of skin and put it over a wound, it generally takes so long for nerves and blood vessels to connect with the tissues of the wound that the skin dies. That is why the pedicle graft was invented.' McIndoe looked at the inert form of Tom Gleave lying on the table and pointed as he spoke. 'I intend taking a piece of skin from Tom's forehead here, and then I'll attach one end of the tube of skin to the nasal area here.' He opened his right hand towards Jill Mullins who swiftly gave McIndoe a scalpel without a word being spoken. McIndoe, Mullins and Hunter, a highly efficient and expert trio, were known as 'The Firm of Three'.

Rob watched in fascination at the deftness of the Maestro's surprisingly short, thick fingers in their surgical gloves as he cut a long strip of skin from Tom's forehead and left one end of it still attached. They all waited as the skin slowly curled. Then with fingers as deft as a pianist's, McIndoe rolled the skin into a tube and attached it to where Tom's nose should have been. Rob was now used to seeing tubes of skin that looked like elephant trunks on the men's faces: skin that was left temporarily attached to the original site so the blood flow would help the graft to take. For the first time since watching the operations, Rob felt that there was some hope for him; one day he wouldn't look like a gargoyle.

Back in the ward, someone shouted. 'Remember the Maestro's story about the Italian surgeon, Fiorovanti, who saw a duel and one of the duellists had his nose cut off –'

'– so the surgeon urinated on it and stuck it back on,' someone else shouted back.

'Thank God McIndoe didn't do *that* in the operating theatre.'

'Imagine having to tell old Tom he's covered in piss.'

The laughter reverberated round the room and Rob felt happy for the first time since he'd been burnt.

*

Rob stood behind Hoke's wheelchair on the grassy slopes of the hospital grounds. At the side of them were Czech pilot, Joseph Capka, also in a wheelchair with burns on his legs and Francisek 'Frankie' Truhlar, a small, dark-haired Czech pilot with 311 Squadron. He had asked McIndoe, in broken English, 'New leeps to kees, pleese,' and pointed to his misshapen mouth. 'She terrible – she no use.' Now Frankie was smiling with his new lips, grafted from his right arm.

Rob, Harry, Frankie and Joe were about to start their weekly race around the hospital grounds.

'Off!' Rob shouted, careering across the grass with Hoke hanging onto the sides of the wheelchair. The Czechs stood at the starting line, astounded by English duplicity.

'Not very British, old bean,' Hoke said, vainly trying to imitate a public school accent.

'Oh, bugger being British.' Rob ignored the pain in his hands as he pushed the chair, determined to hold on to their lead. 'This is war.'

'Ty svindle zasranej!' screamed Frankie, racing after them.

'Goddammit, Rob – he's gaining!' Hoke shouted.

Frankie blinked his new eyelids rapidly as he tore past them, hurling Jo's wheelchair near one of the brown wooden wards. 'Ty hajzle jeden!' Jo shouted.

The Czechs were determined to show their superior speed, whether in the air or on the ground.

Wobbling wildly around the corner, Frankie almost collided with the ample proportions of the Matron who stood in his path. He veered off into the flowerbeds, propelling Jo into a blanket of bright red dahlias.

'Krucifix… ah … Matron,' Frankie said, smiling sheepishly into the granite-face of Matron Hall as she looked at the damage Jo's backside had done to her prize flowers.

*

Rob and the others listened outside the open window of Archie McIndoe's office as Matron harangued him.

'Mr McIndoe – I've turned a blind eye to the barrels of beer on the grand piano in the ward. I've turned a blind eye when my nurses have reported seeing patients climb through the windows at five o'clock in the morning after a night on the town. I've even turned a blind eye when one of my nurses found a mannequin in bed with one of the men … but I will *not,* I repeat, *not* turn a blind eye to wheelchair races which ruin my dahlias. *They must stop!*'

The men suppressed laughter as Rob peered through the window and saw the veins on Matron's neck standing out in supportive indignation.

Archie McIndoe was pinned behind his desk by her anger.

'They will, Matron. Don't you worry.' McIndoe nodded sympathetically.

The men knew that the only person who could intimidate McIndoe was Matron.

'In fact, I can guarantee it, Matron,' McIndoe said, hastily. 'I've got far more important work for them to do.'

A week later they all found out what it was. They discovered that the Maestro had had a directive from the Air Ministry in London informing him that his patients were not wearing the stiff, uncomfortable hospital blue 'uniforms' that the Government, in all its wisdom, had decreed they must do. This unfortunate oversight on McIndoe's part must be rectified. McIndoe had angrily told them that the Air Ministry had obviously never seen a pilot with crippled fingers try to do up the stiff fly-buttons or the boys with pedicles trying to get a jacket on! '*Bloody bureaucrats*!' he'd shouted. They had all cheered.

'This is what I want you to do,' he'd told them when they had stopped cheering.

All the patients who could walk were to collect hospital blue uniforms and with McIndoe's blessing and Matron Hall's tolerance they were to make a bonfire of them with the proviso that they mustn't attract the attention of the Luftwaffe. Rob hadn't enjoyed himself so much for years. It was like a mini-bonfire night when he was a boy.

However, smoke signals somehow reached the attention of the Air Ministry. One week later, an Air Ministry Officer with a posse of Air Force Police in tow descended on the hospital. They were dumbfounded by the scenes they saw: badly burnt men, some using crutches, some completely bandaged from head to foot, some being pushed in wheelchairs, were wearing sports clothes and streaming out of the hospital wards in large numbers. The policemen, all belted and gaitered, wearing high Germanesque peaked caps, stood in a line of astonishment.

Rob, pushing Hoke's wheelchair, walked nonchalantly past them wearing a pair of white flannel trousers and a white sweater from which his clawed fingers protruded.

'*Oi!*' shouted one of the policemen 'Where d'you think you're going?'

'Me?' queried Rob in mock amazement. '*I'm* going to play cricket, old man. And Hoke's going swimming, aren't you, Hoke?'

Hoke, with a face like an undertaker who's in danger of losing a body, showed the policeman two green fish on the blue towelling robe he was wearing.

'Show him your swimming trunks, Hoke.' The American burrowed for some time under the tartan rug that covered his stumps, before bringing out an enormous pair of black swimming trunks that had been knitted in 1880. He looked solemnly into the policeman's face. 'Do *you* like swimming too, officer?' The man didn't answer.

'What are *you* on for, Tom?' Rob shouted to the Squadron Leader who was staggering about on crutches, looking startlingly macabre with a pedicle hanging down from his forehead to his new 'nose'.

'Squash, old sport. Booked a court for 1100 hours. Must dash.' He wobbled past the service policemen, whistling *Rule Britannia* very loudly.

'Well, lovely to talk to you fellows,' Rob retorted as he walked on. 'But as Tom said – must dash. Got to keep fit – *tempus fugit* and all that. Bye.' The injured men, dressed for cricket, squash or swimming, streamed past the policemen who stood, motionless with shock.

They had come face to face with McIndoe's native cunning; he had discovered a directive in the corner of one of his files. All service personnel, whatever rank, must dress in sports clothes when going to participate in sport. By order of the Air Ministry Authority.

The service-police never returned.

Chapter 6

It was a brilliant March morning as Colin drove through the tapestry of Sussex scenery. He was pleased with his new red MG sports car, bought for twenty pounds - a fortune, but money didn't have much meaning for him now. He was singing loud enough to frighten the birds. Bridget joined in enthusiastically. Kate, sitting squashed in the back seat, saw the glow on her brother's face as he sang, constantly glancing at Bridget. He'd fallen in love and she should be so happy, but all she felt was fear: fear of meeting Rob again, the man she was supposed to love. She stared at the snow coating giant cedar trees at the side of the road. She'd always found March a mercurial month: leaning Janus-like towards the snow-laden branches of winter and the hope of spring-yellow primroses. This March she felt only winter.

Bridget and Colin finished the last verse of *When Irish Eyes Are Smiling* as Colin swept up the curve of the hospital drive and parked conspicuously in front of the main entrance of the rectangular hospital.

'Well, here we are then,' Colin said, as they all got out of the car. 'Kate?' His sister was staring into the distance at the snow, her face reflecting its colour. 'You all right?'

'Fine,' she said quickly, folding her handbag over and over in her hands.

'Rob's ward is at the back of the hospital. Follow me.' Colin marched off along the path that Rob's mother and Charlie had trod every week for nearly nine months, the shield of a reedy whistle escaping his lips.

Bridget put her arm through Kate's. 'I'll be all right. Charlie said Rob was much better now, didn't he?'

Charlie had told Kate she wouldn't recognise Rob any more. When she'd shuddered, Charlie realised what he'd said. *'No, I mean he looks better.'* He told her about the wheelchair races and Kate had laughed. As she walked along the path with Bridget she tried to block out the memory of her last visit to see Rob in a hospital: his grotesque features filling up the room. She swallowed the bile that flowed into her mouth.

'I'll stay here, Kate,' Bridget said. They had arrived at the door of Ward Three where Colin was waiting, too tense now to whistle. 'Remember what Charlie said. Rob laughs now.' Kate gave Bridget a small smile.

'You can wait with Bridget if you'd prefer,' Colin told his sister. Kate shook her head. There was a slight tremor in Colin's hand as he opened the door. He wanted to remember Rob as he was: a man with a face women wanted to touch. They tried not to react as the clammy heat and smell crawled into their nostrils.

'You sure about this, Kate?'

'Yes.'

At the end of the long rectangular room a young man with bandages over most of his face was sitting at a grand piano pumping out a tune that was better suited to the four-ale bar in the town. A crowd of young men, in various stages of surgical repair, were drinking beer from the barrel on top of the piano and singing to the tune of *The Bells of St Mary*.

'The balls of t'Squadron Leader are wrinkled and crinkled. Capacious and spacious as the dome of St Paul's. They crowd, they do muster, to gaze at the cluster, they stop and they stare at that glorious pair of the Squadron Leader's Balls, Balls, Balls –'

One of the young men turned to see Kate and shouted. 'Lady present, chaps!'

The singing smouldered to a mere hiss of 'balls' as they all twisted to stare at Kate. In front of her were the jawless, the noseless, the ones with holes in their heads through which the bones obtruded, the pedicled, the bandaged and the one lying in bed covered by a network of large mesh soaked in Vaseline and antiseptics to prevent it from adhering to the scorched remains of a man. A nurse suddenly appeared from nowhere, pulled back his bedclothes and watered the navigator's shrivelled flesh with rainwater from a watering can. It had a rose on the end.

Suddenly, the surge of familiar chords from the piano. The sound of men singing in celebration. *'Mary, Mary, quite contrary, how does your garden grow?'*

Kate's tears fell down onto the front of her new blue dress.

*

'We've formed a club, Col – the Guinea Pig Club. One of the chaps said we're all guinea pigs here for the Maestro's ghastly experiments and it stuck. We've got an honorary secretary who can't write because of burnt fingers and an honorary treasurer who can't walk because of burnt legs. So no minutes to read and plenty of money to spend as the treasurer can't run off with it.'

Colin and Kate laughed on cue.

'The Maestro, that's Archie McIndoe, is our President and old Tom Gleave over there is our Vice President.'

Rob was effervescing with excitement. Stories about the ward and the men poured from him. Just like the old days, Colin thought as he listened to him. Then held himself rigid as Rob tried to smile. He'd become a caricature of himself. The lopsided smile which had attracted people in the past was now a grimace, and the network of red scars criss-crossing his face reminded Colin of a train junction after a crash. Only his dark brown eyes were untouched. He concentrated on Mrs Adams' account of Rob's deep depressions; depressions that bordered on psychosis, but each gruelling operation brought him a little closer to normality. Whatever that was in wartime. 'Without Charlie...' she'd said, not wanting to finish the sentence.

'So America's come in to help us, then?' Rob said.

'Yes.' Colin sounded mournful. 'You ought to see the Mess dances now. The girls make a beeline for the GIs. All they want are stockings, chocolate and chewing gum. No time for us British lads at all.'

'Rubbish,' Kate said. 'Try saying that to Bridget, Colin Brazier.'

'*Phew* – wouldn't dare, not without reinforcements.' He raised his eyes skyward as if God was going to provide them.

'Who's Bridget?' Rob asked quietly.

'Kate's WAAF friend. Smiling Irish eyes and a mane of copper hair.'

'He's smitten, Rob. He even brought her with us today.'

Rob stared around the ward before speaking. 'Oh, yes? Where is she, then? Why didn't she come in? Other people's friends do.'

They sat in silence as his questions wafted round them like insidious nerve gas. There was a welcome flare of argument on the other side of the ward.

'Always this noisy?'

'Yes,' Rob said, brusquely. 'I like it.'

'Ah.'

A longer silence as they studied the floor. Then Kate jumped up, clearing her throat. 'I'll just go outside to see Bridget for a moment, Rob ... let you and Colin talk about old times. You know. Back soon.' They watched her rapid retreat, her wedge heels sparking off the stone floor.

Old times? Colin thought. Their time in school? Their holidays? Their life in the squadron? The last time he'd mentioned the RAF to Rob he'd seemed angry, rather than interested. Could he chance it?

But before Colin could introduce the subject, Rob said, 'Remember that mission with Sandy when he led us through those Messerschmitts before they attacked London, Col? The enemy between 12,000 and 30,000 ft. Us climbing astern of the bomber formation and engaging the fighter escorts.'

'Hundreds of Me 109s flashing about.' At last, Colin thought, common ground.

'Brought down twenty, didn't we?' Rob said, excitedly. 'You, me and Sandy.'

'And only one of our kites got pranged.'

'Then the rest of the 109s opened their throttles wide and were on the run. Remember?'

'Thin black smoke trailing from their exhausts.'

'Tails between their legs.'

They laughed, but Colin knew he'd have to tell him. 'Sandy' Lane was their brilliant Number One who had led them on many missions; his rapid-fire reflexes, innovative flying formations and easy manner had made him a well-respected and well-liked leader. Just one mission too many.

'Sandy's dead, Rob.'

Rob's hands contracted with pain. 'Christ.' He spread out his hands on the bed and did the finger exercises the physiotherapist had taught him. After twenty he spoke again. 'And the others?'

'Potter's been missing for a month. We've just discovered he's a POW. The rest are fine. Send their regards and told me to tell you they'll descend on the ward in force the next leave they have.'

Rob stopped his finger exercises. 'Tell them to look after *Sirius* for me.' They had painted the word *Sirius* on the side of Rob's plane whilst he was convalescing after parachuting down into a forest full of oaks. Colin hadn't told Rob that an eighteen-year-old pilot with only twenty hours' experience was flying his beloved Spitfire now.

'Listen, Rob –'

'I'm coming back.'

'What?'

'I'm coming back to the squadron. I'm going to fly again.'

Colin looked at Rob's clawed hands; hands that had difficulty in letting go of a cup. Rob followed his gaze.

'I'm having another op on them next week. It's Dupuytren's Contracture, that's all. It draws the fingers together. Lots of the pilots have it, but the Maestro's perfected a new technique. He cuts the lesions adhering to the tendons here, you see and –'

'Stop.' Colin had always hated anything that entailed cutting into a body, dead or alive. Rob had even had to cut a sheep's eye in Biology for him when they were at the Grammar School together.

'Still squeamish?'

'No, I just don't like to talk about blood –'

'Or bone or burnt flesh or scars.' Rob looked closely at his old friend. 'Tell me honestly, Col. What do I look like?'

'Honestly?'

'Honestly.'

Colin studied him for some time before saying. 'Bloody awful. But not as awful as the last time I saw you.'

77

'I knew you'd tell me the truth, but I'm getting better. Each op I have, I can see an improvement.'

'How many have you had?'

'Nine.'

'*Jesus*. You're braver than me. I couldn't face one.'

'You could if you'd looked like me.'

Colin sat back in the chair and closed his eyes, exhausted by all the emotions flooding his body.

'You're tired,' Rob said.

'Bone-tired. In fact I don't know which is more tired – me or my bones.' He opened his eyes to look at Rob. 'You've heard of the raids over Germany?'

Rob nodded.

'Night flying over Essen last week. The Krupps works. My God, I hate night flying. Visibility's lousy getting off the deck. Terrifies me. Wouldn't tell anyone but you.'

'I love night flying. Wish I'd been there.'

'*I* wish you'd been there. I wouldn't have had to go then.'

Rob smiled and Colin wanted to weep at the twisted wreckage the fire had left on his friend's face.

'Hear we've got new bombers,' Rob said.

'You ought to see them. Bloody great lumbering things with four engines. A nightmare to protect. Carry 4,000 lb bombs.'

'You're not serious?'

'I am. Things have moved fast since you left the RAF.'

'I haven't,' Rob said.

Colin didn't answer.

'Well?'

'Well what?'

'What are your objections?'

'I haven't said a word,' Colin protested.

Rob stared at him.

'Oh come on, Rob. Be realistic. You know how fast you have to be in a Spit. Lightning reactions and all that.'

'Don't tell me what I already know.'

'Well, then.'

'Well then, what? My reflexes weren't burnt, Colin. Just my fingers. They need good pilots more than ever since the Baedeker raids started. Exeter. Bath's all rubble. What city will be next? Oxford? York? People and architecture are disappearing daily.'

'Rob, you need terrific flexibility to fly a Spit. I was flying all over the shoot when I had to protect the bombers over Le Havre two nights ago.'

'Don't tell me about fucking flying tactics!' Rob was shouting. 'I've flown hundreds of missions. Successful ones. *I know how to fly!*' Startled faces turned towards the anger in Rob's voice.

'Sorry … I didn't mean …' Colin breathed deeply, knowing Rob wouldn't like what he was going to say. 'You're a good pilot and I'm sure you're getting better. But you've done your bit for King and country, haven't you? There *are* other ways of helping the war effort apart from flying.'

'Such as?' Rob's twisted lips flecked with spittle.

One summer's morning in 1940 they had met an old school friend on a train travelling to the West Country. Colin recalled Rob's contempt when the man had told them in a whisper about his office job in a small village, away from the war.

'Well, there's always a great demand for people who know about flying –'

'Yes, they're called pilots.'

'– in control rooms.' Colin was determined to remain calm. 'You could advise the bigwigs on planning missions – that sort of thing.'

'You mean sit in an office all day talking to elderly men who haven't a clue about flying or flying tactics and listen to them prattle about things completely outside their knowledge or understanding.'

'Well, that's why you'd be useful, wouldn't you – you stroppy bastard!' Colin shouted. 'Why do you always have to be so bloody arrogant?'

Suddenly, all other conversation in the ward ceased.

'Because I want to fly!'

'But what if you *can't*, Rob?'

'Christ! You always were a defeatist moron in school, weren't you?' Rob got up and started pacing round his bed. 'You haven't changed at all. Remember who couldn't pack his satchel properly? Remember the boy who always had *me* fighting his battles for him? Remember who couldn't cross the road *without me* going first? So don't bloody tell me what I can or cannot do!' Rob's voice rang around the ward. 'Look, do me a favour – piss off!'

Colin got up from the chair and pushed through the patients who found something fascinating to look at on the ceiling of the ward.

The sky was darkening; wind was scattering snow from the branches of a sycamore, dandruffing Colin's shoulders as he leaned against it, shaking. He lit a cigarette and watched the smoke swirl up in the air. He didn't notice Bridget and Kate walking over the grass towards him.

'How's Rob?' Kate said, worried by the expression on Colin's face.

'Rob …' Colin inhaled deeply '… is bloody.'

'Oh, no,' Kate whispered, 'you haven't had a row, have you?'

'Well, I don't know what you'd call it.' Colin's anger eased a little when he saw his sister's fear. 'It was just a disagreement about flying, that's all. Go on in, he'll be fine with you. Just don't mention the RAF, will you?'

'So, you're enjoying yourself here on the ward then?' Kate inwardly groaned at the stupidity of her question.

Rob was the only man in the room who wasn't staring at Kate's legs as she sat down. His face frightened her. What was he thinking about?

'Did you know I'm in charge of a balloon unit in Cardiff now? Quite good, really. Lots to do.'

Rob stared at the sheets on his bed as if they were about to reveal something important.

'The food's good in the restaurants. The authorities don't seem to bother about the five shillings restriction in Tiger Bay … that's the dock area of Cardiff. '

'Oh, *really*?'

'Sorry.'

His gaze shifted to the other end of the ward as if longing to be free of her. Something to make him laugh. The night of the French letters. She waited for his reaction after she'd finished the story.

'That's supposed to be funny, is it?' He was almost snarling. 'Are you such an experienced woman now that men's private parts are passé?'

'No, of course not. In fact, I didn't know what they were until …'

'Yes?'

'Until someone told me.'

'Who? A man?'

'Yes.'

Kate watched him vigorously exercising his fingers.

'Who?'

'Just someone I met in Cardiff.'

'Just someone?'

'*Yes!*' Again all conversation around them anchored. 'Why the inquisition, Rob? We haven't seen each other for nine months. You don't own me.'

'Who does?' Rob asked in a murderously quiet voice. 'Someone with a handsome face? Someone who can satisfy your needs? Remember that night in the boarding house? You couldn't wait to get into bed with me, could you? I was told once that a woman can only stay faithful if her lusts are satisfied every night. Who's satisfying yours? Someone with no scars?'

Kate was rigid with shock. It took her some time to speak. 'You've no idea what love is, have you? I loved *you* once. Not your face. Not your hands. *You.*' She swayed as she stood up, then turned to face him. 'You know what you make me feel like? A piece of grass you stamp on. You know something else? Once upon a time I would have exchanged the gift of sight for you. I won't come back.' She walked down the ward, followed by the covert glances of injured men.

Rob felt as if someone was pulling out his entrails through his nostrils.

Chapter 7

'German anti-personnel bombs, boys.' Mr Smedley, Charlie's new teacher creaked up and down the classroom in his new, polished, brown shoes. Everything about Mr Smedley was brown, Charlie thought: his suit, his tie, his socks, even his voice. He sounded as if he swallowed soft-centred chocolates every morning before school. His age had been determined from two physical oddities: large pendulous bags under his eyes which reminded Charlie of the toads that lived in the Anderson shelter in his garden, and a spectacular stoop which had developed in his first year of teaching. *'Having to bend down to the level of illiterates is not conductive to good posture, boys,'* was the first of Mr Smedley's many baffling sentences. The boys had decided he was eighty-five. In fact, he was only forty-eight and lived with his mother in a house full of silent birds.

'And what do these bombs look like, umm?' Mr Smedley creaked to the blackboard to draw numerous pictures of all the objects the bombs might resemble: sardine-tins, cigarette packets, bottles, canisters, bars of chocolate. The boys helped him by shouting out suggestions. 'Hitler's moustache, Sir? ... Mrs Humphries' dog, Sir? ... the Headmaster's cane, Sir?... Mr Smedley ignored them all until Ian shouted out: 'What about birds, Sir?' Mr Smedley stopped chalking to look at Ian, a snotty little boy.

The classroom was bleak: a Victorian relic with endlessly high ceilings, small windows and the subsequent problems with heating and lighting. It was October and the boys could feel an icy slice of approaching winter slide under the door as they waited for Mr Smedley's response. The classroom's one redeeming feature was a gilded cage in which two green finches with red speckles on their wings sat listening to their master for hours. They whistled only when Mr Smedley told them they might. He worshipped them.

'Birds?' glowered Mr Smedley, smothering Ian with his stare. 'Don't be ridiculous, boy. How can a bomb resemble a bird?'

'Don't know, Sir. A pilot could cover it in feathers or something, couldn't he?' The classroom filled with laughter.

'Ian Walters.'

'Yes, Sir?'

'You are perhaps the biggest ignoramus I have *ever* had the misfortune to teach.'

Ian's face flushed. 'Thank you very much, Sir.' He puffed out his chest like a pigeon and looked around the class.

It was at that moment Mr Smedley decided to ignore Ian Walters for the rest of the term.

'The Germans,' Mr Smedley hissed in sonorous tones that instilled more fear than the Luftwaffe could ever do, 'are trying to win the war by foul means, boys.'

The boys shrivelled.

'They have failed to win the Battle of Britain; they have failed to knock out London by night bombing, so what do they do? Resort to anti-personnel bombs! *Anti-personnel bombs, boys.* That is not how war should be conducted! War should be honourable. There is the Geneva Convention to be followed. Now, boys, I want you to listen carefully. *This is important.*' Mr Smedley creaked carefully around the classroom, savouring each word. 'I don't want you to pick up anything you see lying about on the ground.' He paused to create the maximum amount of drama. He had always wanted to be an actor as a young man, but Mother knew best. 'It could be a disguised bomb. Don't touch it and don't kick it. It might explode and blow off your legs.'

The boys gasped. It was very, very gratifying.

*

It was the afternoon of their bicycle ride to the Fairlight Cliffs, a mile outside Hastings. The boys only had lessons in the mornings, in the afternoons they were kings of the countryside, no matter how cold it was. They wheeled their bikes with their heavily masked front lamps onto a grassy slope which ended in a precipice, falling headlong to the sea. Ahead of them was the crater of a recent bomb which the Luftwaffe had jettisoned before flying over the Channel. Mr Smedley's words were fresh in their ears.

In the distance a man was throwing a tennis ball at a black Alsatian. The ball came to rest at the foot of a crater. They watched in horror as the dog came bounding towards them, scattering a couple of baked-bean tins and a cigarette packet with its feet. It skidded to a halt before the rigid boys, gulped the tennis ball in its salivating mouth and raced back towards its master.

'Hey – you ought to keep him on a lead – we could have been killed!' Charlie yelled.

The man lifted up his right hand and gave a two-fingered signal with the back of his hand facing him.

'What's he making a victory sign like that for?' Ian asked, wiping the snot off his nose with his cuff.

'Nutter!' they shouted, when the man was out of earshot.

'It's not much fun any more, is it?' Tubs muttered. 'Like living in a minefield. Can't touch nothing.'

'Well, what do soldiers do when faced with a minefield?' Charlie said.

'Run?' Tubs asked, hopefully.

'No – they clear it – systematically.'

'You don't expect us to clear the cliffs?' Tubs and Ian looked at him as if he'd asked them to climb Mount Everest.

'No – not all of them – just the area over there.' Charlie pointed to a large section of the cliff path.

'How?'

'You got an air-gun last Christmas, didn't you, Tubs?' Tubs nodded. 'Then listen.'

The boys looked at Charlie with growing enthusiasm as he told them the plan.

It was another week before they could cycle up to Fairlight again. Charlie had brought Uncle John's binoculars, Tubs, his air-gun and Ian, a note pad. First they drew up a list of all objects they would have to deal with: old tins, cigarette packets, bundles of shining white material which came from land-mine parachutes, shrapnel and the deceptively innocent looking bits of rubber which were littered all over the cliffs. They were the worst, Charlie told them. You never knew what Germans put in rubber. After writing out their list, they looked for suitable hiding-places some distance away from the objects.

The rest of the afternoon made Charlie almost delirious with happiness. As leader, obviously he'd have the air-gun, he'd told Tubs. Naturally, Tubs had agreed. Charlie lay on the grass behind a gorse bush, his sights set on a particularly nasty piece of black rubber and fired. Tubs quickly rested the binoculars on his knees to see if he'd scored. He jumped up in excitement.

'A hit, Charlie!'

Ian, from the safety of a nearby elder tree, ticked off one potential deadly bomb from their list. As the afternoon wore on, his ticks became more and more frequent until he rebelled.

'I'm fed up with ticking, Charlie. When's it my turn with the gun?'

'Hey!' Tubs objected. 'Whose gun is it, anyway?'

Tubs, after half an hour, hadn't hit one of the targets, so Ian was allowed to shoot. He managed to hit a piece of newspaper floating along in the freshening wind.

'Brilliant,' Charlie said. 'How are the Germans going to plant bombs in newspapers?'

'That might be their most cunning plan yet.' Ian nodded in agreement with himself.

Tubs and Charlie shook their heads in silence. Then Tubs said, 'Let Charlie take over. It'll be dark soon.'

Charlie discovered that he was a natural saboteur. He managed to puncture every object in the section they had marked out. It was dusk when it was finally cleared. Charlie fired a triumphant salvo of air-gun pellets into the darkening sky before the boys raced like Apaches up and down the slopes they had cleared, yelling war-cries. They had liberated part of Britain. They finally collapsed from exhaustion and lay on the grey grass, staring up at the storm clouds above their heads.

'We'll tackle the other sections of the cliffs next week,' Charlie announced.

'*What*?' Tubs and Ian shouted, suddenly realising that liberation entailed a great deal more effort than they had anticipated.

*

One moment the road along which Charlie was pedalling was dark, the next, it was illuminated by hundreds of sizzling, blueish-white flames making gentle plopping sounds as they landed on the pavements and roads. Incendiary bombs. Charlie zig-zagged expertly around them. Soon the roads were full of people manning stirrup pumps, desperate to stop the incendiaries igniting their homes. A fire engine clanged up towards Pevensey Road and Charlie pedalled after it. This was turning out to be an incredible day. He skidded to an abrupt halt when he saw the fire engine stop outside the burning ruin of Mrs Bates' home. Firemen, dragging hoses, poured out of it and water cascaded over the now blazing bombs. The house next door was already a cloud of rubble and broken pipes.

A man was standing in front of the collapsed frontage of Mrs Bates' house, listening intently. Charlie ran over to him.

'Where is she?'

Sidney Oak saw a boy with tousled hair and enormous, terrified eyes staring at him.

'Go home, lad – this is no place for you.'

'*It is* – Mrs Bates lives here. Where is she?'

Sidney Oak was the leader of one of the Civil Defence rescue parties. Since he'd been on duty for six hours, he was tired and his uniform was stiff with dirt. All he wanted was to go home and have a bath, even in five inches of water.

'I don't know, lad. Now go home and leave us to do our work.'

'I'm not leaving until you've found Mrs Bates … *Mrs Bates! Mrs Bates*!' Charlie screamed, tearing at the rubble.

'Stop that!' Sidney shouted, holding Charlie's arm. 'There might be an unexploded bomb!' He turned to one of the rescue party. 'How long before the bomb disposal boys are here, Alf?'

'Half an hour, they said – busy night.'

Charlie became rigid, watching the last incendiary flame, smoulder and die. The firemen climbed wearily into their fire engine and sped off towards the next blaze.

'Sorry. Didn't think,' Charlie said.

'Be quiet.' Sidney Oak was listening. They all listened. 'Down there… I think I can hear something.'

Charlie stopped breathing. A curious sound which no one could identity was heard in the rubble. Charlie pressed his ear to the ground.

'What the hell's that, Sid?'

'Blowed if I know.'

Charlie shouted. 'It's Percy. Good old Percy.' He suddenly couldn't stop laughing.

Mr Oak held Charlie's shoulders tight. 'Calm down. Who's Percy, lad?'

'Mrs Bates' parrot.' Surely everyone knew Percy? 'Mrs Bates will be with him. Come on, let's start digging.'

'Look, lad. I've told you before. Go home.'

'And I've told you I'm not. Percy'll listen to me. I can help.'

Sidney Oak looked into Charlie's resolute eyes. 'All right, but don't get in our way.'

'*Percy*,' Charlie shouted. 'It's me – Charlie. Who's coming then? Who's coming, Percy?'

They all waited for a response. There wasn't any. Then a muffled squawk from beneath the rubble.

'Right. We dig here,' Mr Oak told the men.

Ten minutes later they had dug a small tunnel in the direction of Percy's intermittent squawks. Then Sidney Oak, covered with a sheet as his only protection from falling debris and dirt, crawled towards the sound of a woman's groans. The squawking had stopped. The other members of the team carefully cut their way through floorboards and joists.

Eventually, Sidney Oak discovered old Mrs Bates lying in a coffin of wood and stone in the cellar of her house. She was semi-conscious and covered with rubble and dust. The timbers around them groaned repeatedly as he gave the old woman water and tablets to ease her pain. Her leg was lying at an odd angle and the smell was getting worse.

He shouted down the tunnel. 'Hurry up – a gas pipe's fractured down here and …' The effects of the poisonous fumes were making it difficult to think. He shook his head. Near one of his feet lay a yellow pear with eight metal fins. Why were these important?

Half an hour later, Charlie was looking down into the crumpled, dust-covered features of old Mrs Bates as she lay on a stretcher after being rescued by Sidney Oak and his team. She had broken one leg, but the oxygen she'd been given had helped her recover from the effects of the gas. Percy hadn't. He lay like a board on the bottom of his cage. Tears poured down Charlie's face.

'I'm all right, Charlie. Don't cry, son.' Mrs Bates' eyes briefly opened.

'I'm crying for Percy, Mrs B. He's dead.'

'Poor old Percy. Saved my life, didn't he? Good job Fred was away. Ruined his roses. Best go home, son.'

Mrs Bates' eyes closed as they moved her stretcher into an ambulance. Charlie was left crying in the ruins of her house. In the darkness beneath him, lay an unexploded butterfly bomb.

Chapter 8

'Good Lord – *of course*, I remember the first time I was shot
down, old boy.' Twenty-five-year-old F.O. Harris, a veteran of
forty missions, was 'entertaining' a new pilot-officer who had
never flown in combat; had never used a razor. Harris was
sprawled in a chair in the Mess drinking whisky. 'Got me this
Me109 nicely lined up in the gun-sight. Gave the Spit full boost.
Accelerating at about 350 mph but still out of range of von
bloody Hun, so had to wait a few seconds. Suddenly von bloody
Hun dives at me – hell of a bang – Spit flicks into a spin – deuce
of a job getting out of it – then find my starboard engine's on
fire. No R/T. Impossible to inform Duty Pilot on ground. Bit
tricky, I can tell you ...'

At that moment Rob walked into the Mess. The men who'd
been playing cards and billiards froze in a variety of Caravaggio
tableaux as they took in their first sight of the much heralded
burnt pilot. The C.O. Squadron Leader Denham left his card
game to greet him, a stiff smile pasted onto his face. The hair
protruding from his nose and ears, made him look as potent as a
goat.

'You must be F.O. Adams. Welcome.' He saluted smartly.
Rob saluted back. The C.O.'s eyes traced the arc of Rob's
fingers.

'Come into my office. I'd like a word.' Denham marched off, his footsteps echoing round the silent room. Rob followed him, aware of the leech of eyes fastened to his face.

'Close the door and sit down.' The C.O. sat in a small, grim room which contained an inactive oil stove, a heavily burdened desk, an overactive telephone, and two chairs, leaning at angles which would have interested Picasso.

Through a window, Rob glimpsed a square of runway. He sat and waited, building a barricade behind which he could hide.

Fatigue had smudged charcoal over the C.O.'s face. He rubbed his hands over his eyes. 'I'm not going to beat about the bush, Adams. I asked for two replacements, preferably experienced; one is eighteen, the other –'

'is *very* experienced, Sir.'

'I've read the reports, but how the hell are you going to be able to fly a Spitfire with those … hands.'

Rob slowly opened his fingers and placed his hands carefully on the desk. Almost flat. 'My hands are fine, Sir.'

The C.O. was aware of the effort in Rob's demonstration. 'They look inoperable to me. How are you going to shoot down a Messerschmitt?'

'I'll manage, Sir.'

'Will you? Will you, indeed?' Denham drummed his fingers on the desk.

Rob moved his hands onto the arms of his chair and stared intently at a smear of congealed blood on the C.O.'s chin where he'd cut himself shaving.

'Yes, Sir.'

The C.O. shot forward in his seat. 'Look here, I've been *persuaded* to have you in the Squadron. I can't say I'm happy about it. Only way to prove you're capable of flying a Spit is to test you. Are you prepared for that?'

'*Test me?*' Rob jumped up from the chair, his heart thumping erratically. 'You're going to *test* me! Christ, I've flown hundreds of missions. How many have *you* flown? How many has that schoolboy in the Mess flown – the one listening to that self-opinionated prat?'

'That "self-opinionated prat" happens to be one of our best pilots.'

'Not any more,' Rob said, looking steadily at the man sitting in the chair.

'Really?' There was a long silence. 'Well, you can prove it tomorrow morning. You'll fly as my number two and you'll stick to me as if we're joined at the hip. 700 hours. Just hope you're up to it.'

Rob had a sudden violent image of himself kicking Denham hard in the bollocks.

*

He throttles back over the airfield, tries to lower the flaps. No response. He'd have to go for a belly-land. Christ! He lines up with the runway. Sparks from the concrete! He goes around again and lines up parallel with the runway this time, ready to

belly-land on the grass. Craters. Bomb craters everywhere. One
hand moves in slow motion towards the throttle. Speed down to
just over 100 mph on the approach. The airscrew into fine pitch,
better for belly-landing. 50 feet. Sirius shudders as it hits the
grass. The engine crashes to a halt as one blade of the prop
buries itself in the ground; the deceleration smashes his body
forward; the straps crushes the breath out of his chest. Clouds of
dust. Then the flicker of a flame inside the cockpit. The fight with
the straps. The jamming of the cockpit cover.

As usual Rob's bedclothes were drenched in sweat. He
glanced at his clock. Only two hours' sleep. Four more hours to
kill. In the darkness he practised his finger exercises and
visualised the cockpit instruments of the Spitfire until it was
time to fly.

It was a cold morning when he waddled towards his plane,
his breath curling in the air. It was his first flight since he'd been
burnt and he'd forgotten how heavy the flying gear was; how
thin he'd become; there seemed to be yards of waste material in
his flying suit. He climbed into the cockpit, aware that Denham
was standing by his plane a short distance away, watching him.

'Morning, Adams.'

'Morning, Sir.'

'All right. Let's get going.' The C.O. climbed swiftly into
his Spitfire V. Seconds later, he was calling across to Rob.
'Don't forget – stick to me like glue … *Contact!*' he shouted to
an *erk* before slamming his Plexiglas canopy shut. He was
speeding down the runway before Rob had had time to test the
magnetos.

Every nightmare Rob had ever had came back to him as he accelerated down the runway after Denham, with his canopy wide open. No time to make the necessary checks. His hands were clenched on the stick, his back slammed against the contoured seat by his accelerating speed.

Denham was flying fast towards the refuge of cumulus. Rob knew he was trying to lose him in the cloud. These were the most difficult and dangerous conditions to fly in as number two. If he misjudged the distance between them he could either crash into Denham or lose him completely. It was a tactic which Rob had seen employed hundreds of times before by Messerschmitt pilots, but by now he would have been firing his cannon into their fuselage. Rob's thumb instinctively touched the firing button, resisting the violent urge to press it as Denham shot through his gun sights. The sweat dripped into his eyes as he tried to concentrate on anticipating the C.O.'s every manoeuvre. Suddenly, Denham disappeared into dense cloud. The pain in Rob's fingers was becoming difficult to ignore. Grey opacity engulfed him. He was forced to fly on his instruments and looked at the altimeter reading. Rob had discovered that the Luftwaffe, when flying through cloud, invariably changed altitude in an effort to throw off British fighters. Rob anticipated that Denham would do the unexpected. He concentrated on maintaining the same altitude. Immediately he was out of the cloud, he saw Denham directly ahead of him.

'*Got you!*' Rob shouted into the freezing air.

Denham was weaving erratically in front of him. Rob paralleled his every move, but the pain in his fingers was punitive. Denham made a signal for him to fly in close formation. In that instant 'Butch' Morton's words came flooding back. Butch had the reputation for flying so close to planes in formation that pilots felt he was breathing down their necks.

'How do you do it?' Rob had asked him. Pilots had to spend hours exerting continual sideways pressure on the stick to counteract the 'tip' from the vortex round the leader's wings which tended to push the wing-tips of the Spitfire upwards. The strain on the hands was monumental.

'There's no strain if you push your wings in behind the leader's,' Butch had told him. 'It catches the downward flow of air nearer the wing root. No pressure, then. Clever stuff, eh?'

Rob accelerated until the tip of his wing fitted into the curve of Denham's wing-root. Immediately the pain in his hands disappeared. There was no pressure on the stick. Rob could feel the adrenaline surge through his body as he imagined the look on Denham's face.

Ten minutes later, Rob disengaged from Denham's wing root to fly starboard. The C.O. waggled his wings. Through the Plexiglas canopy he saw Denham smiling. He turned to Rob and gave him the thumbs up sign before heading back to base.

'*I've done it!*' Rob shouted, his Spitfire carving a large circle in the sky.

Rob was flying cross-wind in preparation for landing; he 'blipped' the throttle and found the propeller wind-milling. The engine was dead. The mechanic who was detailed to fill the petrol tank had been suddenly taken ill. The plane had half the petrol it should have had. In the flurry of his take-off Rob hadn't checked the petrol gauge. His hands locked onto the stick as he surveyed the landscape. Near the end of the runway were a number of hedges. He knew he'd have to overshoot, rather than undershoot. Hitting the last hedge after landing would be better than hitting the nearest one at full flying speed. But Rob was tired. His hands were stiff. He found he was crossing the first hedge at fifty feet and slammed the Spit into a side-slip, trying to pull out a last moment. His hands wouldn't respond quickly enough. At ten feet he was half way across the field, travelling too fast to land. In the distance the electrified Southern Railway line hurtled towards him. He attempted 'fish-tailing' to work off some speed but his hands would hardly move. The ground rushed up to meet him; the sound of breaking metal screeched in his ears as the undercarriage tore away. He could see the lights of the train winking towards him. No time to say he was sorry to Kate or Colin. He took his hands off the control stick. There was nothing he could do now. No one would ever see his real face again. The plane screeched towards the end of the runway and the oncoming train. Suddenly, the deadly helter-skelter of its slide was halted by great oedemas of waterlogged mud which clamped themselves to the sides of the plane like outsize sores. The Spitfire was sucked into a broadside, stopping with one wing above a boundary line on a short post. Rob sat in the cockpit, unable to move.

'What the hell happened? It was a perfectly straightforward landing, man*? What the hell happened*? The Spit's category four. Absolutely bloody useless!' The C.O. was pacing up and down his small dingy room, almost incoherent with anger. They were two Spitfires short in the squadron already; Rob's accident had cost them another one.

'Well? Speak up, man?'

Rob slumped into a misshapen chair.

'It was your hands, wasn't it? Your arrogance and your *bloody* hands!'

Rob felt the pain shoot up his arms as he hit the table. 'You're right, Sir. It was my bloody hands! My bloody hands and my determination to fly again against all the odds. To show you that I *can* fly and I *can,* can't I?'

Denham stopped pacing to look at Rob. 'Not in this squadron, Flying Officer Adams. You leave tomorrow. 1000 hours.'

*

It was 1 a.m. when Rob walked towards the Spitfire on the runway. He was wearing an Irvin jacket and trousers over his pyjamas, a sweater, flying boots and a blue silk scarf which his mother had bought him. It was a cold, starry night. The flare path was merely a single line of flim lamps, shaped like oil stoves and spaced at 100 yard intervals. A torch bulb was mounted in the centre of them with a small metal disc over each one to prevent the escape of any upward directional light. Looking around to make sure he wasn't seen, Rob climbed into the Spitfire and checked the instruments, ensuring that the petrol tank was full this time. Everything ideal for a quick getaway. Only this would be his last one and it wouldn't be quick.

The long broad engine cowling in front of the Spitfire cockpit reduced forward vision so much that Rob could only see out at an angle of about 45º on either side which was one of the reasons why Colin hated night flying. This limitation had never disturbed Rob in the past and would certainly not do so in the future. He zigzagged up to the runway where he could see the chance light, lined the Spitfire to the right of the light and opened the throttle. The line of lamps to his left was too close, so he eased up on the right rudder. Then accelerating fast, he brought up the nose of the Spit and immediately he was alone with the stars.

The night was black velvet. Below him, isolated patches of cumulus were gathering together into a large bank of cloud, growing larger each second by wisps coming in from the sea. The whole scene was lit up with an exquisite iridescence by the moon above him. For once, Rob wasn't concerned with the enemy. Below him, the flying-bird shadow of a Spitfire was reflected over convolutions of cloud. Above him, Sirius, the brightest star in the sky. As a boy of ten he had read about Sirius B, the white dwarf star which orbits around Sirius every fifty years. He would never see it through his telescope now. He would never see Kate's face again. Why had he never told her he loved her? What was he frightened of? His last flight and he still didn't know.

Rob had been flying into retrospective time for almost half an hour when a black Heinkel 111 glided into view beneath him, travelling towards the coast. The Heinkel couldn't see the Spitfire flying its last journey above him. Rob suddenly looked down and saw the familiar shape of its wings caught in the moon's light.

'*Can't fly, can't I?*' He screamed into the canopy. 'Watch this, Denham!' The Spitfire shuddered violently as Rob slammed the stick forward into a dive. A surprise attack. The German crew would never know what hit them. There was little space between the planes when he jammed his finger on the firing button. What did it matter now? The bullets hit the bomber's central section like small dancing fireflies. Rob veered off starboard, fighting the Spitfire into a tight circle. He was going for a head-on attack, ignoring Malan's doctrine, the C.O. of 74 Squadron. Never fly straight and level for more than thirty seconds in combat. Fire short bursts. Brace the whole body. Think of nothing else. *What the hell did he know?*

Rob flew straight at the bomber until it filled up his entire vision, firing tracer after tracer into it. *Why didn't it go down?* At that instant, the Heinkel's undercarriage descended: a sure sign that it was badly damaged. Tracers cascaded around the Spitfire as the rear gunner retaliated. Momentarily, Rob glimpsed the contorted features of a young German face before flicking the Spitfire into an instinctive spin. Gradually, the huge aircraft started to roll up on its port-side wing-tip, like a primeval creature dying in slow motion, oil and vapour streaming from its engines. Rob watched dispassionately from a distance as the plane continued to roll. All at once, without warning, the whole vault of the night sky burst into light. There was a gargantuan explosion and the sky reverberated as the bomber convulsed into thousands of fragments. The stars fired an apocalypse of colour over the white cumulus cloud beneath.

Then Rob released his prehensile grip on the control stick and started to weep.

Chapter 9

It was a bright day with a hint of spring in the clear air. Mary decided to walk to the seafront, under the Gothic arch of the North Lodge and through St Leonards' Park. A little fresh air before the exhaustion of the Samaritan Centre would revive her after another sleepless night. As she entered the top end of the park, a tall oak threw the path into dank shadow. Here, out of the sun, the grass on the verges was still glistening with frost. She thought of the host of bright-yellow celandines, violets and bluebells she had seen there last spring. A yellow hammer trilled *a-little-bit-of-bread-and-no-cheese* from its perch on the turret of the Gothic-style Clock House in the park and her heart lightened a little. Perhaps Rob would be better in the summer. A sharp wind hit her face as she left the park and walked down the hill towards the shops on the seafront. One of the windowpanes of a butcher's shop had been blown out by a bomb. Some wag had written *I HAVE NO PANE NOW, MOTHER DEAR,* inside the shop window. At least we still have a sense of humour, Mary thought, smiling.

Bracing herself against the wind, she crossed the road to walk along the promenade. White caps on the waves danced through the iron spikes of barbed wire entanglements.

Mummy! Mummy! Don't! It's cold! She could hear Rob's childish screams of laughter as she threw water over his startled,

103

beautiful face one summer's day, light years ago. Mary found herself hastily rubbing the memory away with a large white handkerchief. She remembered their visits to the hospital all too clearly; she knew he hated them coming, but how could they stay away? All they wanted to do was to remove his pain. She and John hadn't seen Rob since he had gone back flying. What would he be like now? Physically? Mentally? Would he cope with flying?

Mary walked in front of the austere statue of Queen Victoria at Warrior Square. A few more bullet holes on her gown, she noticed. In the distance, a number of boys were playing in the blackened rubble of a bombed house which had been hit by a landmine. She crossed the road, the pungency of charred wood and cordite strong in her nostrils, as she walked towards the house. All that was left was the intimacy of one bedroom wall, papered with pink flowers and lacerated by the black line of a chimney snaking up into the sky. A washbasin dangled on twisted lead-piping, hanging in space. In the remains of a garden, a wheelbarrow, half full of water, had three sodden petals floating in it.

The boys ran off after she'd told them the wall was unsafe, stopping only to pull faces at her from a safe distance. Only one small boy remained. He looked at her before picking up a stone and hurling it at the bedroom wall. It rattled down the flowered wallpaper. The boy turned to watch Mary's reaction, then walked with exaggerated slowness in the direction the others had taken. His hands stuffed in his short trouser pockets.

'You cheeky monkey,' Mary shouted, knowing that two years ago that boy would have been Charlie.

*

104

The Samaritan Centre was crowded with the homeless and confused when she arrived. The smell of unwashed bodies wafted round the room. Sitting on a bench, insensible to her surroundings, was nineteen-year-old Alice Rodgers whose husband had been killed aboard HMS Hood. She was seven months pregnant. Mary sat down at her desk, looking at all the forms waiting for her.

'Alice?' Mary called across to the girl. 'Please come over.'

The girl who dragged herself towards her was no longer the golden innocent girl she had been a year ago, helping them pack parcels for the troops in the WVS. Her eyes were pinpricks of red, her hair, dry straw. She didn't look at Mary as she sat down heavily.

'What's happened, Alice?'

'The house was bombed. Mum was in it. She's in hospital.'

'Oh my dear. I'm so sorry. I didn't know. Where've you been living?'

'In the rest centre – up the road.'

Mary instinctively wanted to tell the girl she could stay with them, but she couldn't cope with any more trauma in the house, not when she was still waiting to hear from Rob.

'Have you got any of your cards?'

'No. All burnt. Mum looked after them. She looked after everything.' Alice stared unseeingly across the room. 'If only I'd listened to her … she asked me to leave … again and again. I wouldn't listen. The only time I didn't. Wouldn't leave the sea … my Frank …' The girl's words trickled away like a river bed in a drought.

'You've got the baby to think about now, Alice. You must listen to me.'

The girl stared at the floor.

'Don't want the baby – not with Frank gone.'

'Stop that, Alice!' People turned in surprise towards Mary. She hadn't realised she had raised her voice. 'I know it's difficult for you, my dear, but there are lots of people who will help you.'

'Don't want help.'

'Of course you want help. That's why you're here, isn't it?' Mary shuffled through the mass of forms on her desk, trying to sound dispassionate. 'Let's see – you'll need a new identity card. You'll have to apply to the employment exchange in Priory Street; the old offices were bombed last week. Your mother can receive the new injury allowance … where's the form? Ah, here it is. You can claim twenty-four and sixpence for your mother and –'

Alice looked vaguely around the room.

'Alice – you *must* listen. You must be strong for the baby's sake. There's a lot to sort out, dear. Your mother can get compensation for the loss of her house, but you must register a claim with the housing board. And you can get new clothing coupons from the assistance board in Wellington Square.' Mary suddenly stopped speaking; she saw that Alice wasn't taking in any of the information at all. She waited a long time before saying, 'I'm sorry, dear, there's nothing I can do to help you.'

Alice raised her red eyes, looking as vulnerable as her unborn child. 'I thought you said I could get lots of help.'

'Not if you don't listen to me, Alice.' Mary looked around the room, desperate for someone who could assist the girl in sorting out the complicated arrangements she had to make. She saw Hilda in the distance, dealing with an old man whose clothes were in tatters. He was covered in a thick layer of dust.

'Stay here, Alice. I'll find someone to help you.' Mary walked over to Hilda.

'I don't know where your wife is, Mr Griffiths,' Hilda was saying. She looked up at Mary and gave her a quick smile. 'Have you looked on the casualty lists?'

The old man nodded, holding his left arm to stop a tremor.

'Then you'll have to go to the Central Information Bureau.'

'I can't walk far,' the old man murmured.

Mary wondered if he could walk at all.

'Hilda, sorry to interrupt, but Sylvia could go for him, couldn't she?' Hilda nodded, only too grateful for a solution. She wished now she'd stayed helping in the WVS. The faces in the Samaritan Centre stayed with her in bed at night.

'Sylvia?' Mary called a seventeen-year-old girl who had volunteered to help with the homeless until she was conscripted. 'Can you help this gentleman?' The girl nodded. They left the old man in her care and moved to the other end of the room.

'I didn't know how lucky I was until I came to work here, Mary. We've got it easy compared to these people, haven't we?' Hilda suddenly looked at Mary's gaunt features and cursed her insensitivity. 'Oh, I'm sorry, my dear. The worry must be awful for you.'

Mary spoke briskly. 'Yes, it is... Look, I've got Alice Rodgers over there. Remember she and her mother worked with us in the WVS?'

The women looked over to where Alice was sitting with her arms folded over her head, slumped awkwardly over the desk.

'Yes... poor girl, doesn't look well enough to have a baby,' Hilda said.

'She's not and her husband's dead.' Mary glanced wearily at the long line of people still waiting for her help. 'Hilda, can I ask you a favour?'

'Course you can.'

'Look after her for me, will you? I'm worried about what she might do. If only she could think about her baby it would console her.'

'Not if she can't afford to have it, Mary.' The women stared at each other across the great divide of money.

Three hours later, Mary gratefully passed on the responsibility for the homeless to a retired schoolmaster who had time and expertise on his hands. Mary knew he welcomed finding solutions to the thorny problems which presented themselves daily.

Mary decided to walk home; she needed the fresh air after the cloying problems which seemed to coagulate in the room. She couldn't feel the wind on her face. All the time she was walking she tried not to think; tried not to think of anything. Flocks of migrating birds: skylarks, lapwings, golden plovers were flying west over the street lamps, heading for warmer climates and safer shores. If only she could join them, instead of remaining here encased in confusion and worry. In the distance she spotted three boys squatting down on the ground. What on earth were they doing? She suddenly recognised a familiar flicking movement of a head: Charlie, his light brown hair as usual sweeping over his eyes, was pointing animatedly at something on the ground. Oh no, what had he found now? Mary strode across the road, determined he wouldn't bring any more shrapnel into the house. But the boys weren't looking at pieces of shrapnel, but at strips of stiff metallic paper lying all over the grass verge.

'Hello boys? What have you found this time?'

They jumped up in surprise. 'Don't know, Mrs Adams,' Tubs said, feeling relieved. For once, they weren't doing anything that any adult could object to.

Charlie's eyes were shining as he contemplated their discovery. 'Look, Auntie Mary.' He bent down to pick up a strip of paper.

'Don't touch it, Charlie!' Mary warned.

'Yeah – remember what smelly Smedley said.' Ian slurped as the snot dripped down his lip before he had a chance to wipe it away. 'It could be an unexploded bomb.'

Charlie stood up quickly. 'Don't be stupid! – how could *that* be a bomb!'

'A *disguised* bomb,' Ian said in a theatrical whisper. Tubs and Charlie laughed at the melodrama in his voice.

He turned to Mary for support. 'What do you think, Mrs Adams?'

Mary inspected the stiff metallic paper which was black on one side and silver on the other. 'I don't think it's a bomb, but you'd better let the ARP have a look at it before you touch it. Who's got a bicycle?'

Ian's hand shot up. 'I'll get mine, Mrs Adams. My Dad's a warden. He'll know what to do.'

Ian, racing against time, sped up the road towards his house. He was in the forefront of a battle against the deviousness of German inventors.

'Come on, you'd better come home, Charlie, before you get into any more mischief,' Mary said. 'You haven't picked up any more shrapnel, have you?' She turned to Tubs who preferred his nickname to his real one. 'What have you collected today, Gerald?' Tubs winced. Charlie made faces at him behind Mary's back.

'Only parachute cord, Mrs Adams – nothing else.' He brought out yards of shining white cord from his bulging trouser pocket.

'Good heavens, you could make lots of clothes lines with that, Gerald.'

Tubs looked stunned by the sudden knowledge that he could make money by selling the cord to housewives. He darted off down the road, making a wide circuit around the strips of metallic paper, shouting. 'Bye, Mrs Adams. See you tomorrow, Charlie.'

'Why did he run off so quickly?' Mary asked.

'Don't know,' Charlie said, knowing exactly what Tubs was going to do. He was going to flood the market before

Charlie had a chance to sell the cord bulging in his pocket. 'Have I *got* to go home now, Auntie Mary. I was just going to go for a ride up the West Hill.'

'You're not. You haven't dug up the vegetables for tea yet.'

'But I can go tomorrow, can't I?' Charlie said, his eyes disappearing under a heavy lock of hair.

Mary pushed his hair back over his forehead. 'It needs cutting.'

'You know you like it like this,' he said, smiling up at Mary.

She got out her handkerchief and rubbed a large smudge of dirt off his left cheek. She wanted to hug him; to tell him he must always stay close; to tell him how much she loved him.

'Come on, Charlie, let's go home.' She felt the sudden warmth of a rough hand in hers and gave it a squeeze.

Mary found two letters waiting on the hall mat when they walked in; one covered with a friend's familiar writing; the other made her stomach constrict; it was official. She had seen so many of these in her work.

'Make us a cup of tea, Charlie.' She walked into the lounge and fell into the first chair she could reach. *Dear God. No!* She opened the letter very slowly; perhaps if she couldn't see the words it had never happened. The paper was a blur.

'Charlie. Get my reading glasses from my bedroom, will you?'

She heard his heavy hurtle up the stairs and thought that her life was just about to be nullified. She waited, looking out of the window at the red orb of sunset sparking the beech trees with fire, hearing the muted song of birds.

'You all right, Auntie Mary?' Charlie said, putting her glasses on a table by the chair. Mary's face was leaden. 'Shall I get you a brandy?' He knew that Uncle John always used brandy for medicinal purposes.

'No, thank you, Charlie. I'm all right. You go to your room. I'll be up in a minute.'

Charlie hovered at the door; demons were attacking the inside of his stomach. 'What's the matter?'

'Nothing!' Mary shouted at him. 'Now do what I say!'

Charlie bolted up the stairs, his heart thumping too hard against his chest. He threw himself under his eiderdown and curled up into a ball.

Mary put on her glasses carefully and opened the letter, amazed at her control.

Dear Dr and Mrs Adams

It is with great regret that I have to write to tell you ...

The white paper fell from Mary's fingers. She watched it flutter to the floor, black words waiting to destroy her. She remained still for one minute, listening to the calm ticking of the clock. Then at last, she reached down to pick up the terrifying piece of paper.

... that Alice Slater of 114, Farleigh Road, Deptford, London has recently died of TB. We understand that you are fostering her son Charles Slater. The social services will be contacting you in the near future to ensure the best course of action for Charles' future. We have been unable to ascertain any knowledge of Mr Slater's whereabouts. It is believed that he has been posted overseas.

Unfortunately, as you will be aware, the problem of bereaved children is becoming more and –

The letter fell again to the floor. Mary couldn't stop laughing. **It wasn't Rob. It wasn't Rob. It wasn't Rob.**

Charlie lay frozen under the eiderdown listening to the awful sound of Mary's laughter.

Chapter 10

There wasn't a sound in the lounge when Charlie crept down the stairs. He waited outside the door, his heart pounding. Mary's laughter was still lingering in his head. He pushed the door open with a tentative finger. She was sleeping on the settee – the letter lying at her feet in front of the fender.

'Auntie Mary?' he whispered.

She didn't stir. His eyes clung to the letter like a limpet. He'd once asked Rob what bravery was. Doing something that frightened you, he'd said, but knowing you must, because it would help someone else. Charlie knew that he *must* read that letter, but he wasn't brave; he wasn't doing it for anyone else.

He inched towards it just as the large front door creaked open.

'Hello – I'm home!' John shouted, before walking into the lounge. Mary's eyes fluttered open, then widened in horror as she saw Charlie staring at the letter.

'It's not Rob, is it?' John's voice was hardly audible as he saw the letter.

Mary shook her head vigorously. 'You'd better read it.'

Charlie thought he was going to be sick over the carpet as John picked up the letter.

'Come and sit down, darling,' Mary said to Charlie in a whisper, but he couldn't move. She swallowed hard, trying to find the right words. 'I'm afraid I've got some bad news. It's your mother. You know how ill she's been? Well, she died of TB last week. I'm so sorry, Charlie.'

Mary wanted him to do something. To cry. To scream. To look at her. Instead he continued to stand completely still, staring at the wall as if he hadn't heard.

The silence was monstrous.

'She was very well looked after in hospital. Would you like to see the letter? ... Charlie?'

He shook his head slowly, before turning to Mary. 'She wasn't my mother – *you* are.'

All the complicated questions Mary had ever thought about heredity and environment, were answered in his words. She opened her arms wide to her second son.

That evening Mary did an unprecedented thing: she rang Rob's squadron. She had a valid reason, she told herself. Urgent family business. She was told about the crash; about Rob's subsequent night flight. He'd been found wandering in a field in the early hours of the morning suffering from shock, but unhurt, physically.

Mary had clung to that last word all through their interminable drive to bring him home. Rob had been silent after his initial greeting, then had fallen into a restless sleep in the back of the car, his head lolling against Charlie's rock-like shoulder. It was a nightmare journey of murky, restricted vision as car owners were required to mask their headlights. John had found it impossible to drive any faster than twenty mph, even outside built-up areas. Mary was suddenly struck by the similarities between their journey and their war-torn lives.

*

It was more than a week before Rob began to speak a little, but most of the time, he stared out of the window with a rigid expression in his eyes. He wouldn't go out. Mary relied more and more on Charlie to bring Rob back to them. Each day Charlie brought him news. He had even made him laugh once, talking about school.

'You know what happened this afternoon, Rob? Ian, that's the snotty boy I told you about, started whistling in class at Mr Smedley's finches. Remember me telling you that old Smedley's trained them to be quiet when he's talking? You ought to have seen his face – it went purple. He rolled his eyes up to the ceiling and said:

"Happy the hare in the morning, Walters, for he cannot read the Master's thoughts." Tubs and me nearly died laughing. Then Ian said: "What hare, Sir?" And he was *serious*, Rob. There's more light in a number 8 torch battery than Ian. Old Smedley was padding up and down the room like a caged animal. He couldn't get his words out, he was so angry. He sputtered: "Walters, you have the most open mind I have ever encountered… ideas fall *out* of it, not in."

Rob laughed. Briefly. Then stared out of the window again.

*

Charlie had taken up cycling to Fairlight every day. He didn't want to see the other boys now. They'd only ask about Rob or his mother. He didn't want to talk about either. The house was silent as he crept down the stairs, aided by the moonlight streaming through the hall window. He stopped suddenly, listening to the familiar tapping on glass. Rob had started doing finger exercises against the large window in the lounge. In the half-light, Charlie padded across the carpet and stood at the door, watching Rob. He was systematically drumming each finger in turn against the glass, increasing his speed slightly with each repetition.

'Rob?'

The noise stopped instantly, but Rob didn't turn round.

'I'm going for a bike ride. Come with me. No one's up yet. Just you and me.'

There was no response.

'Rob – come on – you'd love it on the cliffs when the dawn comes. I saw some porpoises in the bay yesterday.'

At last Rob turned to Charlie, a flicker of interest in his eyes. 'Did you?'

'I'll bet they'll be there again today. Come with me, Rob … it'll be like old times.'

Rob walked over to the mirror to stare at the network of scars on his face. If only I could rub out words as easily as I do at school, Charlie thought.

'They won't go away, Charlie.'

'Bet Mr McIndoe would get rid of some of them.'

'I've had *fifteen* operations.'

'Some of the chaps have had over thirty. I asked them.'

Rob walked back to the window and stared out. Charlie joined him. The sky was lightening.

In the distance, two herring gulls were wheeling circles in the air before descending on a roof-top. A male and female. The male stood like a rock as the female walked around him, pausing as she reached his front to brush his chest feathers with her beak. They heard a plaintive mewing call.

'What they doing, Rob?'

'The female's enticing the male.'

Charlie looked at him, puzzled.

The male suddenly rocked forwards on his legs and bobbed his head up and down, making a choking call. The female did the same. Suddenly the male mounted her; she rubbed her bill on his chest as he uttered a hoarse call. Then it was over. They flew off over the town together.

'Is *that* mating? … Doesn't last long, does it?'

'No,' Rob answered. 'As Humphrey Bogart said, "it doesn't add up to a hill of beans." Bit like life.' Rob's lips twisted in a grimace.

Charlie stared up at him, remembering how Rob's smile had lit up his face before the accident.

'Do you think the streets will be empty?' Rob started his finger exercises against the window again.

'Yeah, no one around for hours.'

'What about coming back? They'll be crowded then. People all wanting to stare at the Phantom of the Opera.'

'Other people have problems too, Rob. Stop feeling sorry for yourself. Remember Bill Foxley and Hoke and Geoff Page and Squadron Leader Gleave?' Charlie waited for Rob's reaction. Terrified. This was the longest conversation they had had since he was burnt.

After a few minutes, Rob said, 'All right. We'll take Dad's car. Come on.'

The dawn was breaking golden shards of light over the sea when they arrived at the sandstone cliffs. The calls of gulls and kittiwakes crowded the air. Rob and Charlie stood side by side on the edge of the cliff, leaning against the wind as a fulmar glided past, buoyant on the up-draught. The sea below them changed from green to midnight blue, then as the bird-calls diminished, they heard a sharper whistling note, faint at first, becoming stronger. Suddenly, below them, a school of porpoise: fifteen to twenty gleaming black backs, swimming in close formation like a squadron.

'They've come, Charlie! They've come!' For the first time in over a year, Rob sounded excited.

'Told you!'

A flash of bright white bellies as the porpoises arced up into the air, over the surface of the sea in a majestic display of prowess before diving back into the depths. Almost as if aware of being watched, they gave Rob and Charlie two repeat performances. Then, all at once, they disappeared from sight, leaving only the empty epidermis of endless blue and green.

Rob gazed down in wonder at the surface of the sea. 'I've only seen that sight once before in my whole life.'

'You can't sleep late if you want to see porpoises,' Charlie said, pragmatically.

On the beach below them, a rock pipit, the size of a slim sparrow, was scavenging for food. Ignoring the large gulls and kittiwakes, it hopped delicately towards some bladder-wrack to probe for sand-hoppers and small worms. A tiny wind-blown fluff of feathers at the edge of the surf.

'He's not bothered by the big boys, is he?' Charlie's voice trailed away as Rob studied the sea fixedly.

'Come on, Rob. I'll race you to that –' In the distance Charlie saw a two hundred foot high steel lattice mast silhouetted against the sky. 'What's that?'

Rob knew about the secret Chain Home Radar Stations which had been installed along the south and east coasts. He just hadn't seen one before. 'It's some sort of radio or television mast, I think ... they were working on them before the war.' Rob felt the first stirrings of interest as he looked at the mast towering in the distance.

'What's it for?' Charlie asked as Rob raced off towards it. 'Blimey, Rob – what's so important about a mast?'

'It can detect an aircraft well over a hundred miles from the coast.'

'Well, why don't we just shoot the Luftwaffe out of the sky at sea, then?' Charlie was beginning to believe that Churchill ought to change his policies on aerial warfare.

But Rob was way ahead of him, striding off into the distance.

'Hey, wait for me,' Charlie shouted.

They raced along a path above an overhanging slab of rock on which a lovers' seat was set: a magical precipice where hundreds of lovers had sworn eternal love into the winds of the sea. Three years earlier, on a beautiful summer's day, he and Kate had carved their initials into the seat. But Rob had forgotten. He was mentally occupied with the problems involved in installing a chain of radar stations along the coast. He didn't speak, but felt happy. The fresh air made him feel alive again. They turned into a clearing.

A middle-aged man with a shock of wavy hair was standing by himself, peering through a pair of wire-framed spectacles and writing rapidly in a notebook. He was wearing a fawn raincoat, although it was a cloudless morning.

'Bugger,' Rob whispered. 'Come on, Charlie.' He started to turn away from the man towards the concealment of a dense clump of hawthorn bushes, but they had been seen. The man turned towards them, a sudden gust of wind sweeping his hair around his face. In that instant, Rob recognised that this was the face, although much older now, which had stared at him from the mantelpiece of his bedroom since he was a boy. It was John Logie-Baird. For the first time since his accident, Rob was the one to stare.

'What's the matter? Do you know him?' Charlie couldn't understand Rob's interest in this man.

Rob didn't take his eyes off Logie-Baird. 'Not yet,' he said to Charlie before walking towards him. He had seen this man's work in 1936 when his father had taken him to the Crystal Palace. Logie-Baird's television sets were being demonstrated before an astonished crowd of people. He knew instinctively that the scientist had some connection with the work being carried out at the nearby radar station.

'Good morning, Sir.' Rob stopped a few paces away from the alarmed man. In his excitement, Rob had forgotten how shocking his face looked.

It took Logie-Baird a few moments to recover before he answered in quiet Scottish tones.

'Ah ... good morning to you.'

Rob went to shake his hand, but stopped when he saw the man's embarrassment. 'I'm sorry to intrude but I wanted to say how much I admire your work.'

'What work?' Logie-Baird asked him abruptly.

It was Rob's turn to be embarrassed. 'Well, your work on television ... but I imagine you must be involved with something else now there's a war on.'

The scientist studied Rob's face, but for some reason Rob didn't feel self-conscious.

'I was burnt trying to bale out of a Spitfire.'

'Ah... I'm sorry to hear that. So how did you recognise me?'

'I've had a photograph of you since I was a young boy. Taken in 1923. You were experimenting with what I think was object-detection apparatus on the West Hill in Hastings.'

Logie-Baird looked amazed before bursting into a wide smile. 'Was I, indeed?'

'I believe so, Sir… Has it got anything to do with that mast over there?'

The scientist turned to stare at the mast as if he hadn't seen it before. 'And where did you get such a photograph?'

'My father was walking on the hill and was intrigued by the apparatus. He took the photograph and gave it to me.'

'A man with an enquiring mind,' Logie-Baird said.

'Yes, he has, Sir. Could I ask you …' But before Rob could press him further about his work, the strident voice of a retired Colonel reverberated through the air. Into the clearing walked an elderly couple: both wearing mud-splattered stout shoes and carrying walking sticks. They stopped abruptly when they saw Rob's startling appearance. The Colonel, in the loud tones of the deaf, shouted to his wife.

'Told you it was dangerous, Margery. That man's been underneath that steel monster. Rays coming from it. I told you. It's a national disgrace. I'm writing to the Government. Has to be removed. Danger to all of us. You must ask for compensation, young man,' he shouted over to Rob. 'Come on, Margery. We're not walking here again.'

Within a second, the wife was whisked off by her husband who obviously thought Rob's scars were contagious. They watched the couple disappear down a cliff path, eager to get away from the source of contamination.

'That's exactly the sort of bigotry I've been fighting all my life,' Logie-Baird snapped, tapping the tip of his pen on his notebook repeatedly to underline his anger. He turned for the first time to Charlie. 'Don't you grow up with cramped vision, young man. Look beyond the ordinary.'

'Yes, Sir,' Charlie answered, wondering what on earth he was talking about.

'And what are you doing now?' Logie-Baird asked Rob, calming down a little.

'He's getting better,' Charlie said, quickly.

The scientist examined Rob as if he had a microscope hidden behind his glasses. 'Are you indeed?'

There were a few moments of silence before Rob answered quietly. 'Not really. I've been told I can't fly any more, you see.' He lifted his hands for Logie-Baird's scrutiny.

'Really? You've been told you can't fly in any capacity, have you? ... A man once told me that opportunities look for you when you're ready to see them ... Well, I must be going. Good day to you both.' Logie-Baird tramped off down a footpath towards the mast, stopping briefly to write something in his notebook, before continuing on his way.

'Blimey, he's more eccentric than Mr Smedley.'

'Geniuses usually are, Charlie.'

*

Slowly, after the meeting with Logie-Baird, Rob began to change; imperceptibly at first, then his walk became more vigorous; he ate more and started to take an interest in what was happening to the war. When he wasn't walking with Charlie, he was studying textbooks in his room. Rob wouldn't tell them what he was studying, but Mary knew he was now strong enough, mentally and physically, to support her in what she was determined to do.

She waited long after Charlie's bedtime one evening when Rob and John were talking in the lounge about the latest raid which had happened two days earlier. FW190s and ME109s had been seen flying low over the rooftops of the town before they dropped their bombs.

'One of my patients told me he saw a bomb fly straight through a house at the top of Spa Hill and out the other side. It was old Carstairs. Probably drunk, of course.' John looked at Rob who was sitting on the settee drinking a glass of Chablis. 'Not possible, is it?'

'It is if the bombs are dropped from a low level and the pilots are flying at high speed. Makes missiles act in odd ways.'

'One bomb exploded near Alexandra Park. The rescue services were busy all night apparently.' John yawned widely.

'So were you, Dad.'

'It's this blasted flu epidemic. Hospitals are full. Worst bout since 1937. The Government has even stopped conscription for young doctors.' He yawned widely again.

'You can't keep up this pace much longer. Not at your age.'

'Well, thank you very much, Robert. That makes me feel much better. Did you hear that, Mary?'

They looked over to Mary who was sitting quietly near the fire, deep in thought.

'Sorry?'

'You haven't listened to a word we've said, have you?'

Mary breathed deeply. She knew that John would object. 'I've been thinking about Charlie.'

There was a long silence as they waited for her to continue.

'Yes?' John said, warily.

'I want us to adopt him.'

There was a stunned silence before John and Rob spoke at once.

'What?'

'We can't!'

'Why not?' Mary could feel the colour flood into her face. She was determined to win this argument.

'You're not serious?' John looked at Mary in amazement.

'Charlie's father's still alive, Mum.'

'And what sort of father *is* he? How many times has he come to visit him? How many times has he written?' Mary started pacing up and down the room.

John stood up and caught her hands. 'Mary, Mary. Listen. We *can't* adopt Charlie. He has a father.'

'But you know what Charlie was like when he came here. Infested with lice, undernourished, traumatised. You know what Rob told us about his father beating him. He's not going back to him. He's not!' She broke away from John. 'Anyway, how do we know he's still alive? No one's heard about him for years.'

'How do you know that?'

'I've written to the social services.'

'Without telling me?' John looked hurt.

'I knew what you'd say.' Mary turned to Rob. 'You can't want him to go back to him, Rob?'

'Of course I don't. Do you think it's possible?'

Mary was radiant. 'Yes.'

Rob looked at the glow on his mother's face. If she thought it was possible, it was. 'You're right. It's a good idea.' He jumped up excitedly. 'No, it's not!'

'What do you mean?'

'It's not good, Mum. It's great! In fact, it's the best idea you've ever had.' Rob walked over to hug his mother for the first time since he'd been injured.

'Well, that's decided then,' Mary said, looking triumphantly at John.

'Don't be ridiculous the pair of you.' John spoke angrily. 'Have you any idea how difficult it is to adopt a child, even in peacetime, let alone in wartime.'

'I know it will be difficult, but if we can prove that Charlie's father hit him –'

'How?'

'What?'

'How can you prove his father hit him? You can't ask Charlie's mother. Charlie hasn't said a word about his father in eighteen months. And we don't know where his brothers are.

'Anyway, I doubt whether any court would ask them to testify against their father.'

'Oh, don't be so defeatist, John! Other people in the street must have known about it.'

'Not if I know anything about families. Most have secrets they don't mention outside the four walls of their house.'

Rob saw the radiance on his mother's face fade.

'Oh, come on, Dad. You don't know if that's true. It's worth investigating, isn't it?'

Charlie, standing frozen in ice in the hallway, strained to hear John's answer. Charlie had known this discussion was going to happen for weeks. He'd seen a letter from the social services and heard Mary's discussions with them on the phone. Since that time his work at school had been perfect. He didn't mind if the other boys thought he was sucking up to Smedley. Smedley had told them that one transgression in life could blight one's life. He knew that Smedley was exaggerating because Charlie had committed many in the past, but he wasn't taking any chances now that his future was in the balance. But the thought of someone knocking on doors in his old street asking what his father did to him made him feel sick. Charlie heard Mary question John again and heard the silence as they waited for an answer.

'Listen to me, the pair of you. I'd like nothing better than to have Charlie as my son ... I'm proud of him ... but ... '

Charlie thought his heart would explode as he held his breath.

'There are *major* difficulties.'

'Oh, you're always the same, John. If someone sees a glass half full, you see it half empty.' Mary's voice was shrill with bitterness.

John was deeply hurt. 'I didn't realise I'd been so difficult to live with all these years.'

'Mum doesn't mean it, Dad. It's just that she's set her heart on this adoption. You know Mum.'

'Yes, I do – that's why I don't want everybody's hopes raised up to the roof to be suddenly dashed to the ground. Imagine what it would be like for Charlie. And isn't there something you've both forgotten?'

'What?' Mary said.

'How do you know Charlie *wants* to be adopted?'

Years later, Charlie would still be able to recall the shocked expressions on their faces as he walked into the room.

'I do,' he said quietly.

'How long have you been listening?' John asked, rather shaken, trying to remember what he'd said.

'I don't want to go back there, Uncle John – ever. You're not going to make me, are you?'

They all stared at John who absent-mindedly lit his pipe and puffed. He always smoked when he was worried. It was difficult enough to convince Mary to be rational, but now Rob *and* Charlie were involved, he doubted whether he could bring any common sense into the house at all.

'Of course, I'm not, Charlie, I'm just trying to be objective about this.'

Mary jumped up and hugged Charlie so hard, he couldn't breathe. 'Well, I'm not. I love Charlie and I want him to live with us forever. It's as simple as that.' Then Mary smiled and all the beauty of her youth was in her face. 'If we present a united front to the social services, we'll win, John. I know we will. *Please* support me … How could they refuse you?'

John shook his head, wanting to wipe out the strain of the last eighteen months from their lives. 'Oh, my dear love, if it will make everyone happy I'm prepared to do battle with Satan himself, but it won't be me who'll persuade them, will it? It'll be you and Charlie.'

'But you *are* with us, John?'

He saw the apprehension on their faces and realised how much he had changed since Rob's crash. 'Of course, I am.' He spoke empathetically. 'I'll help you as much as I can.'

Charlie, eyes like August light, threw his arms around John and squeezed. A memory surfaced in John's mind: he was eight years old; sitting on the pier with his father, eating ice-cream. Another world before two world wars. They were listening to an orchestra playing Bach's *Goldberg Variations*. His father had leaned over to kiss his forehead. "I'm embalming this moment, John. Just you, me and Bach." Now there was Charlie. Capable of preserving them all.

'I know this is premature and not at all rational but … go on, Rob. Get me that bottle of Krug 20 I've been saving for a special occasion, would you?'

'There's something you should know first, Dad, especially if we're celebrating.' Rob moved the muscles of his face into the semblance of a smile. 'You know the studying I've been doing?

… I've been learning about radiolocation. I wrote to a few people in the RAF and explained the circumstances of my crash and injuries. Told them about my studies. The long and short of it is … I've just heard I've been accepted on a navigator's course. I start next week.'

Charlie blinked very rapidly. He was almost a man now. He certainly wasn't going to cry in front of his family.

Chapter 11

Kate felt she could almost forget the war as she drove along the Welsh lanes on her way to one of the balloon sites on a crystal clear morning. The picture of patchwork fields and mountains in the distance dazzled her. She knew now why Richard Llewellyn had called his book *How Green Was My Valley*: a kaleidoscope of green spread out around her: vibrant leaf-green trees, avocado fields, olive-misted mountains, greengage streams and moist sage moss. She stopped the jeep to indulge her eyes. Then suddenly, in a distant field, she saw an all too familiar shape. A rogue barrage balloon. Sighing deeply, she started up the jeep and drove towards it. It seemed she couldn't escape the frieze of war, wherever she was.

The balloon was miles off course: its cable barely within reach of the ground. Kate ran and grabbed it just as a light breeze became a gust, and she was momentarily lifted into the air. The steel of the cable bit into her hands as she hopped along the ground, looking desperately around for something to tie it to. The only thing in the field besides her was a cow. Kate bounded towards it while it peacefully munched the luscious green grass. It looked up in surprise when its flanks were assaulted with cold cable as Kate hastily secured it round the cow's stomach.

'At least it won't get tangled up in telegraph wires with you hanging on it,' Kate said, patting the creature.

The gusty breeze became a sudden gale, and the bewildered cow was lifted into the air – its brown eyes reproaching Kate. It attempted a mournful moo as it levitated across the field towards an elderly lady who was out walking her Welsh terrier. She looked up to see the shadow of the cow, hanging in the air, masking the sun.

'Good heavens,' she said to her dog. 'Time for new glasses, I think, Morgan.'

Morgan, the terrier, in a paranoiac frenzy, leapt higher and higher, desperate to bury his teeth in one of the cow's hooves which dangled tantalisingly just out of reach. Kate ran over to the lady and explained what she had done. They watched helplessly as the cow swayed in the vagaries of wind and Morgan continued his battle with gravity. After enduring minutes of bellicose sounds which Kate had never believed a cow could make, the wind died down enough for the two women to grab hold of the cable and pull the confused creature down to earth. It stood beside the debilitated dog, trembling, as Kate cut the cable.

The old lady, whose long life had not been weighed down with the confusion of logic, turned to Kate. 'Well, thank goodness it was a cow, that's all I can say, dear. I can't afford new glasses. Not with the war on … Well, we certainly showed that German what we're made of, haven't we?'

'What German?' Kate asked in confusion. She didn't mean the cow, did she?

The woman pointed her walking stick up at the barrage balloon. 'The one sitting in that balloon, dear. If those Germans think they can frighten *me* by sitting in those balloons all day, they're *very* much mistaken. I was in the last war, you know. Come on, Morgan.' She nodded knowingly at Kate before walking off, dragging the exhausted dog behind her. Kate stood in the field, unable to stop laughing.

It was almost five o'clock by the time she finished her duties at the balloon site. She scrubbed the exhaustion of the day away in a warm, shallow bath before knocking on Bridget's door. Bridget was reading a letter from Colin.

'Bridge – you'll never guess what's –' She stopped when she saw Bridget's face. 'What's the matter?'

'It's from Colin.'

'Is he all right?'

'He's asked me to marry him.'

Kate couldn't speak. Colin had only known Bridget for a few months. She and Rob had known each other for years.

'I know – it's ridiculous, isn't it?' Bridget studied Kate's face. 'Say something then.'

'I don't know what to say … it's … so unexpected.' She looked down at the bulky sheath of pages on Bridget's lap. 'He doesn't usually write much.'

'Doesn't he?' Bridget frowned, trying to think of the right words. 'Does he always ramble in letters?'

'No. Not when he writes to me, but then he's not in love with me. People do odd things when they're in love.'

Bridget smiled. 'Oh, do they? Thanks for that piece of philosophy, old Mother Murphy. I'll remember it.'

'You know what I mean … what are you going to tell him?'

There was a sudden flurry of feet outside the door, a loud knock. Before they could answer, the door was flung open. Two white-faced young WAAF privates stood shivering with shock.

'Come quickly, Ma'am. It's Freda.' The girls ran off in the direction of the ablution block with Kate and Bridget racing behind them.

They could hear the groans from over a hundred yards away. The privates stopped in their tracks.

'It's awful, Ma'am.' They wouldn't go any further.

Kate and Bridget were infected with the girls' fear as they walked towards the sound.

'What d'you think's happened?' Bridget asked her.

Kate shook her head, wild visions of disasters swirling round her brain. If she hadn't become an officer she wouldn't have to cope with whatever was waiting for them.

The groans were coming from the bathroom at the end of the block. They were a few feet away from it when they saw the blood oozing underneath the door.

'Holy Mary Mother of God,' Bridget said, crossing herself.

Kate steeled herself to walk forward into the blood. It sucked at her soles. 'Hello? Freda? It's Section Officers Adams and Reilly here.' There was no answer. She tried to push the door open. It wouldn't budge.

'What shall we do, Kate?'

'Get a chair. Quick.'

'There's usually one in the other bathroom. I'll go look.'

Kate stood in the blood, trying to remain calm while Bridget brought a chair.

'Who's it going to be?' Kate asked, when she returned.

'You. I'll die of shock.'

Kate climbed on the chair, her nerves tingling with tension. Standing on her toes she could just see Freda, an eighteen-year-old girl from Somerset who had never been away from home before the war. She was spread-eagled on the floor, soaked in blood. Whiter than marble. Her head was twisted at right angles, blocking the door.

'Oh, God, Bridget. I think she's dying.'

'Oh, Holy Mary –'

'Shut up! Go and see if the MD's about. NOW.'

Bridget raced off towards the medical block. Kate held herself tight. Like her mother, she hated the sight of blood.

'Freda? Can you hear me?'

The girl on the ground moaned.

'Listen, you must move away from the door. *Please*. I can't get in to help you.'

The girl trembled, then struggled to move. Each minuscule movement brought more blood leaking from her body. At last, after numerous attempts, there was enough room to open the door a fraction.

'Good girl, Freda. Now lie still.'

She didn't need the instruction. She wasn't moving. As Kate squeezed into the bloody bathroom she saw a small blood-stained bundle wrapped in a once-white towel. One miniature, perfect finger protruded. It had a crescent fingernail. Translucent. Lying next to the four-month-old foetus was a large knitting needle, covered with a shredded piece of placenta.

Kate fainted.

She was in her own bed when she woke up, dressed in a blue silk nightgown. She looked down in wonder at her body. There was not one drop of blood on it. Perhaps it hadn't happened. Then Bridget crept in, her face anguished.

'Oh, Katie.' She sat down and held Kate's hand. 'That poor, poor girl. What a terrible way to die.'

'She's dead?'

Bridget nodded vigorously.

Kate couldn't speak.

'Squadron Officer Virtue and I cleaned you up. You were a bit of a mess. She's a grand lady that one. I can't stop thinking about that girl and the ... '

'Don't, Bridget. I don't want to talk about it. Can you ask the Squadron Officer if she'll come to see me?'

Bridget looked hurt. 'Of course.' She walked out of the room and Kate was left staring at the ceiling of the old stables. The carpenter's chisel was clearly visible in some of its wooden beams.

The door opened quietly. Squadron Officer Virtue's perfume, *Evening in Paris,* wafted round the room.

'Hello Katherine. Are you feeling better?'

Kate nodded.

'You've been asleep for hours. May I sit down?'

'Please.'

'If only she had come to you or me. We could have helped her.' Squadron Officer Virtue sounded troubled.

'How? We'd have thrown her out of the WAAFs like Brenda and Bertha, wouldn't we?'

The Squadron Officer looked at Kate, startled. 'Do you think us that heartless?'

'Yes.'

'That's not true. It's a tragedy that two young lives are lost. I could have helped her. I've helped others in similar positions.'

Kate looked at the Squadron Leader for the first time since she'd entered the room. 'Have you? How?'

The S. O. hesitated. 'I have friends who have found them positions.'

'You mean as servants.'

'No. As companions. I didn't realise you had such a low opinion of me.'

'I'm sorry. I don't. It's just that today's been …'

The S.O. leaned over and touched Kate's fingers. 'Hush, I know.'

Kate was bewildered by the brilliance in the S.O.'s blue eyes as she looked at her.

'Katherine. I want to tell you –'

'Please, don't. Don't tell me anything. I'd like to ask for some leave, Ma'am. Starting immediately.'

The light died in the Squadron Officer's eyes. She stood up. 'Of course. After what's happened.' She walked out, leaving the room full of her perfume and presence.

*

Kate couldn't believe all the changes she saw in Hastings on her return. She had been home a week and had traversed almost every road, field and country lane. Everywhere was full of the noise and dust of military vehicles and equipment. There were even POW camps in an old school and in Normanhurst, a grand manor house where her mother had worked as a maid when she was thirteen.

She got on a bus near St Nicholas' Church in the Old Town. Soldiers were busy loading the church with the machinations of war. Out of rain-splattered windows, she saw distorted reflections of bombed buildings on the puddled road. The last time she was in this area she'd been thirteen. A sunny day in 1935 had turned into the blackness of the swastika. She and her mother had walked straight into an open-air meeting of

Blackshirts by the lifeboat. She remembered the stones thrown by hecklers; the terrifying anger on people's faces; her mother's hand gripping hers as they fought to get away from the multiplying crowd; one policeman frantically trying to calm a mob. The next day a national newspaper had run the headline: *Hastings Policeman Draws Truncheon On Blackshirts.* If only they had understood the dangers then. They'd had the warnings. But they couldn't have known how powerful the machinery of Hitler's propaganda war would become, nor how effortlessly he would invade so many countries. But Kate couldn't believe the World Service reports of mass exterminations in concentration camps. They *must* be exaggerating. No one was capable of such barbarism.

Out of the bus window, she saw signs stating: DANGER MINES all along the beach. A barricade of iron stakes stabbed the sands and rolls of thick barbed wire enclosed the top end of the beach. Marching along the promenade were hordes of Canadian soldiers, billeted in any undamaged hotel they could find. There were bombed buildings everywhere and the gaps were filled with Army lorries. How would the town ever be able to recover?

She got off the bus, keeping her head down against the mutinous rain and wind and crossed the road. Every day she had waited for a visit from Rob. Living only two streets away and not a glimpse. She shivered as the rain dripped from the cherry trees inside the collar of her navy blue raincoat.

She vowed she'd never go to see him again, so what was she doing standing outside *The Beeches* on a day like this? She looked around the Adams' large waterlogged garden, waiting for the door to be opened.

Suddenly Rob stood looking at her in astonishment. The violent red of his scars had faded to a polished pink. His mouth stretched like elastic. He was smiling at her.

'Kate ... I didn't think you'd want to see me again after ... Come in.'

They sat in the large kitchen, overlooking the garden. Kate tried to think of something significant to say.

'Tea?' Rob asked.

'Yes, please ... Shall I make –?'

He shook his head vigorously before bustling round the kitchen: his fingers fighting to open the tea caddy with a semblance of ease.

'Kate ... I ...'

'Yes?'

'I'm sorry. I was unforgivable to you in the hospital. Can you forgive me?' He turned towards her, his mouth a herringbone and Kate's stomach contracted. The first time she'd seen him she was fourteen and he was a dark-haired sixteen-year-old with a devastating smile.

'What – forgive the unforgivable?'

'Yes ... Please. Charlie told me to stop pitying myself. I have. Have you?'

'Your tirade in the hospital knocked pity on the head.'

It was over two years since they had really talked. Kate wondered if Rob felt as displaced as she did. He brought the tea over to the table and they sat looking at each other. Years of love uniting them: years of war dividing. She would never be sitting here if she hadn't seen Freda die.

'I'm going back, Kate.'

'To what?'

'To fight.'

Kate forced herself not to stare at his hands. He lifted them up as if he had read her mind. The scars, tortuous snakes running up his palms towards his wrists.

'Look.' He clasped the teapot and poured the tea into the cup without spilling a drop. There was only a small tremor in his hands as he placed the pot down on the table.

'I never thought you'd be able to use them again.'

'A year ago, nor did I. Amazing what a little will-power will do. And Charlie, of course … I couldn't have done it without Charlie.' A short pause. 'Did you know Mum and Dad are adopting him?'

Kate looked startled. 'But he has a family in London, hasn't he?'

'That's a *very* loose term. His mother's dead and Charlie's father used to beat him with a belt. He told me once when I needed a kick up the backside.'

'He hides it well.'

'He learned to live in a disguise much of the time.'

Kate's eyes darted briefly to his face.

'I'm learning too. Mine is just more obvious than Charlie's, that's all.'

'You're not so … angry as you were in hospital.'

'No. I remember you walking towards me in the ward, wearing a blue dress, looking incredibly beautiful and I hated you. I hated you for looking the same when I was so different.'

'You don't hate me now?'

'I've grown up since I met the Guinea Pigs. You remember the club we formed? I'm still in contact with some of the others. Do you remember the Welsh chap in the next bed to me? Fellow called Owen Parry?'

Kate nodded, although she didn't.

'He's training to become a doctor. Imagine that? After all he's been through. Talk about overcoming obstacles. I didn't realise other people mattered so much before, Kate. *You* matter to me. Very much.'

Kate held her breath. She'd read in a philosophy book in the school-library that knowledge is life with wings. The knowledge that she mattered to Rob made her feel she could levitate higher than the sky.

She laughed and Rob's eyes contracted with pain.

'Sorry. I shouldn't have said anything – not now when I look like –'

'I'm not laughing at you, you silly man. You're still using your face as a shield. I can see *you*, Rob. Not the boy you were. Not a burnt pilot who feels sorry for himself, in spite of saying he doesn't. *You*. I've loved you since I was fifteen and I don't know why. You're arrogant. Self-opinionated. Exasperating. Obstinate. In fact, you drive me utterly insane.'

143

Rob started laughing. 'That's the most negative declaration of love I've ever heard.'

'Well, where's yours?'

He stopped laughing. 'The day I was grounded from flying, I took out a Spit at night. It was going to be my last flight.'

Kate went pale. 'You mean suicide?'

'I knocked out a Heinkel because I didn't care. I should have been blown out of the sky, but I wasn't. I killed the crew because I was angry with life, not because they were the enemy. I was angry that I couldn't get my own way. I wasn't allowed to fly Spits. I was a petulant child. Then I thought of the people I loved. My parents. Charlie. *You.* I saw your face, Kate, as clearly as I can now. You were smiling at me outside the cockpit window and I knew I couldn't do it. I landed in a field.'

'You saw my face outside the cockpit window?' Kate asked, incredulously.

'Yes.'

'It's not possible.'

'I know it isn't, but I did. You made me come back, Kate. I didn't want to.'

'And that's a declaration of love, is it?'

'Well, it's better than yours.'

They looked at each other and suddenly burst out laughing.

They walked along the seafront promenade, listening to the waves crash over the dragon's teeth cemented into the ground

144

along the coast. In the distance, they saw a tall Victorian building, the Queen's Hotel: the adopted home of the RAF in Hastings. Rob hoped he would be accepted there.

It was almost deserted when they entered the Victorian bar. Only a couple of men, one old, one young, neither in uniform, playing dominoes in a corner by the large open hearth. They were too engrossed in their game to look up. Rob tensed as he walked up to the barman to order their drinks, preparing himself for another shocked reaction. The man was calmly polishing the glasses.

'Evening, Sir. And what plane was you flying, then?'

Rob was taken aback. 'Er … a Spitfire.'

'Bad luck, mate. What'll you have? … It's on the house.'

Rob was smiling as he carried the beers towards a secluded alcove where Kate was sitting, staring at an angry sea.

'I'm glad you made me come out, Kate,' he said as he sat down next to her.

'You need to get used to people again.'

'You mean they need to get used to me.'

'Perhaps. You know how difficult you are.' She smiled at him and he knew why he had seen her face from the cockpit of his plane. She gave him the strength to look at a tempest and not shake.

'Who would have thought that flat-chested fourteen-year-old girl would become an officer in the WAAFs?'

Kate frowned. 'Nobody. We didn't anticipate war, did we?'

145

'I didn't mean that. I mean you've achieved so much. I'm proud of you.'

'Are you? I don't know if becoming an officer during wartime is a reason to be proud. I remember Bridget saying that if it hadn't been for the war she would have married a boy from Connemara and had lots of children.'

'And would she have been happier?'

'Well, if she takes up Colin's offer, we'll never know.'

Rob frowned. 'What offer?'

'Hasn't he written? He's asked Bridget to marry him.'

'Marry him! *Bridget!*'

'She hasn't got two heads, Rob!'

'I'm sure she's a lovely girl, but Colin's not the marrying kind – you know that. My God, when I think of all the women –'

Rob stopped, suddenly realising that telling a sister that her brother visited prostitutes when he was in London might not be a good idea. He looked around the bar which was rapidly filling up with people, smoke and laughter.

'What women?'

'Sorry?' Rob said, cupping one hand over his ear. 'Can't hear.'

A number of soldiers on leave came crashing through the doors of the bar and demanded four pints.

'And none of your watered-down stuff, neither!' shouted a very red-faced Sergeant, looking around the room for an appreciation of his rapier wit. The soldiers obliged by roaring with laughter.

'Oh, God,' Rob said.

'Do you want to go?'

'And have to walk right past them?' Rob sank back in his seat. 'I'd rather eat razors.'

'They're too busy getting drunk to notice us. Anyway, I don't think they can see us here.'

Kate prayed that they couldn't. How would they react to Rob? Or he to them?

'Hope not,' Rob replied.

The soldiers were singing *It's a Long Way to Tipperary* at the top of their voices.

'Me old man sang this in the last lot,' the Sergeant shouted, leaning on the bar for support. 'Hero, he was. Learnt me every word.' He looked around the room. 'Come on, you miserable bunch. Sing up!'

People joined in reluctantly at first, but gradually the singing escalated. Soon the whole bar was singing *There'll Always Be An England*. Some people started crying. The men in the corner of the bar continued with their quiet game of dominoes, oblivious to the sentimentality surging around the room. An eighteen-year-old private with a hint of a moustache staggered towards them. 'Come on, gents. "Sing up" our Sarge said.' He leaned heavily on their table, breathing whisky into their faces.

The dominoes shot across the room as the table collapsed. The younger of the two men flushed.

'Why can't you leave people in peace?' the young man said in a shrill voice.

The singing died away as people stared at the dominoes scattered over the floor. No one moved to pick them up.

'Only a bit of fun, mate. Don't get your bollocks in a twist,' the Sergeant shouted across to the man.

'Jimmy, let's go,' the older man said to his son.

'I'm sick of turning the other cheek, Dad. He hasn't got the right to spoil someone's evening just because he's wearing a bloody uniform.'

The Sergeant's face darkened. 'Well, where's yours then, son? In the cleaners?'

'I haven't got one,' the young man answered, looking calmly at the Sergeant.

Kate held onto Rob's arm, frightened for the young man; frightened by what Rob might do.

The Sergeant turned to his soldiers. 'Hear that, lads? This bloke ain't got a uniform. Why d'you think that is?' His face now the colour of ox-blood.

The only sound in the room was the soft shuffle of the young man's feet as he walked towards the Sergeant. His father stood by the hearth, his face crumpling as if his son was walking into gunfire.

'I'll tell you why … I'm a Conchie. A coward. A lily-livered bastard you'd say, wouldn't you, Sergeant?'

'Jimmy!' His father clutched onto the mantelpiece over the hearth for support.

'Yeah – that's just what I'd say, son.' The Sergeant shouted in the younger man's face. 'My old man died for scum like you.' He smashed a beer bottle against the bar. 'What would have happened in 1914 if everyone acted like you, you scummy bastard?'

The young man stood in front of the Sergeant and said quietly, 'There wouldn't have been a war, would there?'

Suddenly Rob stood up and walked out of the alcove.

'Rob – no!' Kate called out to him.

Rob stood at the edge of the tense crowd of people who were looking at the Sergeant and the young Conscientious Objector.

'And I wouldn't have looked like this,' Rob said, holding up his head towards an over-hanging light.

Everyone turned to face him and a loud shock of air exploded round the room. All they saw was a grotesque mask. The Sergeant dropped his broken bottle in disbelief. Rob turned to Kate and she got up. They walked out of the hotel into the darkening twilight sky.

Chapter 12

By the time Rob had finished his course, qualified as a radio and navigating operator, he'd had the opportunity to use the latest AI Mk X radar equipment which could lock onto its target, via radio waves, and send back signals on a cathode ray tube. It was Rob's job to interpret these signals and tell the pilot whether the target was friend or foe.

He had been instructed to report to a Fighter Interception Unit in Middle Wallop. He knew he would be a valuable addition to the unit. But the day he went into the dispersal hut to find a pilot to team up with, was the most humiliating moment of his life. It was like touting for trade in Piccadilly with an overused body. He could see it in the eyes which looked at him, then darted away as they registered the scars.

Most of the officers were already fixed up with a navigator by the time he arrived, but there were a few still looking. They stopped when they saw Rob glance in their direction. He wanted to scream: *For Christ's sake – I'm good. I can fly anything! I've worked on radar! I can get you back home!* He had finished his course, top of the class.

He forced himself to walk towards an older officer who exuded calm competence as he puffed on his pipe. He wore the ribbons of the DFC and DFM and bar on his left breast.

'Good morning, Sir. I'm F.O. Adams. Just retrained as a navigator. Looking for a pilot.'

The man immediately held out his hand and before Rob was aware, his hand was held in a firm handshake. He managed not to wince.

'Squadron Leader Rowley. You could have me, but they consider me past it. Thirty-eight, you see. On the scrap heap.' He smiled. Rob felt an immense surge of warmth towards the man. 'Hear you used to fly Spits. Bloody marvellous kites, but the Beaufighter's not a bad old bus.'

Rob looked around the room; everyone seemed to have teamed up with a navigator. He had a hollow feeling in his stomach.

'Got a new fellow arriving shortly. From a Spit squadron too. Just been posted here. God knows why. Name of – ' Rowley shouted over to one of the pilots. 'Peter – what's the new chap's name again?'

'Brazier, Sir.'

'Brazier, that's it. Not a name I'm familiar with.'

'Brazier?'

The Squadron Leader looked startled. 'You know him?'

'I don't know, Sir, it's a common name in Sussex.'

At that moment the door crashed open, causing the wind to eddy round the room. Colin almost fell in: his enormous kitbag sliding off his shoulder into the mud around the door. He looked around in embarrassment.

'Sorry about that … F.O Brazier reporting.' There was an awkward silence, then Colin's eyes locked on Rob's. 'Good God! Can't I *ever* get away from you, Adams?' He let out an enormous whoop of laughter. The other pilots decided that the newcomers suited each other admirably: one scarred physically, the other mentally.

A quarter of an hour later, Rob and Colin were walking across the aerodrome which consisted of two grassy runways and a straggle of Nissan huts set in one corner of the field. Their quarters were at the end. They had to share until some other rooms became available – by somebody being killed. Inside the hut they saw two sagging camp beds without sheets, two broken chairs propping up a wall and one discoloured mirror hanging from a large nail.

'Bloody hell,' Rob said, looking around the bleak room.

'Christ, I have to share a plane *and* a depressing bedroom. This is stretching friendship a bit too far.' Colin grinned at him.

'Col, I'm sorry about the visit you know … in hospital. I said some lousy things I didn't mean.'

'Oh, shut up. I'm not used to you being apologetic.'

Rob leaned on the bed. It collapsed. 'Like old times. All home comforts.' He hesitated before asking the question he'd wanted to from the moment he'd seen him. 'What are you doing here, Col? Why'd you leave the Squadron?'

Colin immediately lost his veneer. He got up and stared out of the dirty windows which looked out on the runway. 'The night flying, Rob. You remember me telling you?'

'Yes.'

'The last flight. Solid cloud. The landing was…' Colin shuddered. 'I thought I'd bought it. Not a bloody light to be seen until I hit the deck. Sat in the cockpit for half an hour before I could move. Thought it was time for a transfer. This is it.'

Rob walked over and stood beside him at the window, thinking of the Conscientious Objector in the bar of the Queen's. He and Kate had walked home with him and his father that night and talked about the war. Who was more courageous? Rob thought. A man who held onto his principles against all opposition and helped the war effort by driving an ambulance? Or a man who was terrified of flying, but continued?

'How the hell did you get posted to nightfighter unit, Col?'

'Ironic, isn't it?'

'You *are* okay to fly, aren't you?'

Colin didn't speak for several moments. 'I am if you're going to be my eyes, Rob.'

Their first flight in a Bristol Beaufighter with its devastating armament of 420mm cannon was a trial by ordeal. They were sent up in conditions which forced Colin to fly on his instruments. But knowing that Rob could navigate and pilot a plane allowed him to rediscover the confidence he thought he'd lost. He trusted Rob's judgment implicitly.

Like the Spitfire, the cockpit of the Beaufighter was well laid out with all the instruments easily to hand. Of course, it was slower than the Spit, but Colin had had enough of juggling with Jesus to last him a lifetime. The space inside the plane was vast after the coffin-like confinement of the Spitfire, but there was one aspect of the fighter that bothered them both: the lack of heating. Although they could see a red hot exhaust pipe coming out of the port engine six feet away, only a minute amount of hot air reached Colin's right heel, while Rob's heater sent a mere whisper of lukewarm air dissipating into the myriad draughts whistling down the fuselage. They were both wearing bulky Sidcot flying suits, relics from WW1, in an effort to combat the cold. Rob had discarded leather gauntlets in favour of woollen mittens over thin silk gloves. They gave his fingers more mobility.

They were flying through the upper reaches of cumulus cloud where constant corrections had to be made on the controls because of turbulence. Colin relied more on Rob than his instruments to tell him when he was being deceived by centrifugal force: a force which made pilots believe they were flying straight and level when they weren't. But the strain of concentration was monumental. It was an hour before the Controller told them to return to base; they had obviously passed the test. At that moment Colin knew exactly how prisoners must feel on being given parole. Rob plotted their route home and they descended slowly through cumulonimbus cloud, trying to avoid the usual icing on the wings.

'Right on course, Col,' Rob said, through the headphones. 'ETA – 1700 hours. Mine's a double brandy.'

Colin started whistling. Landing ten tons of Beaufighter on a bumpy field held no terrors for him. Rob was on board.

Over the ensuing weeks Colin and Rob practised airborne interceptions with the other planes in their unit. During one practice, the squadron discovered that Rob was invaluable as a 'jammer'. He had changed wavelengths on the A1 and intercepted a German radar operator talking to the pilot of a Ju 88. The pilot was trying to manoeuvre his fighter under a British Lancaster, the one spot which was blind. The radar operator started to give instructions to fire the 20-mm cannon up into the Lancaster's fuel tanks. Before he could finish, Rob shouted: *'Das ist die Stimme des Feindes. Nicht schiessen! Nicht schiessen!'* After Rob shouted these instructions repeatedly, the German pilot became so confused he broke off the attack.

'What did you say?' Colin asked him.

'Don't fire! That's an enemy voice – don't listen to it!'

They both laughed as they flew back to base.

Rob didn't have to pay for a drink for over a fortnight in the Mess. The camaraderie he'd felt in his old squadron and the hospital was returning. His only worry was Colin. He noticed his lack of concentration, his sleeplessness, his occasional bursts of over-noisy laughter at some weak joke: minute, but disturbing signs of combat fatigue. He knew that Colin was disturbed that two 'trick-cyclists', psychiatrists, were going to pay the unit an 'unofficial' visit. The suggestion of one young pilot officer appeared to save him. Peter Oldham, not long out of Initial Training, commented on the fact that all 'trick-cyclists' were bonkers themselves and were obviously looking for signs of it in others. 'So, let's give it to them, chaps.' The unit, all tired from constant night patrols, decided to have some fun.

The day the two psychiatrists arrived incognito, Colin and Rob were in the Mess with a number of other officers playing cards. R.O. Tony Bowles, a goblin of a man with round ruddy cheeks and a wicked sense of humour was dealing. He was wearing dark glasses and accentuated his lack of height by sitting on a low chair so that his five-foot-three-inch body was barely able to see over the table top.

'Good morning, gentlemen,' Tony shouted out over the sound of Glen Miller's band playing *In The Mood* very loudly on the wireless. The psychiatrists had told the S.L. that they didn't want any fuss. They wanted to study the men 'as they really were' and would wander around, merging into the background. They were startled to see an enormous pewter tray on a table in the middle of the room, full of carrots.

'Take one before they all go,' Colin shouted to the psychiatrists, twitching his eyes alarmingly. 'Mad on carrots here, aren't we, chaps?' To prove the point the men got up as one, took a handful from the tray and started munching vigorously. They all sat down at the table again as Tony threw the cards over the table.

'Bloody eyes. Carrots don't seem to be working.'

'What's trumps,' shouted Peter Oldham, twirling an enormous black moustache he had waxed and stuck on for the occasion. 'Not hearts. It's got to be diamonds. I like them.'

'But I don't,' Rob shouted back. 'Not with my hands. I know a hawk from a handsaw.'

'Do you?' They all looked dumbfounded.

The psychiatrists shifted uneasily on their chairs. One of them cleared his throat noisily and everyone jumped, cards cascading into the air.

'Wish you wouldn't do that, old boy,' Tony said. 'Nerves not too good at the moment. It's the flying, you know.'

The men grovelled on the floor, collecting the cards and gave them to Tony.

'Right,' he said when they were all sitting down. 'Diamonds it is, chaps.'

'Goodo,' Peter chortled, twirling his moustache again. 'A boy's best friend. My lead.' He threw the King of Diamonds onto the table.

'Bloody madness, that,' Tony muttered, leaning over the table, trying to see the cards through his dark glasses.

'Ah, but there's method in it.'

'How true, Peter,' Rob said. 'Madness to an observer is often wisdom to the doer. Don't you agree, gentlemen?'

They stopped playing and turned to look at the psychiatrists who were silently creeping out of the room.

'Bye!' everyone shouted.

Rob hadn't heard Colin laugh so loudly or naturally for weeks. He wondered how long it would last.

Chapter 13

One beautiful summer's morning in 1944, Mr Smedley blew a whistle and a hundred boys froze on the hard asphalt playground, blood dripping down several knees from skirmishes with the ground. *Well, what do you think of your little boy now, Mother?* Mr Smedley always thought of his mother on such occasions. He lingered before he blew the second whistle, savouring the moment. Jutting out into the playground at right angles to the school was a cycle shed which backed onto the toilets. One of the doors was banging again. Very irritating. Mr Smedley waited to see if Masters would peer out from behind the toilet door, trying to escape Geography. He must have spent years in that toilet, he thought, recalling the question he'd asked the Geography teacher: 'Please, Sir what street's Brighton in?'

Mr Smedley checked the sky. Several raids had caused havoc with his discipline. Thankfully, today the skies were clear.

'*Did I see someone move?*' he thundered. The boys stood like stones, cemented in rock. No one was falling for that.

He blew the second whistle shrilly and a hurl of bodies transformed into eight lines with each boy placing a hand on the corresponding shoulder in front. The strains of a Sousa march blared over the loudspeaker system and the pupils marched into school like well-drilled soldiers, their gas masks bumping against their legs.

In the classroom, Mr Smedley stared at the pile of papers in front of him. 'Cast your minds back to a windswept day in June last year, boys, when Walters over there was murdering one of Malvolio's speeches from *Twelfth Night*. Those of you with more than four brain cells might remember. *"Some are born great, some achieve greatness and some have greatness thrust upon them."* If Shakespeare had had the misfortune to read the *de*compositions I was subjected to last night he would have revised Malvolio's speech. Can anyone think what revisions he would have employed?' Mr Smedley creaked up and down the rows of desks, waiting for a brilliant answer. The boys looked for enlightenment from the execrable drawing of the *Globe Theatre* on the blackboard. Minutes limped by. Mr Smedley banged his cane repeatedly across the silence.

"Some are born ignorant, some achieve ignorance and some have ignorance thrust upon them." Mr Smedley picked up one particularly dirty, ink-blotched piece of paper from the pile and thrust it into Ian's hands.

'Walters. Contrary to popular belief, a dinosaur is *not* an amphibious vehicle.'

The class laughed for exactly ten seconds.

It was very, very gratifying.

Three hours later, Tubs and Charlie were cycling home after school past the bombed houses in Gladstone Terrace when they saw an AA unit standing in a sand-bagged emplacement built high on the West Hill to give an unbroken view over the

159

coast. One of the men was wearing headphones, with a mouthpiece strapped over his chest. A young ATS Officer was working a plotting instrument, which stood on a tripod in the centre of the post, and a number of gunners were manning light Bofors guns.

'What they doing?' Tubs asked.

'Trying to work out where the Luftwaffe is, of course, stupid. I think old Smedley's right.'

'Hey watch it, smart ass!'

'Come on,' Charlie said. 'Let's have a look.'

'Can't. Got to be home early after those women complained to me Mum about me trying to sell them those parachute cords.'

'Shouldn't have asked them for fourpence. Asking for trouble. I only charged tuppence.'

'What! That's why they complained to me Mum!'

'All's fair in war, Tubs.'

'Oh *yeah*! You wait 'til I find something important. I won't tell you!' Tubs rode off, planning how he would throttle Charlie with the cord he had left.

Charlie grinned as he wheeled his bike over the hill towards the AA unit. The man with the headphones had heard something.

'5678. South East. Eight. At 10,000,' he said.

'What's that mean?' Charlie asked.

The man motioned Charlie to silence as he listened.

'Hurricanes, I think… Okay.'

He looked pleased before he turned to Charlie and frowned.

'Push off, lad. We're busy.'

'How'd you know they're Hurricanes? They might be enemy planes.'

'Didn't you hear me?'

'All right. All right. I'm only asking.'

'Well, don't.' The man looked at his watch. 'Your shift ended half an hour ago, Mary. You go home. Put your feet up.' He was speaking to the ATS Officer. He sounded much nicer when he talked to her, Charlie thought, picking up his bike off the grass.

'Okay, Freddie. See you tomorrow,' she answered. One of the men took over the plotting instrument as she walked over the hill towards Charlie who was wheeling his bike across the grass.

'He's not usually like that,' the young woman called to him. 'It's been a long day.'

Charlie turned to look at her. She had an open friendly face; the sort you could trust. 'Sorry. I shouldn't have asked. Only I'm interested … my brother was a Spitfire pilot, you see. He taught me about planes.' Charlie suddenly found himself telling her about Rob's crash and his life with John and Mary. He had never spoken about them to anyone before, not even Mrs Bates. But he was going to be adopted in two weeks. The social services had written that his father was missing in action, believed dead. So Uncle John had written some powerful letters to powerful people.

'Your family sound lovely.'

'Yeah, they are. And my brother's better now. He's a navigator. Rob could do anything.'

'Good. My father will be pleased.'

'Your father? He doesn't know Rob, does he?'

'No, but I'm sure he'd like to.'

'Why, what's he do?' Charlie asked.

The young woman smiled disarmingly. 'Oh, quite a lot really. He's the Prime Minister.'

'What?' Charlie's bike crashed onto the grass. 'Your Dad's Winston Churchill! Go on – pull the other one.'

Mary laughed at his disbelief. She took out a picture from her jacket pocket and gave it to Charlie. He looked into a garden full of roses. Three people were sitting at a white table by a large pond having tea: Winston and Clementine Churchill and the young woman standing in front of Charlie.

He was speechless for at least five seconds.

'Wait 'til I tell the others. Winston Churchill's daughter standing with me on the West Hill!'

Mary Churchill looked worried. 'No, please don't. I don't want everyone to know who I am.'

'Why not?'

'Because they'd treat me differently. I don't want preferential treatment.'

Charlie screwed up his eyes. 'What's that?'

'Oh, I don't have to queue up if I don't want to and I have lots of invitations to concerts and exhibitions and parties – that sort of thing. All free.'

Charlie's mouth dropped open. 'Blimey, wish someone would give *me* peripheral treatment.' He suddenly realised that perhaps Winston Churchill's daughter *could*. 'Can I ask you to ask your Dad for something.'

'I can *ask* him,' Mary Churchill said tentatively, not giving Charlie much hope.

'Can you *please* ask him to lift the ban on ice-cream? I love it,' Charlie said, seriously.

Mary Churchill laughed, then suddenly they heard a noise in the air, unlike any aircraft noise they had ever heard before: a deep guttural note, harsh, vibrating, like a cheap, gigantic motor bike. They looked up, trying to catch a glimpse of whatever was approaching, but the sky was swathed in clouds. It was almost above their heads when through a small break in the cloud, Charlie saw his first brief glimpse of a V1 bomb: a deadly black cross slicing the sky, flames belching from its exhaust. The thunder was deafening.

Then suddenly the engine cut.

Charlie looked at Mary Churchill. For a second, neither of them moved, rigid in the silence. Then simultaneously they dropped like stones in the long grass.

Charlie lay with his face pressed into the grass, one hand squashed awkwardly under his hip, his breath a whisper in case he disturbed something. He heard Mary Churchill counting under her breath. *Ten. Nine. Eight.* How long would they have to wait before they were blown up? He opened one eye and saw her staring back at him. People he hadn't seen before were sitting up and looking around in wonderment. Then someone started to laugh just as the bomb hit the roof of a house, shattering the windowpanes, blowing the doors off their hinges, killing a wife and husband as they ran, too late, to their Anderson shelter.

Soon, the papers were awash with news of the pilotless planes, quickly renamed 'doodlebug' or 'buzz' bombs by the people living in south-east England. Within weeks, the area changed its face. Shooting galleries of light and heavy AA guns, American 88s, British 3.7s and lines of Bofors on high ground were placed all along the coast. Overhead, a formidable barrage of hydrogen balloons floated in their hundreds to deter the track of the unnerving pilotless bombs. The War Office sent out a directive to all the coastal towns. *Capture one.* They wanted to examine it.

Charlie and the other boys were desperate to be one of the first to 'discover' one that hadn't blown up. They didn't have long to wait. They were cycling near a field in Wishing Tree Road in St Leonards when the now familiar harsh grating sound of a doodlebug was heard coming towards them. They waited for the awesome sound of silence. Charlie felt as powerful as Alexander the Great when the sound cut off directly over his head. If a doddlebug's engine cut out overhead there was no danger. Pilotless planes without power drifted sideways. The boys watched the bomb glide down into a field a hundred yards away from them and waited for the explosion. Nothing.

They raced past oak and birch trees, trampling through tall grass until they found it. A black monoplane, with a wing span of just over seventeen feet and a length of twenty-five feet, was pitched nose-down into the ground. One broken wing lay close by. On its tail, a curious tube jabbed into the air.

'Is that all it is?' Tubs said, speaking for them all. It seemed impossible. Houses, hotels and churches were being destroyed almost daily by these small robots.

Charlie was determined to take part of the broken wing home with him. He started to move towards it just as they heard the sound of army vehicles speeding towards them.

'Oh, bugger,' Charlie whispered. 'Now I'll never get near it.'

'Well, I don't think you should anyway,' Ian said. 'My Dad knows all about these. One touch and it could blow you to kingdom come, he said.'

'Oh, shut up. You sound like old Smedley,' Charlie muttered. The treasure of a lifetime was being cordoned off by a troop of soldiers who swarmed over the field, pushing the boys back from the bomb.

Charlie hopped over the cordon and sauntered towards an officer. 'We found it. Do we get a reward?'

'No,' the Captain shouted. 'Now get back with the others or you'll get a clip round your ear.'

Charlie stuffed his hands in his pockets and stomped back towards the boys. 'That's what you get for being patriotic, is it? Cleared Fairlight cliffs *and* found a buzzbomb,' he shouted when he was out of range of the officer.

Within five minutes the field was full of subdued people, staring in awe at the bomb. This time they were lucky, but what about the next? The tension lifted as a squadron of Spitfires flew overhead. A cheer went up. People started shouting:

'Hitler's bomb's no bloody use.'

'Yeah! The candle went out.'

'Forgot to put in the wick.'

'He ain't got no wick, has he?'

A tremor of laughter rippled through the crowd. Then the bomb disposal team arrived and everyone was directed off the field before they began.

The boys stood at the edge of the operations for over an hour, waiting for the bomb to explode. To their disgust, it didn't. And soon they were watching an army convoy disappear with it.

'Makes you want to take up spying for the Hun, doesn't it?' Charlie almost wept as the convoy snaked round a corner. 'Not even a thank you.'

'I'm going home. Nothing doing here,' Tubs said with disgust.

'Wait a minute, Tubs … got something to show you.'

'Oh yeah? – parachute cord, is it?' he muttered.

'Oh, come on. That was ages ago. Wait 'til you see this.' Charlie took out a bottle of luminous paint he had discovered on a shelf in Woolworths.

'Paint! … That's it? I'm off.'

'Got something much more exciting than that.' Ian stared up at Charlie and Tubs, hardly able to contain his excitement.

The boys looked at him without interest. The last time Ian had showed them something exciting it had been Mrs Humphries' bloomers blowing in the wind.

'Can't wait,' Tub said.

Ian, squirming with anticipation, produced a magazine from under his jumper. Charlie and Tubs had never seen it before.

'*Health and Efficiency!* Worse than bloomers.' Tubs got on his bike.

'Wait,' Ian said. 'Look.' He turned over a page and the boys gasped as they saw a dark-haired girl in a cornfield. She was naked.

'Blimey,' Charlie couldn't stop himself blushing as he grabbed the magazine off Ian. 'Where'd you get this?'

'Careful – it's my Dad's.'

'*Your Dad's?*' Charlie couldn't imagine Uncle John even looking at such a magazine, let alone buying one.

'Why hasn't she got any hair?' Tubs whispered.

'She *has*,' Charlie said, puzzled.

'Don't be daft. *You* know …down there.'

The boys looked at him and Charlie's colour heightened even more.

'They've painted it out, 'cos it's ugly,' Ian said, with all the knowledge of an innocent thirteen-year-old.

'Oh, yeah,' Charlie drawled, hoping he sounded as if he'd seen millions of pubic hairs.

'They've painted out what's underneath too. Look,' Tubs whispered. He had seen his older sister in the bath, but she'd never looked this exotic, even with all her 'bits' intact.

'They'd have to, wouldn't they? To pass the censor.' Charlie put one hand over the front of his trousers to subdue the movement. The girl was standing in the middle of the cornfield; her dark brown nipples pointing at him. Did mating feel as strange as this?

'Wouldn't mind meeting her on a dark night,' Tubs said.

'Don't suppose she'd want to meet you, though, Tubs,' Ian sniggered.

Suddenly, a rotund man Ian dimly recognised walked around the corner and saw the boys with the magazine. He advanced on them, looking disgusted.

'Hey – where did you boys get that from? Dirty little buggers!'

'Found it, Mister,' Charlie shouted. 'Over there.'

Ian hid behind the boys, petrified. He suddenly recognised who he was: Mr Baker – one of their neighbours.

'You better give that to me. Shouldn't be looking at filth like that. Not at your age anyway.'

Ian turned pale. His father would strangle him slowly if he found the magazine missing. Charlie shoved it in his hand and whispered, 'Get going.'

Just as Mr Baker drew level with them, Ian jumped on his bike and sped off down Gillsman's Hill.

'Hey, you little – I'll report you.' He turned to Tubs and Charlie. 'I'll report the lot of you.'

'Who to?' Charlie said.

'You're a cocky devil, aren't you? The police.'

'But we haven't got anything, mister, so it's your word against ours. Two against one. And *my* Dad's a doctor. Bet we'll win in a court of law.'

'Who said anything about a court of law? I'm just saying you shouldn't be reading such stuff, that's all.'

'Well, we're not, are we?' Charlie said, with the confidence born of high expectations.

'You better be careful with your tongue, kid. You might cut yourself.'

Charlie studied the man carefully. 'Not on you, I won't. You're too fat.'

'I told you to be careful, kid.' His eyes were now broken bottles.

Tubs raced off on his bike as the man went to hit Charlie across his head. He didn't see the hostility on Charlie's face – the aggressive kick aimed at the groin – the man's face contorted in agony as he collapsed onto the road. Charlie stood over him, breathing heavily.

'No one will *ever ever* hit me again, Mister. Remember that.'

Charlie got onto his bike and raced down the hill, leaving the man lying on the ground.

Chapter 14

'Remember the last time we were in London?' Rob said to Kate. They were walking against the turbulence of wind towards Shepherds, Rob's favourite pub in Mayfair. He and Kate had two days' leave.

'Don't.' Kate *did* remember it all too clearly: the dirty room at the top of the boarding house. The knowing look of the landlady as she over-charged them for one night. The appalling squeaky bed.

'I didn't mean our abortive night of passion. I meant walking in Hyde Park on a beautiful summer's day with you.'

Kate looked up at him, remembering how the walk had been eclipsed by the fear of losing her virginity later that night. The memory was distorted, like notes from an underwater orchestra.

Rob's heartbeat accelerated as he opened the green and yellow door. This was his first visit since the crash. He always came here to catch up on events from Oskar, the short dark Swiss who ran the pub, as he had more news than the World Service.

As usual the pub was crowded with service personnel: British, American, Australian, Canadian, Pole, Czech, stood in a swirling cacophony of noise and smoke, exchanging exclusives. Kate's eyes started smarting as she tried to see across the room.

'You *like* this?' she asked Rob.

He disappeared under the weight of pilots who'd flown with him. They'd all heard about his crash and a long line of beers suddenly frothed along the bar. Kate sat, ignored, in one corner of the long room. A dapper little man wearing immaculate clothes - grey striped trousers and a black jacket - walked over to her.

'I know you.' His voice was unsteady.

Kate flushed. 'I'm sorry. I'm with –'

'Robert showed me your photograph a long time ago – in this room.'

Kate smiled. 'Oh, you must be Oskar. Rob's told me about you.'

He stood in front of Kate, whispering. 'I heard about his crash, of course. A miracle he survived, but his *face*.' Oskar spread his hands apart, looking as if he was about to cry. 'I always envied Robert his good looks. He only had to look at a woman and ...' He stopped short. 'Not that he did, of course.'

At the other end of the bar Rob was chatting to old friends, oblivious to the fact that Oskar was traumatised by his disfigurement. 'How can he ...'

'How can he what?' Kate said, sharply.

'Look in a mirror?'

Kate felt dizzy as blood flooded her brain. 'He doesn't need your pity or disgust or whatever else you feel!' Faces turned towards them. She hadn't realised she'd been shouting.

At the other end of the bar, Rob was looking round for her. His face contorted into a smile when he saw Oskar standing near her. He walked over to them, carrying some drinks.

'So that's where you've been hiding, you old reprobate. After my girl, are you?' The beer slopped out of the glasses as Rob banged them onto the table. He went to shake Oskar's hand. There was a fractional hesitation before Oskar, his small face beaming, thrust his hand into Rob's.

'Robert. I know now why you've been hiding her for so long.'

'Kate, meet Oskar. Oskar, meet Kate.'

Oskar and Kate smiled at each other as if they'd never spoken.

'Hello, Oskar. Rob tells me you know everything there is to know about the RAF. So what's happening?'

Oskar was still telling them a quarter of an hour later. 'Naturally, you've heard about the Australian, Kenneth Collier?'

Rob shook his head, knowing the delight Oskar would have telling him.

'One of the Australians over there – 91 Squadron,' he pointed across the room where a noisy crowd of Australian Spitfire pilots were propping up the bar, 'said his friend tipped a V1 off course with his wing tip. Can you imagine flying next to a bomb? My God! You don't think he invented the story, do you?'

172

Rob put down his beer. Would he have the courage to fly alongside 300 pounds of dynamite moving at 330 mph and tip it over? He'd never know now.

'No. It's possible if he was flying the new Spitfire XIV, but bloody dangerous.'

They were silent for a moment while they drank the beer, contemplating the absurdities of war. Then Oskar, looking around the room as if he suspected Hitler to walk in at any moment, whispered, 'And the V2.'

'What about it?' Like most of Great Britain, Rob had only just discovered it was capable of flying faster than sound.

Oskar wiped his forehead with a large handkerchief. 'It's far worse than the V1, Robert. Ten times more destructive. It comes from deep inside Germany. I have it on good authority. These Germans! And after the V2 – what next? V3s? V4s? Even if the Russians swamped Germany from the east there would still be the Bavarian mountains, and these rockets could be fired off from caves, secret valleys, the Berchtesgarden, even. They could destroy Paris, Moscow, London … my God – what would happen to my business then?'

Rob and Kate exchanged smiles. Rob had always suspected that Oskar wanted life to be reduced to a mere balancing of books. He suddenly realised that there were far worse ambitions to have.

'And you know what they're doing with the Spitfire now, don't you?' Oskar continued.

Rob shook his head.

'Turning it into a bomber.'

'What?'

Oskar motioned him to silence with his fingers. 'Walls have ears.' He leaned forward. Your old friend, Hugh Dundas, came in last month. Asked after you, of course. He told me in *strict* confidence. I am now telling you in strict confidence. It concerns the V2. He told me the Spitfire is the only plane capable of accurate bombing of the V2 sites because they're so small. Special training for pilots has been set up to instruct them in precision bombing. They desperately need experienced Spitfire pilots.'

Rob's longing to fly flooded through him with such force, he couldn't speak. His hands clenched round the glass; his gaze fixed on the sparks of amber in the beer, caught in November light. Oskar looked at Kate nervously. This was not the Robert he knew.

'You shouldn't be talking about things told you in confidence, Oskar,' Rob said, his voice like flint.

'I'm only telling you because you're an old friend of Hugh's.' Oskar squirmed under Rob's disapproval. 'I haven't told the others.' He gave a nervous cough. 'Well … it was good to meet you, Kate. I hope we meet again.' He stood up and gave her a small bow. 'Formidable … I must get back to work, Robert. Au revoir.'

He scampered across the room to supervise the new wine waiter.

Kate took a sip of beer before saying: 'You were a bit hard on him, Rob.'

'He was hard on me.'

'How?'

'Talking about Spits.'

'You still miss them?'

'Of course I bloody miss them!'

They were silent while Kate drank her beer, noticing the servicemen staring first at her, and then at Rob.

'Sorry. The ugly spectre of self-pity again.' Rob turned to smile at her.

She was just about to ask him about Colin when three heavily made-up women came in wearing the tight clothes of their profession. They tripped over to the Australians on the far side of the bar. A loud shout went up.

'Are those the sort of women you were talking about, Rob?'

'When?'

'You know when. When we were in Hastings talking about Colin. Does he go with such women?'

Rob nodded after finishing his beer.

'Why?'

'I think because it's uncomplicated. It's just sex without strings.' He glanced at Kate, trying to judge her reaction.

'Is that what men want?'

'Some men.'

'You?' Kate's eyes burned into him.

He inhaled deeply. 'No.'

'Then why the hesitation?'

Rob took Kate's hand into his and told her about a night he had spent with a girl called Billie, a nightclub singer. The avalanche of sex before a bombing raid. It seemed like prehistory now.

Kate's face went very pale. 'You made love five times in two hours?'

'Yes.'

'Why? … Why so many times? Did you need the practice?'

'She seemed to like sex … a lot.'

'I see. And you *had* to oblige her.' Her voice was so low he was lip-reading.

'Kate – it was nothing like the feeling I have for you.'

'So it meant nothing? Just sex without strings?'

She moved her hand away from his as he struggled to find the right words.

'It's difficult to explain.'

'Try.' Her voice was hard.

'She was unlike any girl I'd met before. She had this great gift for … embracing life. To enjoy it totally. We seem to have forgotten that with the war.'

'You mean she slept with any man she wanted?'

'I don't know … I never saw her again. I … suppose she did.'

'And that's all right, is it? That's *embracing* life? Sleeping with anyone who takes your fancy?'

'I didn't say that, did I?'

'So it would be all right for me to go up to one of those officers who've been ogling me since I walked in and suggest we sleep together?' Kate snapped.

'Don't be ridiculous!'

'Well, when that girl did it, it was "embracing" life. Why can't I "embrace" it?'

Rob could feel his heart racing. This was their first day together and already they were arguing.

'Keep your voice down, Kate. You're being ridiculous.'

'You've already said that! I'd better go since I'm so ridiculous.' She got up hurriedly, spilling her drink.

Rob jumped up and put his arms on her shoulders. 'No! You're not leaving. She was a minute's excitement, Kate. *You're* my love. My only love. There's a *hell* of a difference.'

'And how do I know that? I didn't know about *her* before today.'

'Because I've never asked someone to marry me before today – that's why!' Rob shouted at her.

Everyone around them stopped drinking, waiting for Kate's reply.

'And that's a proposal, is it?' she shouted back.

'Yes!'

'Well, I don't think much of it!'

'Well it's all you're going to get Katherine Brazier, so what's the answer?'

Kate suddenly looked around to find everyone in the bar staring at her, their glasses poised in the air. Her face flushed as she looked from them to Rob. 'I must be mad, but *yes*!' she shouted.

Oskar was standing on a chair, tears dripping down his face. 'The drinks are on Oskar, gentlemen. It's not often we can celebrate such a noisy engagement.'

The room erupted into wild cheers. Oskar's whisky was unrivalled, both in quality and expense. There was a stampede towards the bar.

Oskar felt suddenly faint as he contemplated the folly of sentimentality from the giddy heights of his chair. His bar-stewards were a blur, rushing around the room, giving away every penny of his profits.

Kate was looking out of their hotel bedroom window after an extravagant meal of Boeuf Bourguignon and a rare bottle of Chateau Margaux. The room and the dinner had cost Rob two weeks' wages, but he was determined the awful experience of the cheap boarding house was not going to be repeated. He came and stood behind her, putting his arms around the blue chiffon dress he had bought her from Dickens and Jones.

The black of the night was criss-crossed with moving parallelograms of lights: searchlights sweeping the skies for enemy aircraft. Far in the distance they could hear the tattoo of heavy ack-ack fire.

'Not the quietest night for romance.' He nuzzled into her neck and kissed it. 'No regrets, then?'

'About what?'

'Marrying me.'

'Not yet. Give me a week.' She laughed, leaning against him. The wine made her feel indomitable.

'I *do* love you, Kate. Very much.'

'That's the first time you've ever –'

She turned towards him and at that moment, the searchlights swept across the window, highlighting each knotted scar on his face. He inhaled noisily, before moving back into the shadows.

'How can you bear to look at me?'

Kate walked into the shadows and touched his face, tracing the path of his scars with her fingers. He tried to pull away.

'Don't,' she whispered.

'No one's touched them like that.'

'Come back to the window, Rob. I want to remember everything about this night.' She took his hand and they stood again, looking at the black lake in front of them as the searchlights seared another part of the sky. 'Tell me something … if you hadn't been burnt, would you have asked me to marry you?'

She waited for his reaction. She had learnt to read his body movements as once she used to read his face. He twisted his feet on the floor. 'You wouldn't have, would you?'

'I don't know. Before the crash, I always wanted everything – like a child. To *be* a child in a Spitfire fighting the Hun and have all the girls fighting over me – the conquering hero.'

Kate frowned as Rob took her hands. 'I said *before*, Kate. Being burnt shred more than my skin. I'm not a hero. Not by anybody's definition. Charlie is. My mother is. You are.'

'Me?' Kate looked at him, astonished. 'I haven't done anything heroic in my life.'

'You've helped bring this wreck back to life. Stopped him destroying himself and his family's lives. You're here after I told you I had sex with another woman.'

'That's not heroic, that's stupidity.'

He laughed. 'No, it's not. She frightened me to death.'

*

Rob wanted to feel every inch of her skin, but his fingers felt nothing. His nerve endings had been burnt away. But he could taste the tang of his tears and so could Kate.

'Hey, stop that.' Kate kissed his face. They were lying on a large bed which had been covered with ornate drapes, now heaped on the floor. 'It's not that awful being with me, is it?' They smiled at each other. Kate concentrated on the immense depth in his dark brown eyes. 'I've got something to tell you.'

His body tensed. That's why he'd never wanted to fall in love. Too much like having an open wound.

'I've slept with someone too.'

The incredible pain of English euphemisms, Rob thought.

'When? Who?'

Kate told him about the night she'd spent with a Canadian called Mike. The night she'd drunk lots of cider. The night she regretted.

'I'm not saying I went with him because I was drunk, Rob. That's an easy excuse.'

Rob lay on the bed looking up into blackboard darkness. The scenario reminded him of a passage in *Tess of the d'Urbervilles*. Tess confesses that she's had a child, thinking her new husband will forgive her as she's forgiven him for earlier liaisons. He doesn't. But that was the nineteenth century and he's not Angel Clare. So why can't he speak? Why this pain constricting his heart?

Kate reached over to turn his head towards her. 'Rob, remember what you said to me in the pub? She was a minute's excitement? It wasn't even exciting for me. I could only go through with it by pretending he was you.'

'Poor man.'

'Do you think he knew?'

'Yes.' There were tears in Rob's eyes. 'Oh Kate. I wanted to be the first to love you.'

She felt her own eyes pricking. 'You are, my *dear, dear* love.' The searchlights suddenly swept the window. Closing her eyes, she kissed him on his lips, his eyes, his scars. Rob watched her chestnut hair spark gold fire before the lights moved, changing it to ebony. He reached out for her in the darkness.

Chapter 15

Charlie had been up since dawn to see what the war had left him in the night; he had to get there before the other boys. He had his booty spread out on his bed: pieces of shrapnel, twisted metal torn off an exploding AA shell or a German plane. One piece interested him. It had lettering on it, some sort of code in black on a shiny silver surface. It gave him an idea. A peace offering for Tubs. He'd never been the same with him after he'd undercut his prices.

Half an hour later, Charlie had finished inscribing the word on the largest piece of black shrapnel he had. He put out the light. In large luminous letters on the smooth side of the metal was the word GEORING in the gothic script he had copied from Uncle John's German dictionary. It was a masterpiece. He couldn't wait until he saw Tubs in the graveyard that night.

He heard Mary coming up the stairs and hastily hid the paint behind his Beano comic before she walked in.

'Charlie?' Mary put on the light to find him sitting on the bed holding the unique piece of shrapnel in hot, innocent hands. The odour of paint, pungent in the room.

'You'll never guess what I found, Mum,' Charlie said, bright as butter.

Endorphins raced round Mary's body at the sound of one word. 'What?' she asked, smiling.

He held it out to her, waiting for her stunned admiration. She burst out laughing.

'That's unique, that is! Could fetch thousands on the open market.' Why was she laughing? Rembrandt couldn't have signed it better.

Mary managed to stop laughing. 'I never knew Goering had a problem with spelling, Charlie. Come on, it's time for tea.' She started to walk out of the room, but couldn't resist adding, 'I think you'd better write another one if you want the thousands.' Charlie could hear her laughing as she walked into the kitchen.

He sighed as he looked at his flawed masterpiece. He couldn't give it to Tubs now. Then he remembered what Tubs had got for his last spelling test. Two out of twenty. Whistling loudly, Charlie followed Mary down the stairs.

*

Charlie was sitting on a tombstone near the bombed nave of St John's Church. Only the tower and spire were still standing. Meeting in the graveyard had seemed a great idea that morning. The shadows of the dead made it less attractive at night. His torch, covered with red tissue paper, directed the shadows into devious shapes. He wished he hadn't bought luminous paint now. He heard a faint moaning sound from behind a tombstone and went rigid with fear. They had come for him. Then a sniff. Unmistakable. Ian.

'Very funny, Masters … Are you dressed in black?'

Ian came out of the shadows, wiping his sleeve across his upper lip. 'You weren't scared then, Charlie?'

'Naw,' he answered, nonchalantly, looking Ian up and down. It didn't take long. For once Ian had remembered what he had to do – wear black. Suddenly Tubs was there too, crashing over the rubble in a desperate attempt to be quiet.

'No one would know you'd arrived, Tubs.'

'Well, I can't help it, can I? Can't see nothing.' He fell over a large section of the church wall to emphasise his point and groaned loudly.

Charlie and Ian walked carefully over to him. He was lying twisted in the rubble, apparently in agony.

'You all right, Tubs?' Charlie said, worried that this might be the end of their friendship completely.

Tubs sat up suddenly. 'No, I'm not. Anyway, Slater – this is a daft idea. Meeting in a churchyard dressed in black.'

Charlie shone the torch onto the piece of shrapnel he was holding. 'No, it's not. Look what I've got for you, Tubs. Found it this morning. Guess whose plane it comes from?'

'I don't know, do I?' Tubs got up, brushing the dust of his black clothes before reluctantly walking over to Charlie. He looked at the shrapnel. The word GEORING shone out into the darkness. The boys gasped. 'Where'd you get that?'

'From that bombed house in our road. What d'think?'

'It's not from that fat Kraut's plane, is it?' Ian yelled.

'Yeah … shhh. You'll wake the dead.' Charlie suddenly wished he had left the dead in peace when he saw the boys looking in horror at the tombstones.

'Tubs, it's for you. A sort of present … you know.'

Tubs looked as if he was suffering with goitre trouble. '*For me*? Gordon Bennett! Thanks, Charlie. It's …' Tubs couldn't think of an adequate word.

'The best thing you've ever had?' Charlie supplied him with a sentence.

'Yeah! It is. Thanks.'

'Some people have all the luck,' Ian said, kicking pieces of rubble. 'I never get no presents.'

'Well, the next piece of shrapnel I find with writing on it, I'll give it to you.' Charlie grinned as the piqued expression on Ian's face changed to euphoria.

'Promise, Charlie?'

'Promise. Now let's get started. She'll be coming in half an hour.'

Charlie had discovered that Mrs Humphries had peculiar habits; one of which was visiting her first husband's grave at the same time every Thursday evening. Always in the dark. Ian's father was a warden. He had told his son that murderers often come back to the scene of the crime at night. Ian had told Charlie. That's when Charlie decided to take his revenge on all the Mrs Humphries in the world.

Charlie took a brush and a pot of luminous paint out of a bag he was carrying.

'Right – I'll do Tubs first, but you must stand still … Ian, you hold the torch.'

Charlie had been studying skeletons in *Gray's Anatomy:* a book he'd found on one of the bookshelves at home. He drew a luminous skeleton on Tub's clothes.

'My Mum will kill me when she finds out what I've been doing,' Tubs said, already regretting coming.

'How's she going to find out?' Charlie asked. 'No one's going to recognise a skeleton, are they?'

They burst out laughing before Charlie motioned them to silence. He started on Ian's skeleton, then gave Tubs a quick lesson in anatomy before allowing him to paint a skeleton on his clothes.

The boys froze as they heard someone approaching.

'What do we do, Charlie?' Tubs' voice was a strangulated castrato.

Charlie motioned them to follow him. They crept behind the tombstone of Mrs Humphries' first husband.

'*Oh take me home again, Kathleen…*' the strains of a sentimental song drifted towards them. Suddenly, they saw the bacchic features of old Mr Carstairs, flickering in the light of a moving match. 'Wossa matta? … can't keep still? Only wanna a fag.' The match fizzled out. 'Shit!' He stumbled past the ruined church, apologising to Kathleen for his bad language as he fell over a bombed piece of buttress.

'And *he* plays the organ in our church as well,' Ian said, in disgust.

A few minutes later, the boys, shivering with cold and fear, heard another sound: the sound of a woman gibbering nonsense to a dog. They looked at each other. Charlie had told them what to do. Mrs Humphries pointed the dim light of her torch at her dead husband and walked straight up to him. Spot sniffed the air, wondering at the strangeness of the graveyard odours.

'It's certainly not my fault, Eric. You shouldn't have taken it. I didn't force you, did I?'

The boys looked at each other in horror. Then Charlie gave the signal. They rose from behind the tombstone, their luminous skeletons shaking. Mrs Humphries' mouth opened in a silent scream for several seconds before her vocal chords regained their power.

The boys couldn't remember later whether Mrs Humphries' screams were louder than Spot's hysterical barking as he strained on his lead, frantic in his desire to savage the skeletons. Mrs Humphries nearly broke his neck as she yanked his lead and stumbled out of the graveyard, moaning to herself.

Tubs was shaking more than Mr Carstairs.

'Well, *she* won't forget tonight, will she?' Charlie said, chuckling.

'*She* won't. *I* won't. That woman's a murderer.'

'Yeah,' Ian piped up. 'Wait 'til I tell my Dad what she said.'

'You can't. We haven't been here. Remember?'

'Oh, nuts.'

'Look, we better spread out before we're caught.'

'Spread out?' What d'you mean?' Ian asked.

'Go home, stupid. Someone's bound to come to investigate the noise.'

'Oh.' Ian looked at Charlie and Tubs fluorescing in the dark. 'You don't think someone will spot skeletons riding bikes, do you?'

Charlie shook his head as he peeled off his skeleton. 'Course not, Ian. You go home dressed like that.'

'Right, then.' Ian ran off towards his bike before Charlie could stop him. 'See you tomorrow.'

Charlie and Tubs watched in disbelief as Ian's flickering skeleton raced down the hill.

'Where was he when they were giving out brains, Tubs?'

Charlie frowned as he wheeled his bike around to the back of the house. Someone had forgotten the blackout! He could see a light in the kitchen window. Like a beacon for the Luftwaffe, Charlie thought, intending to run into the house after he disposed of the evidence of his luminous clothes in the garden shed. But the stars waylaid him as usual. He looked up into the clear, star-lit night. There was Rob's favourite star, Sirius. He felt the chasm of loneliness as he remembered the nights when Rob was with him, pointing out the stars, letting him use his precious telescope. He traced the contours of the constellation with his finger, wondering if Rob was flying above him now. Sighing deeply, he turned towards the house, knowing he was going to get into trouble for being late, but having a counter-attack ready – the lights were pinpointing targets for the enemy. As he walked up the garden path, he suddenly saw Mary outlined in the illuminated window, her face contorted. Charlie wiped the sudden sweat from the palms of his hands. He had never seen such an expression on her face before. She seemed to be shouting at someone beyond the frame of the window. Sweat soaked his shirt. He could hear her shouting now. He took a deep breath and opened the door quietly. Mary twisted towards him. 'Oh, Charlie...'

He suddenly saw the person Mary had been shouting at. He was sitting in the corner of the kitchen as if he had taken root. His father.

Chapter 16

The train was bombed by a Heinkel 111 outside Tonbridge station, but Rob was lucky. He escaped with bruises. Other people were screaming, trapped in the wreckage, but he didn't stop to help. He had to get back. He ran into the road and hitched a lift from a Canadian soldier who was delivering military equipment to the Royal Sussex Regiment in Hastings. The soldier didn't react to Rob's appearance. His brother was a pilot, he told Rob. He'd been burnt baling out of a Halifax.

In the lorry's masked headlights, they saw the shadowed gaunt faces of *trekkers*: people whose houses had been bombed; people looking for somewhere to live. As the Canadian drove past them, Rob felt an immense surge of hatred build up in his body. He studied the road, noting how expertly the Canadian negotiated a route through craters, fallen trees and rubble from ruined houses: obstacles created by the Luftwaffe's bombing.

'Can't take civilians to the coast any more,' the Canadian said apologetically, 'not now there's a ban on travelling there ... Home on leave, are you?'

Rob told the Canadian he had come back on compassionate grounds. The man asked no further questions.

He arrived at Hastings twenty-four hours after Charlie had discovered his father in their kitchen, and had run off into the night. His mother's phone call had disturbed him deeply. His mother, always so calm, so controlled when he was growing up, had been almost hysterical. He remembered the last time Charlie had run off into the dark because he thought he was going to be evacuated to another family. He had hidden in St. Clements Caves under the West Hill. He couldn't hide there now. People from the Old Town had taken to sleeping in the caves at night for safety. Rob had left Kate at the hotel. He couldn't have stayed with her, knowing how Charlie must have felt the moment he'd seen his father return from the dead.

Rob opened the heavy oak door of his home, expecting his parents to be waiting for him.

'Mum? Dad?' The house was silent.

He ran up the stairs towards his parents' bedroom. His mother was lying on the bed, tangled white strands of hair twisting round her face. Rob was shocked; he had never seen her in bed in the daytime. He sat down beside her. 'Mum?'

Mary's eyes fluttered open. They were bloodshot, as if she had a hangover.

'Are you all right?'

Mary struggled to sit up. 'No. Never felt like this before.'

Rob pushed her back onto the bed. 'Lie down. Is it just Charlie?'

'*Just* Charlie!' Mary whispered.

'You know what I mean. Are you ill?'

'I feel as if someone's taken my stomach away, Rob. I ...'

All his life Rob had had the sanctuary of his parents. Now a relic of a woman was lying in bed, pretending to be his mother. When he was six, a large wave had picked him up and tossed him onto the rocks, drowned him in glassy green depths before spewing him up onto the shingled surface of the beach. He had seen the horror in his mother's eyes as she rushed to gather him in her arms. Now he understood it.

'Where's Dad?'

'Called out on another case. He's never here these days… Oh Rob, what am I to do? That dreadful man came back again yesterday evening. Demanding to see Charlie. I don't know where he is. What am I to do?' Mary started weeping, very quietly.

Rob was six again and his mother was disappearing. He looked out at the beech trees.

'Don't cry, Mum. I'll find Charlie. I did last time, didn't I? Then we'll deal with Slater.'

Rob looked into his mother's bloodshot eyes and wondered how long she would last without Charlie. And how long would he last, without her?

*

The bombed house was overgrown with weeds and tall buddleia bushes that shed greasy leaves onto the crumbled bricks in the front garden. The rescue services had cleared up as much as they could, but there was only so much time in the day. They hadn't discovered the unexploded butterfly bomb buried deep in the earth in the cellar.

Charlie knew every inch of Mrs Bates' ruined house. He'd discovered the cellar was almost intact. It was damp down there, but he felt safe. His father would never find him. He would hide there for ever, if necessary. The first night was the worst. He heard scratching noises and immediately thought of rats. He hated rats. They used to run over his face in the dark when he was lying on the floor under his parents' bed. But the sounds weren't made by rats, but by a scrawny cat, cowering in the rubble, too terrified to go out. He fed it with bits of spam and cereal and called it Pencil. It slept with him at night wrapped in the blankets Charlie had brought from home.

He was curled up with the cat reading one of his Wizard comics by the dim light of the torch. The battery was very low. How long before Tubs came with another one? He didn't want to be in a black cellar with ghosts and a terrified cat. In one hand, he held the polished stone he had once given to Rob. He rubbed it rhythmically.

Charlie was fast asleep when the footsteps came. Pencil leapt up into the air and shot under the rubble. Suddenly, the dark cellar was flooded with torchlight. Charlie screamed.

'It's all right, Charlie. It's me.' Tubs moved the torch under his face and presented Charlie with two bulbous eyes.

'Move the torch, Tubs. Your face's awful.'

'Thanks.' He put the torch down on the ground so that the damp ceiling of the cellar was lit.

'Put it sideways on the floor. Don't want anyone to see the light. You weren't seen coming in, were you?'

'Naw. I did what you said. Waited to see if anyone was following me. Got you a new battery.' He gave it to Charlie who fitted it into his torch.

'You haven't told anyone?'

'Naw. But I think you ought to go home, Charlie. They'll be worried stiff. I know my Mum would be if I was missing.'

'Yeah, but you don't have King Kong waiting at home for you, do you?'

Tubs sat down on the blanket with Charlie and gave him some cakes his mother had made. 'Do you think he's still there?'

'Yeah. He doesn't like losing something he owns.'

'He don't own you, Charlie. He's just your Dad.'

'You try telling him that.'

'No, thanks.'

The boys sat in silence, eating the cakes.

'You ought to tell your Mu … Mrs Adams though. I don't think it's fair, Charlie. She's nice.'

'Don't tell me what to do – she's *my* Mum!' Suddenly Charlie started sobbing. 'Would have been if that bastard hadn't shown up. I hate him! I hate him! I hate him!'

Tubs was stunned. Charlie was their leader. Leaders don't cry. He finished the last of his mother's cakes to take his mind of the sounds of the sobs.

The sobbing stopped as abruptly as it had started. 'Never going back, Tubs. Never.'

Tubs looked around the damp cellar. 'You can't stay here for ever, Charlie. It's horrible. Listen, shall I go round your house and ask –'

'No!'

'– if anyone's heard about you? I can find out if your Dad's still around, can't I?'

Charlie studied Tubs in the torchlight. 'If you squeal, Tubs, I'll take Goering's piece of plane back.'

'Cross my heart and hope to die, Charlie. I wouldn't tell them if you don't want me to.'

'Okay, but come back and tell me what they said.'

Half an hour later, Charlie heard the sound of footsteps. They weren't Tubs' heavy tread. He swallowed violently to stop himself being sick as he crept behind the rubble. The beam of a torch flooded the room.

'Charlie?' It was Rob. Without thinking, Charlie hurled himself across the cellar into Rob's arms, sobbing uncontrollably.

'You'll have to stop doing this, Charlie,' Rob said, when he had calmed down. 'Always hiding in the dark. Mum's really ill. Worried to death about you.' Rob suddenly wished he hadn't used that cliché.

'I couldn't help it, Rob. It was him. I'm not going back. I'll chuck myself off the pier first.'

'Hey – stop being so melodramatic. I'll sort something out. I promise.'

'You don't know my Dad. If he wants something, he gets it.'

'Well, he's not getting you, all right?'

'How you going to stop him?'

Rob held Charlie's shoulders tight. 'I'll go to the authorities and explain the situation.'

'What if they won't listen to you, Rob? Then I'll have to go with him… I'm not coming out.'

Rob looked down into Charlie's frightened, but resolute face. If only he could give him a guarantee, but he couldn't.

'All right, Charlie. I'll bring you some things. You stay here while I talk to Mum and Dad.'

Charlie's mouth trembled. 'Don't let Mum come here, Rob. I'll want to come out and I can't.'

Chapter 17

They were sitting in the lounge when the doorbell rang. John went to answer it. A small, prematurely balding man with a bony face and a thin pencil moustache stood at the door. A few wispy strands of brown hair were combed over his crown. He wiped his feet carefully on the mat before walking into the Adams' large hall with its antique oak furniture. Bert Slater knew money when he saw it.

'Come in here, Mr Slater.'

Charlie's father walked into the lounge and saw Rob for the first time. He stopped short.

'Blimey – heard yer'd fried but ... sorry. Caught me on the hop, like.'

Rob had vowed that he would control himself in front of this man. He didn't react.

'Lovely house yer got, Dr Adams. Must have set yer back a bob or two.'

Rob wanted to get out of his chair and smash the man's face.

'Sit down, Mr Slater. We've got a lot to discuss,' his father said.

'Ta.' He sat down in a chair, his feet barely reaching the floor. His eyes roved around the furniture as if he was pricing everything. 'Found Charlie yet?'

'No!' Mary shouted across the room.

John and Rob looked at her with concern.

'Let me do the talking, Mary. Charlie doesn't seem to want to be found, Mr Slater. Do you know why that is?'

'Naw. Can't say I does. Allus was a bit of devil. Allus up to something.'

'Really?' Rob shouted, all vows forgotten. 'Perhaps if you hadn't have hit him so much he wouldn't have been!'

Rob regretted the words the moment he uttered them. Bert Slater's face darkened; he looked like a dangerous dwarf.

'Oh yeah? And who says I did?'

'Charlie,' John said, quietly.

'Then he's a fuckin' liar. I never laid a finger on him. Felt like it, mind you, but I never did. Not once. Don't hold with hitting kids.'

'Really? … We must have got it wrong, Mr Slater.' John looked intently at Rob and Mary, willing their silence.

'Yeah. Allus tellin' porkers, our Charlie. Bit of a lad, know what I mean.'

Rob saw his mother's knuckles turn white and tried desperately to control the intense anger he felt.

'But with the Missus gone, Charlie's all I've got left now.'

'What about your other sons, Mr Slater?' John asked.

'Disappeared. Doris – that's the Missus - couldn't read or write, see, so there's nothing in the house to say where they are. What with the war an' that they could be dead for all I knows.'

'So how did you find out where Charlie was?'

'Remember coming to our house to see Doris coupla years ago, Doc? You left a card. Doris thought it ever so grand. She put it on the shelf, like. I found it after she died. Bit of luck that, Doc, weren't it?'

Christ, Rob thought. A simple thing like a card could destroy Charlie's life. His parents' faces sagged; they both suddenly looked very old.

'I want me boy back. I know there's a war on and all that, but the law's the law. He's mine and if yer don't give him back, I'll go to the police.'

Rob jumped up from his chair. '*You'll* go to the police. *We'll* go to the police and tell them how you systematically tortured your son for years.'

'You'll fuckin' do what?' The little man jumped off the chair and looked up into Rob's scarred features. 'Don't yer threaten me, yer bleedin' ghoul. I'll have the law on the whole lot of yer –'

Rob couldn't remember moving, but suddenly he had his arms around the man's body and was squeezing the life out of him. Slater struggled frantically for breath.

'Robert!' His father was trying to tear him away from the man.

Slater slumped onto the carpet.

Rob's mother threw her arms around him and almost wept. 'Oh Robert, Robert. What *are* we going to do?'

Rob's breathing came in short, agitated gasps as he looked down at Charlie's father. He had never wanted to kill the Germans he was forced to kill, but he wanted to kill this man very much.

'Sit down and don't do *anything*, Robert,' his father said, before helping Slater into a chair. The man's breathing was laboured. 'I'm sorry about that, Mr Slater. My son got carried away.'

Slater held onto his ribs, looking at Rob. 'I could have you for assault, you bastard.'

John glanced quickly at Rob and shook his head slightly. All his life he had spoken the truth. 'It would be your word against ours, Mr Slater. Who do you think they'd believe?'

'All the fuckin' same, you lot, ain't you?' The man emphasised the difficulty of his breathing by wheezing noisily. 'You no better than me – just pretend to be. But you live in a posh house an' I live in a fuckin' bomb site. Well, your little display, son, will cost you. Can't leave me lad with a bloke with a temper like yours, can I?'

'What do you want, Slater?' Rob managed to keep his voice level.

'*Mr* Slater, son. Don't forget that. I want me rights, that's what I want.'

'You're in the army, aren't you?' Mary's voice was shrill. You could be posted anywhere. How could you look after him?'

'Got relatives. Only too happy to look after Charlie for me 'til I get back.'

'So you're prepared to take Charlie away from us and give him to some strangers and ...' Mary's face crumpled.

'How much do you want?' There was a long silence after Rob had spoken.

'What?' Shock registered all over Slater's face. 'You're not suggestin'?'

'How much? ... *Mr* Slater.'

John and Mary stared at Rob in panic.

Slater kept a high level of shock on his face as he looked at them. 'Didn't do much of a job with him, did yer? Thinks money can buy me boy. I don't care what you says.' Slater turned to John. 'I'm goin' to the police with this right now. I can see the headlines: *Assault Battery and Bribery. Doctor's Son Imprisoned.*'

'One thousand, *Mr* Slater?'

John and Mary gasped.

'A grand, eh? You lot must be made of money if you can throw that much away.' Slater slowly looked round at the furniture again. 'Mind you, I suppose all these antiques would fetch you a bob or two.' He relaxed back in the chair and looked at John. 'Tell you what. Make it two grand and I'll think about it. I'm a reasonable man.'

Rob shuddered as he stared at Slater. He was actually contemplating *selling* his own son? He looked over at his Mother. Her face was the colour of a terracotta statue. His father had his head in his hands. How on earth could they possibly find £2,000? Rob wanted to crush the little man under his feet.

'All right, Mr Slater,' Rob said calmly. '£2,000. If you sign the adoption papers tonight.'

'Robert, for God's sake!' John said, in horror.

'*Oh no*, son. Weren't born yesterday,' Slater replied. 'I'll sign the papers after the money's in me hands. Not before.'

Rob didn't trust himself to look at the man. 'All right. Come here tomorrow night at eight o'clock and you'll have the money. You can see yourself out.'

'Righto. See you folks tomorrow.' Nice doin' business with you. Nighty night.' Slater sauntered out of the room, fingering the seventeenth-century grandfather clock by the door.

Mary and John sat in shock after they heard the front door slam. Rob went to check that he'd gone before coming back into the room.

'It's simply unbelievable,' John said, shaking his head. 'I wouldn't even have thought to offer him money.'

'The man's a monster, Dad. I just didn't believe he'd travelled all this way out of fatherly love. He doesn't care a fig about Charlie. He's had no contact with him for two years.'

Suddenly Mary seemed to come to life. 'He said he'll sign the papers! Charlie will be ours!'

John slumped back in his chair. He hadn't felt well for some time and had suffered the occasional pain of angina. He shouldn't have stress. Yet tonight had, perhaps, been the most stressful of his life after Rob's crash. He took off his glasses and rubbed his hands over his eyes. They felt as if they had grit in them.

'Dear God, Robert. Where on earth are we going to find £2,000 by tomorrow evening?'

Rob suddenly saw what a quagmire he was forcing his parents to wade through. 'I don't know, Dad, but Charlie isn't going back to that monster. I think I would have offered him anything.'

'But it wasn't your money you were offering. That's about three times what this house is worth.' Worry was etched into the lines of John's face.

'I can sell my telescope.'

'That will bring in about £50 in a pawnbrokers.'

'And I could sell my jewels,' Mary said, excitedly. 'Then there's the paintings and tapestries.'

'And my watch and –'

'Stop it, the pair of you,' John spoke abruptly. 'This isn't a game we're playing here, it's Charlie's life.'

'We know that, Dad. We're trying to think of ways to raise the money to *give* Charlie a life.'

'Robert, it's impossible to raise such an amount by tomorrow. What on earth do we say to Charlie's father on his return?'

Rob started pacing up and down the carpet, thinking what to do. 'I'll find a way, Dad.'

Charlie must remain in the cellar until the papers were signed, he thought. He didn't trust Slater. But the darkness …

Chapter 18

Charlie didn't know how long he'd been in the dark damp of the cellar. Time had disappeared. Sometimes he was back in his old house in Deptford. The house a sponge, absorbing rain; leaking mildew. Nights lying under the sag of his parents' bed, trying to understand the noises.

'Bert … no … I ain't –'

The rhythmic squeal of broken bed springs. His mother's coughs.

'No more –'

That went on and on.

'No!' more urgent.

'You all right, Mum?'

The terror of the silence as he waited in vain for her answer.

'Shut yer mouth, kid or I'll shut it for yer!' from his father.

The returning rhythmic squeal. Then the belt.

The only thing that kept the ghosts at bay was Pencil, curled up in his arms in the darkness. Rob had told him he was sorting everything out, but he didn't believe him. No one could sort his father out. The cold was seeping into his bones and his chest hurt. How much longer before Rob came?

*

Rob followed the light of Slater's torch down Pevensey Road and into Highland Drive. He watched him turn into Maze Passage and go into the Horse and Groom pub. Celebrating his future wealth, no doubt. Rob stopped himself punching a nearby stone wall. It wouldn't help his damaged tendons. He stood in the doorway of a house and waited in the darkness.

Two hours later, Slater staggered out. A wave of stale, beer-ridden air wafted out into the night as the pub door swung open. The stark fluorescence of a searchlight suddenly swept the darkness and Rob was immediately awash with sweat and crouching in a doorway. Slater, blinking in the brightness, stumbled along the road, holding onto the houses for support. The blackness seemed even more dense when the searchlight swept out over the sea. Slater muttered to himself as he tried to cross the road. There was a sudden yelp of pain as he fell down the steps of St Leonards Park. Rob waited in the shadows as Slater staggered to his feet and walked on into the park, singing. *'Oh isn't it funny – I'm in the money and everything's sunny again.'* Rob had no idea what he was going to do, but he followed Slater down an uneven path towards the water-lilied pond.

Slater dropped his torch as he stumbled through the long grass: his bony features highlighted in the soft light as he bent to pick it up. He suddenly swung his torch around as if he knew he was being followed. Rob froze behind an oak tree, not breathing. Satisfied, Slater moved on. He was stopped by the moon shimmering in the pond water.

'That's lovely, that is. See that? That's lovely, that is.'

'It is, isn't it?'

Slater jumped as Rob shone a torch onto his face. 'God Almighty. What the fuck' yer creepin' up like that for?'

'Just enjoying the night air, like you, Slater.'

'Balls. You're up to something, ain't yer? Got the money yet?'

'Not yet. Strange to tell, I couldn't find a bank open at this time of night.'

'Don't try an' be clever with me, son. It ain't worth it.'

'Is that a threat?' Rob's voice was very low.

Slater played his torchlight onto Rob's face. 'Ugly bugger, ain't yer? Don't need threats – not now. Yer want something. I got it. That's power, that is, son.'

'Charlie isn't a *thing*, Slater!'

'Nah – he's a fuckin' devil. Glad to be shot of him.' He laughed at the expression on Rob's face. 'And yers givin' us two grand for the privilege. Gotta laugh, ain't yer?'

Slater's drunken laughter took him to the periphery of the pond. Rob watched him teeter towards the water. Just one small push would do it.

Slater stumbled backwards and suddenly his startled face disappeared under the water. He surfaced momentarily to splutter. 'Can't swim! Help us for Gawd's sake!'

Rob's laboured breathing synchronised with Slater's. He watched the man's desperate thrashings to get to the side, knowing that soon his clothes would become waterlogged. Rob was rigid with indecision. Slowly, he held out one hand.

'Hang on!'

'To what?' In his thrashing panic, Slater couldn't focus on the hand that Rob was holding out above his head.

And suddenly, Rob was listening to the man's last phlegmy gargle as he was sucked under the water.

Rob bent down and threw Slater's torch into the pond before walking up the path towards Charlie's cellar. He felt very calm.

*

Charlie was sleeping by the time Rob got to the bombed house. Vulnerability written over the knotted tension in his face. He shot up as the torchlight reached him.

'It's all right, Charlie. I've got something to tell you. Your father's had an accident … he's dead.'

He waited for Charlie's face to light up with joy. But he simply stared at Rob for a long time before saying. 'Dead? … How do you know?'

'I saw him fall into a pond. He didn't get out. You've got nothing to fear again, Charlie. Ever. He'll never hurt you now.'

Rob was stunned by the tears dripping down Charlie's cheeks.

'Didn't you hear what I said? He's dead. Why are you crying?'

'Cos he was my Dad.'

Rob hugged him. He didn't understand, but it didn't matter. Charlie could come home now. He gathered up Charlie's meagre belongings and started to walk out of the cellar.

'Come on, Charlie. Let's go home.'

Charlie suddenly rushed into the corner where the unexploded bomb was waiting to explode.

'I'm not going without Pencil,' he said, picking up the scrawny cat and putting it underneath his jersey. It curled up near Charlie's heart.

As Rob and Charlie walked up the road together, hand in hand in the darkness, a bat swooped near them. Charlie jumped with shock.

'It's all right, Charlie. They've got excellent radar.' Rob looked down at Charlie's exhausted face by the light of the torch and put his arm around his shoulder. 'Come on, let's get you home.'

As they trudged up the road, Rob was suddenly struck by the paradox of his life: *he* was using radar to kill Germans. His country *wanted* him to kill and to continue killing, often innocent people. It was legal.

They were almost home when they heard the sound of the butterfly bomb exploding in the distance.

Chapter 19

Colin and Rob had been flying missions for months without leave. The last one had left an indelible mark on them: the bombing of Dresden. More than 1,200 Allied bombers had come in from the West to support Marshal Koniev's columns advancing in monster tanks on the city from the east, sixty-two miles away.

Their squadron, now equipped with Mosquito Mk XVs, had been on duty, escorting Lancasters which deluged the city with tons of incendiaries and high explosives. They had looked down on an inferno of fire that must have equalled Dante's, Rob thought. He remembered the splendour of the city from a school visit before the war: the beauty of its architecture and art. The people he had met. Now the city was a smoking ruin and an estimated 130,000 people were dead.

'Bomber Harris went too far this time,' Tony Bowles said wearily, echoing what they were all thinking.

They were sitting exhausted in the Mess; some of the men leafing through *Picture Post*; others playing cards. One of the new Pilot Officers disappeared out of the room, leaving the door open. It banged repeatedly in the gale.

'*I'll* close it then, shall I, since nobody else can be bothered to get off their backsides!' Colin stomped across the room and slammed the door shut. He glowered at everyone before sitting down again and shuffling cards repeatedly. No one reacted.

Rob opened his mother's letter which had come that morning.

My dear Rob

We are all thinking of you and pray for your safety every night. Please write to us soon. I know that you have little time, but we worry about you. Charlie ticks off the days on the calendar since your last letter. It's been nearly three weeks as he constantly tells us.

You'll never believe the changes in Charlie since the adoption was finalised. He seems to have grown inches, physically and mentally. He is now taller than me. 'Only three more inches and I'll be as tall as Rob,' he said yesterday. Two weeks ago he told us he wanted to be a doctor. He's been devouring your father's medical books. It's quite worrying finding him poring over pathology pictures. Anyway this week he decided he's going to become a famous artist after looking at some of my art books. What do you think? An artistic doctor or a medical illustrator?

I'm so happy, Rob, in spite of the war. You're so much better and now Charlie is really a member of the family. He is always warning your father about working too hard. I've told him to tell your father about the advantages of early retirement. Please write and tell him the same, will you? He won't be able to resist a pincer attack.

It seems months since they discovered his father in the pond, doesn't it? I still think of those children throwing stones into it and seeing his face under the water. They must have nightmares. I'm ashamed to write it, but I'm so glad he is dead. What a monster he was. Sometimes we have to make our own justice, don't we? Thank you for Charlie. At least he will never know that his father was prepared to sell him.

We're all looking forward to seeing you when you come home on leave. It won't be long now, will it, my dear? Take great care of yourself for all of us. We miss you very much.

All our love

Mum, Dad and Charlie

P.S. You won't believe this, Rob. I didn't. My hair is turning brown again! Your father says that the shock of your crash must be finally out of my system. Sounds like an old wives' tale to me, but he's the doctor.

P.P.S. Kate called in to see us last week when she was home. Has she written to tell you? What a lovely girl she is. I'm so looking forward to having her as a daughter-in-law.

Kate. Rob hadn't seen her since that night in the hotel. The night they had made love for the first time. What a difference it had been from the experience with Billie, the nightclub singer. That was all frenzy; this was all giving. He looked across at Colin's stony expression as he kept shuffling cards repeatedly. He hadn't been able to tell him about his engagement to Kate. Colin still hadn't had an answer from Bridget. She wrote him amusing letters, but no mention of his proposal. Colin swore loudly as he dropped one of the cards. He seemed to have undergone a personality change since they'd been flying together. No light-hearted banter passed his lips any more. Now

Rob understood what his own family must have had to endure after his crash. He had been ten times more difficult than Colin. A brilliant idea flashed through his head and he got up to tell Colin. It would cheer him up. At that moment the phone rang in the ops room. The door suddenly crashed open in the wind and the Duty Officer poked his head round it.

'Rob. Colin. Duty Patrol.'

They had been flying on patrol for two hours and hadn't seen any sign of the enemy. Rob tried to stretch his long body, but there wasn't much room in the cockpit; the front of it was filled with airborne radar: *A1*, *Gee* for navigation, *SCR 729* for picking up homing beacons and blind approach, two four-channel R/T sets. It went on. Rob was grateful that he'd undergone such an intensive course. Radar was a complicated weapon.

Colin hadn't spoken, except to exchange technical details. Rob knew that this wasn't the time to tell him of his idea. He was trying to rub some circulation into his frozen legs when he saw a German signal cartridge firing on the port side. The Luftwaffe had about six different combinations of coloured cartridges: each combination changing every four hours as a recognition signal. Once the British discovered this fact, of course, the changes inadvertently helped the British identify enemy aircraft. However, now friendly planes also had a supply of these *ESN* cartridges to use in an emergency to dupe the Germans. What if this was one of theirs in trouble? Rob studied the A1 screen and picked up a blip on his radar.

'Left, hard left, Col. Tighten the turn, he's crossing starboard port range about two miles. Ease the turn. He's five degrees port and five degrees up. Dead ahead … now throttle back. We're coming in too fast.'

At 3,000 range they suddenly saw the plane.

'Get right underneath her, Col,' Rob shouted through the headphones.

'I'm bloody trying to!' Colin answered abruptly. 'What do you think it is?'

'Can't be sure …it looks like a Dakota …'

They both knew that from below the Dakota looked very like an HE 111.

'You'll have to get in closer,' Rob shouted.

Colin's hands were slippery with sweat inside his gauntlets as he manoeuvred the Mosquito until it was a hundred yards beneath the other plane.

'Can you see, Rob?' Colin's heart was thumping violently against his ribs. He didn't know how long he could maintain this proximity.

'Christ!' Rob yelled. 'Drop back fast – then fire!' Rob had suddenly seen the unmistakable black crosses of a Heinkel 111 just above them.

Colin throttled back 200 yards and fired a two-second burst into the Heinkel's port engine. There was a blinding flash; then a section of the plane broke away. The German pilot suddenly swung hard port and dived steeply. Colin throttled back again, but not quickly enough; he overshot the plane.

'Where the hell is he?' Colin shouted.

'2,000 range. Well below.'

Colin dived through the haze.

'Can't get him on radar. Lost him in the ground returns …
Shit. It's a no-go.'

Rob looked at his watch. Four hours had disappeared. He
got out his navigation computer and plotted their route home.
The wind had driven them way off course.

'Time to return to base, Col.'

There was no reply. Rob took his eyes off the instruments
to see Colin staring fixedly at the control stick. He switched off
the R/T.

'What's the matter?' Rob's voice sounded impersonal
through the headphones.

'I can't carry on, Rob. I can't fly any more.'

'You mean you want a desk job?'

'Yes. No. I mean I can't fly us back to base… I can't do it.
I can't fly any more.' Colin took his hands off the stick. The
plane started to dive.

'*Jesus Christ.* Trim it up!' Rob screamed at him through the
headphones. 'I'll take over. Just trim it up! COLIN!'

In slow motion, Colin's hand moved towards the elevator
trim. After long, long minutes, the plane was sufficiently
trimmed to fly level. Rob breathed in deep gulps of oxygen. He
hadn't flown a plane since that night. *Could* he fly? Were his
hands capable of it?

'Okay, Col. Undo your harness and parachute and move into my seat. Now!'

Again Colin moved in slow motion. It was a terrifying manoeuvre with the limited space in the cockpit. They removed their parachute packs to enable them to change places, but if one of them knocked against the control stick … After what seemed a decade, Rob had his hands on the controls.

'All right, Col? Now switch the R/T back on.' Rob's voice was deceptively calm.

Colin didn't move.

'Switch the bloody R/T on!' Rob shouted, before taking another gulp of oxygen. His head felt muzzy.

At last, Colin leaned over and flicked the R/T switch.

'Good. Let's get back to base, shall we?' Rob said, his voice calm, his body trembling.

The unbroken row of nine switches in front of him weren't easy to distinguish in the dark and the controls felt leaden after the buoyancy of the Spitfire, but the fact that Colin was sitting beside him in a trance forced Rob to concentrate his mind totally. He was determined to get them back.

He was flying on his instruments through dense fog, thankful he had plotted their course. By his calculations they were now directly over the runway. He couldn't see one light.

'Hello Wagon Leader here. Circling, ready to land, Tower,' Rob said, without a trace of a tremor. 'Do me a favour, chaps, will you? Fire off a few rockets to help me get into position? And can you ask the boys to project the local searchlights horizontally for a couple of minutes. Can't see a bloody light anywhere. Over.' Rob inhaled deeply.

Within minutes, one rocket after another came up through the cloud and fog to help Rob get into position. He descended through the murk, tempting the stars. He looked briefly at the altimeter reading: 1,000 feet and still no sight of the runway. He clenched his hands on the stick bracing himself for the inevitability of death. Then suddenly, he saw the 'goose neck' flares: little cans filled with kerosene oil out of which flared small flames, in parallel lines marking the runway. He moaned softly as he brought up the Mossie's nose, then cut the engine. The plane bounced along the runway towards the mobile Chance light, momentarily floodlighting his welcome home.

An hour later, Rob was writing out a combat report and Colin was with the M.O. His trance-like state announcing far more succinctly than Rob ever could, that he was suffering from combat fatigue. Rob knew that 'combat fatigue' would be translated in many senior officers' minds into L.M.F: Lacking Moral Fibre. It would go on Colin's record. He couldn't change that, but there was something he could change. His own life.

Chapter 20

Kate and Bridget left the long, depressing platform of Paddington station with its vast vaulted skeleton of patched glass to travel by tube to Charing Cross station. Their compartment was nearly empty: a welcome contrast to the hot, incredibly squashed journey from Cardiff. They were both longing for a shower; to be able to change into the dresses they had brought with them to celebrate Kate's birthday after they had met Rob and Colin. This was the idea Rob had wanted to tell Colin before he'd become 'ill'.

Bridget wasn't looking forward to seeing Colin, although he sounded much better in his letters now. The old Colin had returned, Kate had told her. But Bridget wasn't in love with the old Colin. How and when could she tell him? It had to be at the end of the evening. This was Kate's birthday. She couldn't spoil it.

Kate looked at her pale face reflected in an unnetted square of window next to Bridget's. Bridget's reflection suddenly stuck her tongue out at her.

Kate smiled as she turned to her. 'You're daft, you know that?'

'I want a bit more reaction than that, Katherine Brazier. How many times are you twenty-two?'

217

Kate's mouth trembled. She'd have to tell her.

'What's the matter?' Bridget asked.

'I'm late … You know how regular I am.'

Bridget went pale before saying: 'So what? Me Ma's had eight children and she's missed thousands of periods. It doesn't mean a thing.'

Kate loved Bridget's logic. 'Oh Bridge, what would I do without you?'

'Well, it's lucky for you, you don't have to. I'm not having any long faces on your birthday now. Anyway, if the worst comes to the worst you can marry Rob early. There's no problem. No problem at all.'

Bridget dismissed pregnancy with a wave of her hand as she peered through the unnetted piece of window. 'Holy Mary – we nearly missed the stop. Come on.' She dragged Kate and their cases off the tube just as the doors were closing.

They walked past a poster of 'Billy Brown of London Town' in his pinstriped suit. He was admonishing the public for pulling off the heavy netting glued to the windows which was put there for their protection. The girls stopped to read what was written across his face in black ink: *'Owing to the fact that I couldn't see a bloody thing, I was forced to remove a large section of netting. Apologies for any inconvenience caused. W. Churchill.'*

They laughed. 'I love your English humour,' Bridget said, smiling. 'We're going to have such a celebration, Kate. Come on.' She charged up the escalator to the surface.

Once they got out of the station they saw the damage the bombs had created in the Strand: the endless replication of yawning bomb craters; the glass fragments over the road; the broken gas and water mains; the layers of grey dust. Suddenly Kate was back in 1940; the day she'd enlisted at the recruiting station; the day of the outrage of FFI, the 'Free From Infection' parade - hundreds of girls standing naked in lines, waiting like animals for a medical orderly to inspect their bodies. She looked at her watch, shuddering at the thought of what they might find if they examined her now.

'They're late,' she said.

A trolley bus glided silently towards Trafalgar Square.

'Ach – give me an old fashioned noisy tram every time,' Bridget said. 'Sure you could be killed crossing the road with one of those things.'

Suddenly they heard the sound of running footsteps and Kate was swept up in the air.

'Sorry we're late, darling,' Rob gasped, out of breath from running from the platform. 'Bloody train was delayed as usual.' He hugged Kate tight. A number of passers-by glanced at Rob, then hastily away.

Bridget and Colin stood staring at each other. Neither of them knowing what to say for a moment.

'Hello, Colin. Haven't seen you since –'

'You came to Hastings and –'

'Forced you out of your own home?'

'No,' Colin said, looking very shy. 'I was going to say something else.'

'Well,' Rob said, his face stretched into a smile. 'I suggest that we go to Madame Prunier's in St. James Street for a celebratory lunch. What do you say?'

Bridget had seen Rob's autobiography in numerous photographs all over his parents' house: his christening in St. John's church, looking as saintly as a choir boy; a studious boy in a black school uniform; a happy family gathering in a restaurant to celebrate his matriculation; a stunning picture of him as a pilot officer in uniform, smiling at the camera as he leaned against a Spitfire named 'Sirius'. She couldn't believe the ravages fire inflicted on skin.

'A wonderful idea, Rob. I'm Bridget, by the way, since no one can be bothered to introduce us.' She held out her hand to shake Rob's. Kate felt like hugging her.

'Well, what did you think?' Rob asked as they walked outside the select establishment of Madame Prunier's after lunch.

'Lovely,' Kate said.

'Mmm,' from Bridget.

'Do you want the truth, Rob?' Colin's face was sombre.

'Well, you're going to give it to me whether I want it or not, aren't you? You miserable moron.'

'Well, it was intimate. The discreet tinkle of glass. Refined smells. Small slices of cultured conversation. A well-bred menu. That sort of thing.'

'What he's trying to say, Rob,' Bridget said, laughing, 'is he thought it boring and pretentious.' She turned to Colin. 'So did I.' Bridget was beginning to believe she had made a mistake over him.

Colin beamed. 'Right … I choose the next venue. Dancing in Regent's Park. One of the chaps in the office told me they have open air dancing every week now.'

'Wonderful,' Bridget said. She and Colin went off to get a taxi, arm in arm.

'And whose birthday is this, I'd like to know?' Kate said, looking momentarily piqued.

'Oh, come on, Kate,' Rob shouted. 'Colin's right. That place *was* bloody pretentious. Let's really enjoy ourselves and forget the war exists.'

One corner of the park was heaving with service personnel when they arrived. An enormous wooden stage had been set up and young men and women were jitterbugging to the strains of the *Woodchopper's Ball* pumping out from a small orchestra. Rob and the girls looked at Colin.

'Well, I didn't know, did I?'

American GIs were throwing girls expertly into the air and catching them before throwing them between their legs. The girls seemed to be enjoying it.

'Well, you won't catch me being thrown about like a rag doll,' Bridget said, wondering how the girls managed to stand up after such an assault.

The music finished and the dancers came to an abrupt halt: faces glistening with sweat as they roared their approval. After a very short interval, the opening bars of a tune that Glen Miller had made famous before he had disappeared in his *Norseman* aircraft came over the loudspeaker. A male singer with brilliantined hair beamed into the mike as he sang: *'ABCDEFGH'* – everyone on the dance floor joined in. *'I got a gaaaal in Kalamazoo, I don't want to boast, but I know she's the toast of Kalamazoo...'*

The dance floor was an instant mass of jitterbugging, singing bodies. Rob put his arm round Kate's waist and squeezed.

'Want to try?' Rob said.

Kate shook her head emphatically. All at once, a young GI with very short spiky hair, grabbed Bridget's hand. She was suddenly on the dance floor, then in the air. Kate, Rob and Colin watched in horrified fascination. The next moment she was sliding through the GI's legs, missing his hands waiting to pull her up. Her slide continued across the dance floor, knocking people over like skittles. She came to a crashing halt, colliding with a stack of chairs, her skirt round her thighs. The American men stared in stunned disbelief at the sight of her hideous rayon WAAF bloomers. They almost came down to her knees. Blushing furiously, but with her head held high, she straightened her skirt and back and walked with great dignity across the dance hall. The GIs cheered.

'I wouldn't have believed that possible if I hadn't have seen it,' Colin said, laughing.

'I'll choose the next venue,' Kate said, helping Bridget rub the marks off her uniform.

'Well, thank the Holy Mary for that. What's it to be, Katie? A sedate tea dance?' Bridget waved a programme in front of her face to reduce its colour.

'No, I think we ought to go to the pictures and then finish up in a club in the West End that S.O. Virtue told me about. It's under the Rialto cinema in Coventry Street.'

Rob looked at Kate quickly. He hadn't told her that the *Café De Paris* was where Billie, the nightclub singer, had taken him before they'd had sex. What if she was singing there tonight and recognised him? A sharp pain suddenly constricted his chest. She would never recognise him ever again.

'That's two venues, Kate,' Colin said.

'Oh, shut up. Whose birthday is it? Who's still waiting to be loaded down with presents?' She looked at Rob, expecting him to laugh. He was lost in thought. She nudged him.

'Sorry?'

'I said,' Kate spoke slowly. 'I'm still waiting to be loaded down with presents.'

Rob sealed Billie's memory in a vault and smiled at Kate. 'Later, my darling, later. Come on. Let's have a drink and decide what film to see.'

Half an hour later they were in a pub, arguing. Rob refused to see *Gone With The Wind*.

'Listen, you two,' he said, leaning back against the faded fabric of a pub chair. 'Kate forced me years ago to see Lawrence Olivier in *Wuthering Heights.* Melodramatic twaddle. She cried nearly all the way through and said it was wonderful.' He frowned, trying to remember the name of a film he'd been wanting to see for months. 'Lawrence Olivier in something heroic this time – *Henry V.* Come on, Kate, he's your favourite actor.'

The girls shook their heads.

'Well, I am *not* seeing another weepie,' Rob said, emphatically.

'Nor am I,' Colin agreed. '*Definitely not.*' Then he grinned at Bridget. 'Unless you want to, of course.' She grinned back at him. 'Cheers, everyone.' He knocked back his beer and grimaced. 'It *was* beer you bought, Rob. Not rain water?'

'Oh, Ha. Ha. Thanks for your support, old friend.' Rob looked at Colin's grinning face and couldn't help smiling.

'Well, it's Kate's birthday. *She* should choose,' Bridget said.

They all turned to Kate. *Gone With The Wind*, it is then,' she said.

Rob and Colin groaned very loudly.

The moment the auditorium lights went out, Kate's fears about the future resurfaced. Bridget made everything sound so easy, so clear-cut. Just marry Rob earlier and everything would be all right. But she was only twenty-two today, too young to be a mother. She didn't want a baby in war-torn Britain. And what of Rob? How would he react? When could she tell him? And her mother! Kate trembled as the awful scenario of explaining an unmarried pregnancy to her mother loomed large. She huddled up in her seat, trying to protect herself. Then another more dreadful thought drifted through her mind. Her commission! She'd have to resign! After all those months of training, taking exams, gaining the confidence and respect of the men and women under her charge: the pride in knowing that she was going a good job. The fact that she was valued. All would become nothing. She stifled a sob. Rob turned to smile at her, thinking that she was crying at the film. He squeezed her hand.

Kate and Bridget walked through Leicester Square, red-eyed: Bridget from seeing Atlanta burn in the film and Kate from the nightmare of her future.

'We can't go to a nightclub yet, it's too early,' Bridget said, blowing her nose. 'What are we going to do?'

'Frankly, my dear, I don't give a damn,' Colin drawled in an American accent.

'Ah, come on, Colin, you must,' Rob said. 'Rhett Butler and Scarlett O'Hara's contribution to raising the morale of the British public cannot be overestimated.'

Rob and Colin laughed.

'Oh, scoff all you like, you two. We enjoyed it, didn't we, Kate?'

Kate nodded. 'Anyway, Colin Brazier – you make a lousy Clark Gable.'

Colin pulled a long face and chanted. '*Ooooo* – I've upset Sis on her birthday. Sis on her birthday.' He ran in front of Kate and suddenly bent down on one knee and started singing: 'Katie, Katie – I'd walk a million miles for one of your smiles, oh Kaa – aaatie.'

'Shut up, Colin … you're *so* embarrassing,' Kate hissed, her face flaming. The long queue of people, waiting to see the next showing of *Gone With The Wind,* started laughing.

Colin stood up, looking at Bridget to see if she was amused or not. Her face was lit in a smile.

'I think insanity runs in your family, Kate,' Bridget said, walking arm-in-arm with her friend. 'Come on, we're going to get dolled up for the nightclub.'

'And where are you going to get changed?' Rob asked.

'Squadron Officer Virtue's given me the key to an apartment she has in Portland Place,' Kate said, suddenly determined to have a wonderful evening. Something to remember. 'She told me I could use it any time I'm in town.'

'Squadron Officer *Virtue!*' Rob and Colin hooted in unison.

During the taxi journey, they saw fires still smouldering in buildings. The huge new store *John Lewis* in Oxford Street had been reduced to a skeleton of steel and stone. Firemen were hard at work in their tin hats, thigh boots and dirty uniforms directing fire-hoses over its dying remains. From one of the glassless windows on the upper storey, a red dress fluttered, caught on a piece of debris. Kate experienced an unaccountable feeling of desolation as she looked at it.

After a tortuous journey circumnavigating bombed buildings and craters, the taxi dropped them off near

Broadcasting House. A large sheet of tarpaulin covered one section of the building where it had been damaged. They crossed the road to the apartment, helped by a luminous half-moon.

The girls entered the apartment first and were surprised at the starkness of the furniture and walls after the wooden warmth of S.O. Virtue's office in the castle. The walls were painted a brilliant white and four small armchairs were covered in white linen. If there hadn't been a profusion of Matisse paintings on the walls, they would have needed dark glasses to protect them from the glare.

'It doesn't look as if Squadron Officer Virtue designed this at all, does it, Bridge?'

'Perhaps a secret lover did,' Bridget said, looking around.

Colin's eyes lit up. 'Secret lover, eh? What does this Squadron Officer look like?'

'Oh she's beautiful, isn't she, Kate?' Bridget sounded wistful. 'Tall, blonde, willowy. All the things I'm not.'

'Oh *no* – I hate tall, willowy blondes,' Colin said, smiling at Bridget.

Rob was staring at the paintings. 'Look at these, Kate. You know about paintings.' In front of him were *La Danse* and *La Musique*; the people in the paintings were naked and bright red. Rob remembered the paintings in Billie's large bedroom in Bloomsbury: enormous surrealistic canvases painted by Dali. He had hated them. These were marginally better. But only marginally.

'Why on earth would you paint people red?' he asked Kate. He liked people to look like people.

227

'No time for paintings. Come on,' Kate said to Bridget. 'Bath time… see you two in an hour.'

'An *hour!* What are *we* going to do?' Colin moaned.

'Study the paintings, Col.'

Colin grunted. He hated Matisse's heavy-thighed women.

Kate and Bridget marched off to the bedroom, carrying their small cases with their precious change of clothes.

'An hour! … Imagine women in a scramble, Rob? "Sorry Controller, can't fly at the moment. Have to take a bath. Tell the Luftwaffe to wait."'

Rob laughed.

'I never thought I'd ever hear you cracking jokes again, Col, after …'

Colin looked at him. 'After my breakdown, you mean? It's all right. I don't mind people mentioning it. Not now I'm better. Thank God for my Mum, that's all I can say. Two months at home with her cooking and I was as right as rain.' Colin walked around the room glancing at the paintings. 'The feeling of dread has gone, Rob. Every morning I woke with this awful acid feeling in my stomach. As if I was going to be sick at any moment. Only it lasted all day.' He smiled at Rob. 'I can't tell you how much better life is, pushing a pen around. Knowing I don't have to wait for a claxon or a duty officer to shout "Scramble".'

'I didn't know you felt like that.' The friends stared at each other from opposite sides of the room.

'You can hardly tell your flying partner you're petrified every time you fly, can you?'

'No, I suppose not,' Rob said.

'I haven't thanked you yet, have I?'

'What for?'

'Getting me home. Saving my life. All those heroic kinds of things.'

'It wasn't heroic, Col,' Rob said. 'It's called self-preservation. I thought an ugly bugger like Brazier isn't going to kill me.'

Colin grinned. 'Anyway. Thanks. If it wasn't for you we wouldn't be here and I wouldn't be going to ask Bridget to marry me again.'

Rob sat down. 'Again? Perhaps she's not the marrying kind, Col.'

'Well, I wasn't until I met her. She makes me so happy. I wish I could put the feeling in a bottle and take a sniff every day so it stays with me for ever.'

Rob stood up abruptly to look out of the window. 'Turn the light off, Col. I want to look at the stars.'

Colin snapped off the light and the two friends stood at the window. Rob looked up at the stars, remembering how excited he had been two years ago knowing that a spectacular astronomical event was about to occur: the conjunction of Jupiter, Saturn and Earth; a spectacle so unusual it had been last seen in England when Charles II was on the throne. And how ironic, Rob thought. If people saw an unusual light in the sky now, they would think it was one of Hitler's rockets.

Colin nudged his elbow. 'Look.'

A large, dark, shiny object approached a lamp-post in the middle of the road, then receded.

'Is it a taxi parking?' Rob asked.

'Don't know. Bloody funny taxi if it is.'

It hadn't made a sound.

Three workmen, wearing steel helmets, walked across the road, when what looked like a very large tarpaulin descended with the gentleness of a pocket handkerchief. It was about twenty-five feet across.

'What the hell …?' Rob said.

One of the men strolled towards the 'tarpaulin' when a sound like a gigantic fuse burning, sizzled through the air. He raced back to join his mates. Suddenly the street was a large ball of blinding white light with concentric rings of colour: the inner one lavender, the outer violet. Rob and Colin stared in stunned horror as the men were lifted effortlessly up by a tornado of air created by the exploding sea-mine, attached to a parachute. They were thrown like puppets across the street. Pieces of brick, masonry and glass appeared magically on the pavement, making no sound. The grey-and-red bare body of one of the men lay twisted in front of Broadcasting House, blood pumping from a severed leg. His clothes had been blasted away. Rob felt Colin's hand tighten on his shoulder as they saw his leg dangling from a tree. The other two men sat up slowly and started to laugh. The clang of a fire engine resounded in the air, accompanied by the whistles of the rescue services.

'Switch the lights on, Colin,' Rob said, drawing the blackout curtain across the scene. He moved away from the window, almost falling over Kate and Bridget standing behind him.

'God, are we going to enjoy ourselves tonight,' Rob said.

It was nearly 8 o'clock when they arrived at the West End's most glittering nightspot, the *Café de Paris*. It was in a converted basement, beneath the Rialto Cinema and was packed with officers on leave, all determined to enjoy themselves. There were many other faces constructed by plastic surgeons in the club. Rob felt a strong bond of comradeship as pilots raised their glasses to him, then tremendous pride as they turned to watch Kate and Bridget as they swished to a table near the bandstand, looking more like models in the *Tatler* than officers in the WAAFs. He sat down next to Kate, marvelling at the translucence of her skin shimmering in the candlelight, wondering why she still loved him after the way he had treated her. She was wearing the blue chiffon dress he had bought her; it constantly changed colour in the candlelight. He noticed a small red mark at the base of her throat where a pulse was throbbing. He leaned over and put a bent finger on it, trying to imagine how it should feel. He was unaware that Colin and Bridget were watching him.

'What's that? I've never noticed it before.'

Self-consciously, Kate put a hand over her throat. 'Oh, that's the dreaded mark of the WAAF,' she said, smiling. 'That's where our collar button digs into our throats. Bridget has one too.'

The men turned to see Bridget covering her neck. 'I will not have men inspecting me. That's private, that is.' She spoke firmly.

'Oh come on, Bridge. It's hardly that when we're wearing these dresses.'

Both of them were wearing low-cut dresses. It wasn't often they could show off their figures. Colin found his eyes drawn more to the curve of Bridget's breasts than her throat as she removed her hand.

'And you can lift your eyes higher than that, right now, Colin Brazier.' Bridget stared fixedly at him.

Rob smiled to see Colin blushing crimson and stammering an apology. *Colin* – after all the women he'd had! It obviously must be love. He put his hand in his pocket and fingered the engagement ring he had bought Kate for her birthday. It had cost him his telescope. He had asked his mother to sell it for him. He didn't need to study other worlds when he had Kate in this one.

The sleek Rex Morrison sauntered onto the bandstand, wearing a dinner suit and brylcreemed hair so polished, it shone in the spotlight. He took a small bow as the band walked in after him. Everyone cheered.

'Good evening, ladies and gentlemen,' Rex purred in smooth, oily tones. 'I see that we have a lot of pilots here tonight.' Another cheer went round the room. 'So we'll start the evening with *The Spitfire Song*.'

The women in the club covered their ears as the cheering almost took off the roof. Then everyone became quiet as the band struck up the opening bars. Once Rex started on the verse, the men all stood up and joined in.

There's music in the sky,

Can't you hear the engines humming

Prepare to do or die

The British planes are coming.

Steadfast Reliant, The Spitfire or Defiant,

So give a rousing cheer,

The British planes are here.

No one could hear the rest as the pilots did their best to follow the directives of the song.

An hour later, the mood was quieter as people danced to the romantic song *They Can't Black Out The Moon*. Kate was locked in Rob's arms, humming the tune.

'Happy Birthday, darling. Time to announce our engagement formally, isn't it?' Rob whispered in her ear.

'Yes.' Perhaps everything *would* be all right. After all, she didn't know if she was definitely pregnant.

The song finished. They went back to join Colin and Bridget and Rob ordered a magnum of champagne.

'You didn't buy *me* champagne for my birthday, Robert,' Colin said, in mock petulance, as the magnum was put on their table.

Rob and Kate smiled at each other. 'We're celebrating more than Kate's birthday, Colin. We're going to be married next year.'

Kate's eyes darted towards Bridget. She and Rob hadn't discussed dates. Next year! That might be too late.

'What?' Colin asked, ecstatically. 'How long have you been cooking this up, you two?'

Kate felt elated by Colin's reaction. She hadn't known how much she wanted him to be happy about it. 'Oh, since I was fifteen, I think.'

Rob laughed. 'Last month, Col. You know, I'm a slow learner.' He put two boxes on the table in front of Kate: one tiny, one large. 'Happy birthday, darling.'

Kate opened the tiny box first. Inside, nestling on a dark blue velvet cloth was a sapphire ring that fired blue sparks.

'It was the nearest colour to your eyes I could find, Kate. Do you like it?'

Kate was determined not to cry as she put it on. 'It's beautiful, Rob. Thank you.'

'Now the other one.'

Kate opened the box. Inside was a heart-shaped silver locket on a silver chain. The locket was engraved with the initials RA KB.

'Open it, Kate.'

Inside the locket were two pictures: one of her standing on the beach at Hastings in 1940, smiling into the camera as Rob took her photograph; the other was the picture she had taken of Rob on the same day. He was smiling at her and there wasn't a scar on his face.

'I wanted you to have something to remember me as I was.'

Colin and Bridget looked away. Kate was silently crying.

'You silly man – I don't need a picture to remind me. I have you, now, as you are.'

Rob lifted up one hand and brushed her face with his fingers. 'Oh, Kate.'

'Hey, this is worse than watching Atlanta burn in the film,' Colin said to Bridget. She laughed.

Rob turned to Colin. 'All right, how's this for sentiment … I'd like you to be my best man.'

'And I'd like you as one of my bridesmaids, Bridge,' Kate said, still crying. Bridget joined in.

'Oh, God, don't let me start,' Colin said, standing up and pouring out the champagne. '*Mesdemoiselles et Messieurs*', he shouted around the room. 'Please raise your glasses to toast the engagement of Section Officer Katherine Louise Brazier … my sister … to Flying Officer Robert Pickwick Fortesque Adams … my best friend. To Kate and Rob. Long life and happiness.'

'To Kate and Rob. Long life and happiness.' A unified cry vibrated round the room as everyone toasted them.

Kate and Bridget hugged each other as the band struck up the opening familiar chords of If *You Were The Only Girl In The World.*

Rob leaned over to Colin. 'You bastard, Brazier! *Pickwick Fortesque*!'

'Distinguished, don't you think?' Colin laughed before draining his glass.

The bottle was empty an hour later. Bridget and Colin were swaying around the dance floor to a different rhythm from the other dancers.

'God, they must be drunk,' Rob said, staring at them in amazement.

'No, Bridget always dances like that … She's got no … she's got no coordination.'

'I don't think you have either, my darling, at the moment.'

Colin and Bridget came back and collapsed into their seats.

'I know …' Bridget said, then stopped.

They waited for her to continue.

'Yes?' Colin said, helpfully.

'I know what we ought to … Me Ma always said I had a grand memory for forgetting things.'

'I'd like to meet your Ma, Bridge.' Colin spoke with the sonorous tones of the seriously drunk.

Bridget answered him in similar tones. 'And she'd like to meet you too, Colin, if she only knew you …' she looked around for the word, '... existed. There you are ... I've got lots more words ... *and* I've remembered what I want. More giggle water.'

'Giggle water?'

'Champagne.'

'Don't you think you've giggled enough, Bridge?' Kate said, smiling at Bridget's shaking head.

'Did you hear what your sister said, Colin?'

'I certainly didn't. I've spent a lifetime not listening to her. I'm certainly not going to start just because it's her birthday.' He reached into his pocket. 'Oh, before I forget, Sis. 'My present. Just a little something.'

Kate unwrapped the rectangular parcel. Inside it was a maroon box. She opened it and the subtle strains of Debussy's *The Girl With The Flaxen Hair* tinkled round their table. On top of a small red dais, a dancer, wearing a lacy white dress pirouetted to the music. Kate watched her, enchanted.

'Oh, Col ... it's the nicest present you've ever given me.' Kate's voice was unsteady.

'Now don't start the waterworks again. I intend to enjoy this evening.' He turned to Bridget. 'So when are you going to marry me then?'

'Tomorrow. Definitely. Tomorrow. 1000 hours.' Bridget leaned over to kiss him on the cheek.

Colin turned his face quickly to kiss her on the mouth.

The officers sitting at other tables clapped their approval.

'*Mmm.* 1000 hours it is then.' He stood up and shouted across the room. 'Another announcement. Ladies and gentlemen. This beautiful Irish colleen and ... me... no... I ...are going to be spliced tomorrow morning and you're all invited.' Everyone cheered, unperturbed by the lack of location. Colin staggered over to the band leader and shouted in his ear, '*When Irish Eyes Are Smiling.*'

The band played the introduction to the song while Colin stood in front of the microphone clearing his throat noisily. Rob, Kate and Bridget, all feeling ridiculously happy and drunk, joined in noisily as Colin sang.

They didn't hear the bombs tear through the Rialto's roof; they didn't hear anything until they crashed through the ceiling of the crowded, noisy club and everything was plunged into instant screaming blackness. Kate felt as if her eardrums had been perforated by a cataclysmic explosion as the pain was so intense. Later, she wished they had been. She remembered too vividly the screams of dying and wounded people around her. Rob seemed to be calling to her from a vast distance. But how? He had been sitting next to her. Why was she lying on the floor? Why couldn't she breathe? She tried to inhale, then gagged as a smell assaulted her: a rank, acrid smell. One of the bombs hadn't ignited, but spewed its contents over the dead and dying. She couldn't sit up. An enormous pressure lay across her chest. A man gargled out his last word from bloody lungs: *Elizabeth.*

Kate lifted her hand to remove the pressure off her chest and touched the matted hair of the man who had just spoken his wife's name. He was lying across her. Stifling the screams rising up in her throat, she violently pushed him away. Rob was still calling for her in the distance. She opened her mouth to shout, but clouds of thick dust forced its way down her throat. People were coughing, shouting, screaming, everywhere. She heard someone yell: 'Lights! For God's sake! Lights!' Within seconds, the scene was illuminated with torches and Kate was staring into the glazed eyes of the man who had been hit in the chest; the one who'd been lying across her. A large bloody cavity, the size of a boxing glove, had opened over his heart. One arm was bent like a rag doll and the floor was saturated with his blood. She recoiled in horror. Yet all around the room were bodies: bodies lying in impossible positions, next to overturned tables and broken bottles; all covered with layers of dust and the yellow, acrid liquid oozing from the unexploded bomb.

Kate touched her hair and was startled to see her hand covered in blood. She felt no pain. She tried to stand on legs that wouldn't support her. Where was Rob? Her throat was too tight to shout. Then all at once, through the noise and carnage, he was standing in front of her, terror in his eyes as he saw the front of her blue dress covered in copious amounts of blood. He cradled her in his arms. 'Oh, my darling, darling girl. Are you all right? Where are you hurt?' He touched her dress tentatively, expecting to find a large wound in her stomach. There was nothing. She was covered with the other man's blood.

'Oh, thank God … thank God,' he wept.

He lifted Kate to her feet. 'We *must* find them … *Colin?* … *Bridget*?' He shouted their names repeatedly. Then suddenly, Kate saw them. Colin's body was draped down the bandstand, his face turned towards her: a surprised look in his unseeing eyes. And Bridget was lying at the side of their upturned table; her legs at awkward angles; her face pulped into the broken glasses on the floor. Lying next to her was a horizontal bottle of champagne; the one Rob had bought to celebrate their engagement; the one from which Colin and Bridget had drunk to their future happiness. It lay unbroken on the blood-drenched floor.

Chapter 21

Unbelievably, Kate found she still carried the foetus of Rob's child in her womb. Unbelievable after the double trauma of two funerals. Time had become a mirage for her; a collection of distorted images: blood seeping from a severed hand lying on the floor; Rob's tortured face as he held Colin; Bridget's legs twisted in improbable angles; the broken music box lying next to Bridget, the ballerina's once white dress coloured red.

Kate had remained strong all through the long hiatus home in the RAF truck. Strong for her mother. But Hilda had known the moment she had seen Kate. She had insisted on organising Colin's funeral herself. Kate had expected her to collapse. She hadn't. She just sat in a chair and rocked. For hours.

Kate remembered the times in her childhood when her mother disappeared. Her father telling her that 'Mum was resting in hospital'. But two weeks ago, she had found the hidden letters from Hellingly, a mental hospital, stating that they were giving Hilda treatment for recurring nervous breakdowns. Yet she hadn't broken down.

Even after that, Kate had remained strong; writing to Bridget's parents; organising the funeral for them. But sounds seared her sleep: low animal grunts of grief echoed nightly through a crematorium as Bridget's body was consumed by flames. She remembered the small blue urn in which Bridget's ashes lay, the small black letters which blocked out her life: *Bridget Reilly. 1922 –1945. Beloved daughter.* There was no space for anything else. All that vivacity reduced to powder.

Once the funerals were over, she lay awake in bed for days, mourning her brother and her best friend. Each time she blinked, she sandpapered her cornea. She hadn't told Rob about the baby. She hadn't told her family. How could she? Her mother wouldn't be interested in a foetus when her beloved son was lying under the ground. Kate spent hours counting the small green leaves on her wallpaper. She managed four hundred and forty-three before she started again. Rose was keeping the family together now. Her mother spent hours in the graveyard, while her father drank in the pub. And Rose queued for hours and cooked for stomachs too full of grief to eat.

Rob disappeared after Colin's funeral. They had no time in which to grieve together. With deadly dispassion, he told her he'd been posted to another squadron. Death seemed to be shrinking them to shadows.

She had travelled to Cardiff in a stupor, thinking that she could continue her duties. She couldn't. Squadron Officer Virtue had called her into her wood-warmed office in the castle, and Kate had told her she was pregnant. After an initial stunned silence, S.O. Virtue had informed her that she didn't need to leave the WAAFs if she didn't want to: she could have an abortion. Kate wasn't able to speak for a long time. The picture of Freda's perfect foetus lying wrapped in a blood-soaked towel too vivid in her memory. For the first and last time, Kate heard her superior officer stammer as she apologised. Then she knew what she must do. She asked the S.O. to give her the requisite forms for her release from the WAAFs. She was going to use paragraph 42 of King's Regulations; the paragraph all girls who wanted to get out of the services used. There was no patriotism in pregnancy.

So she had come back home. To nothing.

She could hear Rose coming up the stairs with a tray of food as she did every day. And every day she left the food untouched on the plate.

'I've made you some vegetable soup, Kate. You *will* try it, won't you?'

Kate looked at her sister's anxious face, old beyond her fifteen years. Fifteen. An age of innocence. But no age *could* be innocent during a war, could it? Another more frightening thought occurred to her: *would innocence be possible after it was over?*

She sat up and sipped Rose's soup slowly. It tasted of emptiness.

'It's carrot soup – like Mum makes – I've put some basil in it… can you taste it?'

'Yes,' Kate said, continuing to sip under Rose's watchful eyes.

'What time do you think Mum will be back?' Rose said.

'I didn't know she was out.'

'She's been out hours… and Dad.'

'Can't eat any more, Rose. Thanks.' Kate went to put the soup down, but Rose grabbed it off her.

'You've got to eat more. You're too thin. I made it specially for you, Kate. *Please.*' There were bright bubbles in her eyes.

'Don't worry about me. I'm just not hungry, that's all.'

Rose started trembling. 'That's what you said yesterday and the day before and the day before that. You're never hungry. Mum's never hungry. Dad's always drinking... I...'

Kate sipped a little more of the soup until her sister stopped shaking.

'Kate, what are you going to do?'

'About what?'

'About Mum. Always in the graveyard. You don't think she's gone mad, do you?'

'Mad?' Kate said, dully. How could anyone be mad in an insane world? 'No, it's just her way of coping, I suppose.'

Rose sat down on her sister's bed. 'I'm frightened, Kate.'

'Everyone's frightened. There's a war on.'

'No... I'm frightened to go in Colin's room.'

'Why?'

'I don't think he's in the graveyard, I think he's in there.' Rose's eyes were enormous as she stared at her sister.

Kate didn't want this. She didn't want to feel her sister's pain. Her fear. She had too much of her own. She got off the bed. 'That's because Mum's made it like a shrine. Come on, we'll clear out his clothes.' Kate walked out of the room, not noticing the horrified expression on her sister's face.

244

Colin's room was claustrophobic with memorabilia. Shields and plaques from school overwhelmed the shelves, proclaiming his prowess in cricket, football, swimming. The walls were covered with pictures of him growing up with Rob: two sweaty boys, caked with mud, grinning at each other after a football match in the fifth year at school; the school swimming team; a line of grim schoolboys with folded arms across their chests, obviously been told to frighten the opposition; Colin, his carrot hair sticking up like a brush, the only one smiling at the camera. And there was Rob, sitting in the middle of the team, a lock of thick dark brown hair falling over one serious eye, staring at her from the distance of eight years.

'You can't touch Colin's things, Kate. Mum will go mad.' Rose stood at the door, not wanting to go in.

'She's always mad with me anyway, so it won't matter.' Kate opened the wardrobe and Colin's clothes reached out to her. She felt dizzy with smells: sweat, mingled with Old Spice and tobacco were pungently woven into the fabric of his RAF uniform. Kate touched his pilot's wings stitched onto the left sleeve of his jacket: her mother's tiny stitching hardly visible. A long yellow silk scarf Rob had given him when they were flying together smelt of his favourite soap: Pears. This wasn't getting her anywhere. She started to take out jackets and trousers she had never seen him wear. That had no history.

They heard the front door open.

'Put them back, Kate. *Please,*' Rose whispered from the doorway. She darted down the stairs. There were low voices in the hallway, then the sound of her mother's heavy tread coming towards her. Kate's stomach tightened, but she carried on taking things out of Colin's wardrobe until her mother came into the room. She stood at the door in silence for several minutes, watching Kate hold a shabby, brown herringbone jacket that Colin had worn during the months he had been home with his mother, recovering from his breakdown. It was worn around the elbows and cuffs.

'Don't you *dare*! Don't you *dare* touch his things!' Kate saw the discoloration start at her mother's neck and blotch up her face until she looked like a relief map. Kate was frightened. Her mother was a big woman. Hilda quivered across the room and slapped her daughter hard across the face, snapping her neck back. The worn jacket fell onto the carpet between them. Kate held her hand up to her burning face, remembering the last time her mother had hit her. The day she had told her she'd enlisted. A stone age away. She looked into her mother's eyes, bloodshot from lack of sleep and hit her back with all the anger she'd been storing inside her body since she was a child. Hilda slumped, stunned, onto the bed.

'That's for not loving me! *Ever!* And for loving Colin too much!'

And then her mother sobbed. Great racking sobs that shook her large frame; shook the room; shook the foundations of the family. And Kate walked out of the room and out of the house.

She walked for hours, not knowing what to do. Not knowing where she was walking. An old man bumped into her and suddenly she saw the cherry trees lining Pevensey Road. She had been walking in large circles around Rob's house in a trance. She walked up to *The Beeches* without a thought about what she was doing. What she was going to say. She rang the bell and waited.

Mary opened the door and stood there for several seconds before she opened out her arms to Kate. Kate fell into them and started to weep for the first time.

It was ten minutes before Mary could lead her into the kitchen and sit her down. All the sandpaper in her eyes, replaced by the pain of swollen tissues; the constriction in her chest replaced by a dull ache.

'Tea?' Mary said, quietly, noticing that one of Kate's cheeks seemed to be on fire.

Kate gave a small smile and nodded. 'That's what Rob said when I came here to talk things over with him.'

'How are things between you now, Kate?' Mary bustled round the kitchen.

Kate thought about the best way to tell Mary of the monumental chasm that had opened up between them.

'Not too good. Rob was very withdrawn after Colin's funeral, wasn't he? I couldn't talk to him about …'

'Yes?'

'About anything.' Kate took a deep breath. 'I've just hit my mother.'

'What? … But why?' Mary looked at her, stunned.

'Because she hit me. Because … she's never loved me.' Kate could feel tears surface and fought them back. 'Because she loved Colin too much. You've seen the way she treats me, Mrs

Adams. Can you imagine what it feels like not to be welcome in your own home?'

Mary put a cup into Kate's shaking hand before saying, 'Charlie's showed me what it's like not to feel loved... But my dear, I'm sure your mother loves you, perhaps she just doesn't show it. You know what mothers are like with their sons.'

Kate shook her head. 'No, she shows Rose she loves her in hundreds of small ways. She's never shown me any warmth at all.'

Mary looked at Kate's swollen red-rimmed eyes and said, 'I can't understand it, Kate. You're everything that I would have wished my daughters had been.'

Kate looked at her in surprise. 'Your daughters?'

Then Mary told her about the day her twin daughters had died of diphtheria; about the snow falling out of the sky as if nothing had happened. The devastation of the loss.

'It took me a long time to recover. And I could never have any more children, so no more daughters.' Mary smiled at Kate. 'Not until you become Rob's wife, that is. I can't tell you how happy I am that Rob is going to marry you.'

Kate felt that the sun had risen, just for her. 'You mean that?'

'Of course I do. Rob is a very lucky man.'

'He doesn't seem to think so at the moment.'

'Colin and Rob have been close friends since elementary school, Kate. It will take a long time for him to recover from the shock, but he will, I know... and when the war's over you and

248

Rob can start a family and fill up this big house with lots of noisy children.' Mary beamed at the prospect.

Kate sat hugging her cup while the blood drained from her face.

'You don't have to wait until after the war, Mrs Adams ... I'm ... pregnant now.' Kate looked at Mary nervously, terrified of her condemnation.

Mary held onto the table for support. 'You're what? When?'

Kate blushed. 'I ...'

'Oh I'm sorry, my dear. That was very insensitive. It's just that you've taken me by surprise. I mean ... how long ... how long before the baby's born?'

Kate shrunk into the chair. 'Five months.'

'Five months! So soon?' Mary saw Kate's distress and added hastily, 'It's rather a thunderbolt, that's all.' She sat still, trying to absorb the news. 'I'm going to be a grandmother! I might look like one, but I certainly don't feel like one.' She suddenly jumped up from the table and went to hug Kate. 'You're going to be a mother, Kate!'

'*A mother*?' Kate said, as if the word was inexplicable.

Mary smiled. 'Yes, my dear. That's what generally happens after you become pregnant.'

They laughed, both suddenly struck by the miracle of a new life.

'I was so frightened to tell you,' Kate said. 'I didn't think I had anyone I *could* tell, now that Bridget's gone.'

'Well, don't think like that. You've got me now. I'll support you in any way I can. Would you like me to tell your mother?'

Kate's face brightened. 'Would you, Mrs Adams? I couldn't bear to … not after what's happened.'

'It's Mary, not Mrs Adams, Kate. Yes, of course, if you'll do something for me.'

'What?'

'Get your things from your house and stay here with us until things settle down. Will you, my dear?'

'But what will Dr Adams think?'

'He'll think it's a wonderful idea,' Mary said with a determined edge to her voice. 'And so will Charlie.'

Mary decided to walk to Hilda's house to give her time to think about what to say. A bluster of wind buried itself in her dark blue utility coat as she walked up the road. She drew in her belt, shivering. She was entering private family areas which were no concern of hers and Hilda had every right to tell her so. But she was fond of Kate. She was fond of Hilda too, that's why she couldn't understand the discord between them. A mother and daughter hitting each other! It was inconceivable. She thought this sort of violence only happened in families like Charlie's where they were too ignorant to know any better. Not *nice* families. She rehearsed conversations in her head as she walked up London Road towards the Braziers' house: 'Well, Hilda. You and I are going to be grandmothers. Won't that be lovely? Walks in the park with the baby in the summer?' No, far too sentimental. 'Hello, Hilda. Now I don't want you to get upset, but Kate is pregnant and was too frightened to tell you.' No, no, no – that implied Hilda wasn't a good mother. 'What do you think about having grandchildren, Hilda? Would you like them?' But what if she says no?

Mary was full of trepidation by the time she reached Hilda's door. She could hear raised voices. Hilda's husband sounded drunk again. But she had promised Kate; she couldn't go back on her word. She steeled herself to knock on the door. The voices inside abruptly stopped. Rose answered the door, white faced and embarrassed.

'Oh, hello, Mrs Adams... Come in. Mum's in the ...' She looked back in the narrow dark hallway to see if her mother had left her father in the scullery. 'Wait here. I'll tell her you've come.'

Mary stood awkwardly in the twilight of the hall, hearing Rose whisper urgently to her mother. She popped her head around the door. 'Come in, Mrs Adams. I'll make a cup of tea.'

'Not for me, thanks, Rose. I've just had one.'

Hilda was sitting upright on the chair, her mouth tight as a stitch. There was an angry weal across her left cheek. She wouldn't look at Mary.

'Hello, Hilda. Are you all right?'

'Suppose so.' She lifted her hand to her cheek. 'Sit down. Kate did this, you know.'

'Yes, I do.'

Hilda turned to look at Mary. 'How?'

'Kate's at my house, Hilda. She's very upset.'

'*She's* very upset. *I'm* very upset. She was only trying to get rid of my Colin's clothes! I'm surprised she didn't rip up his photographs as well. Rose tried to stop her, but no – madam knows best.'

'I know how you must be grieving for Colin –'

'Do you? How? *Your* son's still alive.'

Oh no, I'm doing this all wrong, Mary thought, looking into the pain on Hilda's face.

'I'm sorry, Hilda … I … only meant … as a mother I know the pain of losing children. You remember my baby girls.'

Hilda's face softened a little. 'Oh, yes.'

They were silent for some time, both lost in their own personal tragedies.

'Would you like to see his room, Mary? I'd only show it to you. No one else. Not even him.'

All the time they had been talking, noises permeated the conversation. Noises from the scullery. Snufflings. Grunts. Whistles. Hilda opened the door, her face contorting as the sounds became more audible.

'Drunk! At half past two. You're a bloody disgrace! And our Colin not …' Mary put a hand on Hilda's shoulder as Rose came out of the scullery, staring in alarm at her mother. 'Your mother is going to show me Colin's room, aren't you, Hilda?'

Hilda turned away from the sounds and trudged heavily up the stairs. 'Come up, Mary,' she called.

Mary gave Rose a small smile and followed Hilda up to Colin's room.

Mary's first impression was of a room only just vacated: a room waiting for the imminent return of its occupant. A brown Harris tweed jacket and beige corduroy trousers were laid out on a meticulously stitched bedspread, embroidered with aeroplanes. Hanging on the outside of the old pine wardrobe was a newly ironed cream shirt; the smoulder of a flat iron mingled with a hint of male perspiration.

'He always wears those clothes when he comes home on leave. I like to have them ready for him just in case he drops in. He's always been one for surprises, has my Colin.'

Mary suddenly understood why Hilda was so angry with Kate. She was telling her mother that Colin was never going to walk through their front door again; was never going to eat his mother's gastronomic dishes magically conjured up from wartime rations; was never going to wear the clothes overflowing out of his wardrobe. Mary was furious with herself. What right did *she* have to interfere with Hilda's window-dressing? Her subtle subterfuges to get her through the day? But what of Kate? She needed her mother. And so did Rose.

She took a deep breath and said calmly: 'He won't be needing these clothes any more though, will he, Hilda? You should give them to the Samaritan Centre. He's not coming back. He's dead.'

An agitated pulse throbbed in Mary's left temple as she saw the effect of her words on her friend. Hilda's face seemed to waver out of control. She stumbled over the carpet and collapsed onto Colin's bed, burying her head in his clothes and wailing uncontrollably. Mary was momentarily rigid with horror. Then she shouted for Rose, giving her a message for Dr Adams. He must come to the Braziers' house immediately. It was urgent. Mary sat on the bed beside Hilda, her hands hovering superfluously over her convulsing body.

An hour later, Mary and John were driving home, exhausted, and Hilda was asleep in her bedroom, heavily sedated.

'I can't believe what an awful mess I've made of things, John. I told Kate I was going to tell her mother about her pregnancy and all I've succeeded in doing is making Hilda hysterical about Colin's death.'

John slammed his foot down on the brake. Mary shot forward, almost hitting her head on the windshield.

'What!' he shouted.

Oh no – I've done it again! Mary thought. What is the matter with me?

John looked at her, stunned.

'Pregnant? My God, what a time to choose!'

'I don't think she chose it, John. It's not all Kate's fault, you know. Rob had something to do with it.'

John started up the car again. 'My God – a war baby with the V1s and V2s dropping.'

Mary was silent.

He turned briefly to look at her. 'It's a bit of a shock, Mary.'

'But far more for Kate. She's had to leave the WAAFs and come home.'

'And what a home to come back to,' John said, remembering the raucous drunken snores coming from the scullery.

'Hilda can't give her any support so I've asked her to stay with us until things settle down. That's all right, isn't it?'

She had to wait for his answer as he crashed the gears, turning the corner into Pevensey Road.

'Yes,' John said, 'as long as it's not our bedroom.'

Mary touched his arm affectionately.

'Remember that night when we talked about Mary Wollstonecraft with Kate and Bridget?' Mary said.

'I remember you saying women should have control over their bodies.' John slowed the car down to let Mrs Humphries and Spot cross the road.

'Well, Kate's lost all control now, hasn't she? No job. No husband –'

'Yet,' John interrupted. 'Let's plan for Rob's next leave.'

'I feel so guilty about Hilda. I shouldn't have said anything, should I?'

'She had to face Colin's death sometime. You've just forced her to face it sooner, that's all.'

'Too soon, do you think?'

'I don't know, but someone needs to look after that child. Rose looks years older than Charlie and they're the same age, aren't they? She's grown up too fast. I'll call in on them tomorrow and see how they are.'

'I'll come with you.'

John suddenly put his foot down on the brake again.

'I wish you'd stop doing that, John,' Mary said in alarm. 'What's the matter *now?*'

'Good heavens, Mary. It's just struck me … I'm going to be a grandfather!' John started to laugh uproariously as he accelerated off up the road.

*

The next morning Hilda dragged herself round the scullery trying to make John and Mary some tea.

'I'll do it, Mum. You sit down. You don't know where anything is any more, do you?' Rose's fingers fluttered over her mother in a magical incantation as she motioned her towards a chair.

They sat in silence in the Braziers' small scullery as Rose laid the table with their best white china cups and saucers and four small plates, each bearing a white paper napkin. Then came four small knives at the side of each plate. Everything an echo of her mother's past efficiency. She took a cake out of the oven and placed it on the table. The smell of warm ginger wafted round the room.

'You made that, Rose?' Mary asked her, inhaling the spiced aroma. Rose's face glowed.

'Haven't had home-made ginger cake for years,' John said. 'Mrs Adams doesn't like cooking.' Mary kicked him under the table as Rose cut a large slice of rich ginger cake and put it in front of him. 'Thank you, Rose,' John said, rubbing his ankle. 'Ummm.' Ginger exploded over the taste buds on his tongue. '*Absolutely* delicious.'

Mary glanced at Hilda, wondering whether to apologise for yesterday, or to do what John said and not mention it.

'Hilda … I'm sorry about …' Mary stopped short when she saw what Hilda was doing: folding her napkin into the shape of a bird's wings.

'Mum?' Rose looked from her mother to their guests in embarrassment. 'Eat your cake.'

'My cake?' Hilda said, vaguely. 'Who made it?'

'I did, Mum.'

They all watched Hilda take a small piece and roll it round her mouth expertly. 'Needs more ginger, Rose. Did you follow my recipe properly?'

'Yes, Mum.'

'*Mmm,*' Hilda said, dismissively. 'Well, pour the tea, I've got to go out soon.'

Mary and Rose looked at John.

'I wouldn't go out today, Mrs Brazier,' he said. 'Not after the sedative I gave you … you'll feel a little groggy.'

'Oh, I'll be as right as rain after a cup of tea. Don't you worry about me, Doctor.' She carried on making the bird sculpture.

'Mum, *please* listen to Dr Adams,' Rose begged. 'Anyway, you don't need to go out. I'll do the shopping. You rest.'

'No, I've got to have a chat to Colin. He'll be waiting.'

There was a stunned silence as they looked at Hilda's impassive face, unaware of the effect of her words.

'Where will he be waiting, Mrs Brazier?' John said, quietly.

Hilda stopped making her design and stared at John. 'In the graveyard, of course, that's where they put dead people, don't they? And Mary told me yesterday he was dead.'

John looked at Mary, knowing exactly what she was feeling.

Chapter 22

'Mary, this is becoming ridiculous. The house is bursting at the seams. Kate, now Hilda Brazier and Rose! What other waifs and strays are you intending to bring here from your Samaritan Centre?' John was striding noisily up and down their kitchen, making Mary's pulse throb in her temple. 'I'm not a charitable institution, you know. I'm not made of money and I've got work to do.'

'John, do sit down. It's only until Hilda feels stronger. Sit down ... *please.*'

John sighed heavily, then sat down opposite Mary, drumming his fingers on the table.

'Are you doing that deliberately?'

He folded his arms across his chest and glowered at her. 'That any better?'

'Yes. Now look ...'

Suddenly Charlie's agitated face appeared in the doorway. '*Shhh.* They might hear you arguing upstairs.' He closed the door quietly behind him and sat down at the table.

'Why are you always arguing?' he said. 'You never argued when I first came here.'

Mary and John looked at each other, knowing Charlie was right. They had only started arguing after Rob's crash. They hadn't heard from him for months since Colin's funeral.

'Sorry, darling,' Mary said, looking at Charlie's worried face. 'You don't think they heard, do you?'

'Hope not.' Charlie turned to John. 'Rose's Mum isn't very well, is she? But you'll make her better, won't you, Dad?'

Charlie had only been calling John 'Dad' since the adoption, although Mary had been Mum for months. Charlie thought John was capable of curing the world.

'She needs a lot of help, Charlie. She's had a tremendous shock to her system, but she's got Kate and Rose.'

'And us and the new baby to look forward to.' They had only just told Charlie about the baby. He was embarrassed at first, remembering all the noises he had heard in his parents' bedroom. But he knew it couldn't be like that between Kate and Rob. Now he was euphoric. He was going to be an uncle. That meant he had to help the baby learn things. He had decided to teach him to swim when he was three.

'She doesn't know about the new baby yet, Charlie,' Mary said.

'Why not?' Charlie said. 'It's her grandchild too, isn't it? Why hasn't any one told her?'

Charlie's expression was puzzled. His logic was always faultless, Mary thought, but so often he didn't understand the complications of other people's lives in spite of the complications of his own. Mary looked into his angular, almost adult face which hid a child's monochrome view of the world.

'Kate should be the one to tell her and she's nervous, that's why,' Mary said.

'But Rob and Kate love each other. Is it because they aren't married? Will she be angry? Can't you tell her that they love each other, Mum? It's all right if you love each other, isn't it? And they *are* getting married soon.' Charlie looked at John and Mary, desperately wanting them to agree.

'Yes, it's all right for Rob and Kate, Charlie,' John said. 'But it's not a good time to have a baby during a war, is it?'

'I think any time's all right if you love it,' Charlie said.

John and Mary looked at each other, thinking how often he had mentioned the word 'love'.

'Perhaps you're right,' Mary said, smiling at him. 'Now go and get the vegetables from the garden for dinner, will you?' She suddenly clamped a hand to her mouth. 'Oh no. I've just thought – I'll have to cook for *everybody*.'

Charlie grinned at John, then stuck out his tongue in mock horror.

It was a difficult meal with everyone working hard to appear relaxed – everyone except Hilda. She was tearing off tiny pieces from her paper napkin. Mary had decided to have dinner in their large kitchen, more informal she'd thought, but the gathering couldn't have been more formal if they had been sitting round a table at Buckingham Palace. Kate and Rose looked as if they had been bound in buckram as they struggled to eat Mary's latest culinary effort: fried spam and a multitude of Charlie's fresh vegetables, all overcooked. Everything tasted of salt. She'd put enough salt in for ten people. Usually John and Charlie would have laughed, but the Brazier family's presence didn't allow for levity. They ate in silence: listening to the attack of clashing cutlery. Kate wanted to scream as her mother continued the slow shredding of the napkin.

'Your garden's going to look lovely in the summer, Mary,' Kate said, wearing a stiff smile as she looked out of the window. An abundance of labels were tied onto the plants, shrubs and flowers that Mary and Charlie had planted on a bright autumnal morning.

'I hope so.' Mary answered in the same stiff tones. 'If only spring would come and the war would end.' She cringed as her vacuous words echoed into silence.

Charlie was sitting opposite her, his head bent down to his plate to avoid seeing Hilda's actions. Normally Mary would have told him to sit up, but not today. Next to him sat Rose, her face pink with embarrassment as she covertly watched her mother. She shouldn't have to cope with so many problems at her age, Mary thought, but there was a war on.

'How do you think it's going, John?' Mary said, desperately.

'What?' John looked startled, lost in his own thoughts. He had to see one of his patients the next day to tell her the results of her tests. Her husband had given her VD It wasn't going to be pleasant.

'The war? How do you think it's going after the Yalta Conference?' Mary thought that John would utter some words of hope. The success of the conference seemed the most encouraging sign for a post-war world that Mary had read about since the war started. Stalin, Roosevelt and Churchill agreeing on the zones of occupation of Germany; sketching the future map of Europe.

'Our Colin always liked green,' Hilda said, looking out of the window. She suddenly found that there was no more napkin left to shred and stared aimlessly around the room.

'Please eat your meal, Mum,' Rose pleaded with her mother. She got up and walked around the table, placed a knife and fork in Hilda's bewildered hands, then pierced a potato for her. Hilda put it in her mouth and groaned.

'Oh, that's awful.'

'Mum!' Kate and Rose were rigid with embarrassment.

'No, you're right, Hilda,' Mary said, putting down her knife and fork. 'It *is* awful.'

'You've put far too much salt in the water, Mary. Shall I cook tomorrow? I like cooking,' Hilda said, looking at them as if seeing them for the first time.

Everyone stopped eating.

'That might be a good idea.' Mary turned to John. 'What do you think, dear?'

'No *might* about it, Mary,' John answered. 'If Mrs Brazier taught Rose to make ginger cake like that, I can't wait for her meal.' He beamed at Rose and Hilda encouragingly.

Only Charlie noticed the small furrow of pain appear around Mary's eyes. 'Well, I *like* lots of salt in my food,' he said, valiantly putting a large salted portion of spam in his mouth and swallowing it quickly.

Three days later, their kitchen had been transformed into an Aladdin's cave of community cooking. Hilda supervised the troops; Charlie provided the vegetables from the garden; Rose did the shopping using their ration books and Kate and Mary helped prepare the food.

Mary and Kate were peeling the vegetables for the evening meal while Hilda minced some pork in a mincer which had lain unused in one of Mary's cupboards for years. She was going to make a rich Bolognese sauce with Charlie's home-grown tomatoes, Rose's herbs and Bisto gravy. The atmosphere in the kitchen was light with melody: Henry Hall's orchestra was playing dance music on the wireless. It was the first time Kate had felt happy since the bombs had crashed through the roof of the *Café de Paris*; happy, peeling potatoes, after all the years of excitement and challenge in the WAAFs. But she still couldn't find the courage to tell her mother about the baby, and she still hadn't finished the letter she'd started seven days ago to Rob. She was just washing the potatoes when the pain hit her. She felt a warm gush between her legs and hung onto the sink for support.

'What's the matter?' Mary said.

'I think I'm bleeding.' Kate looked terrified.

'Lie down at once.' Mary raced to get a blanket out of a cupboard and threw it on the floor. 'Lie down, Kate!'

An ashen-faced Kate lay down on a blanket on the kitchen floor, too frightened to breathe in case she displaced the baby.

Hilda watched in bewilderment. 'What's all the fuss about? It's only her period.'

'She's pregnant. Call John quickly. He's in his study.'

Hilda's face became as white as Kate's as she bustled out of the room and shouted for John.

Within minutes he was leaning over Kate, his face creased with concern.

'I'm not going to lose the baby, am I, John?' Kate lay on the floor staring up at him as he examined her. Part of the placenta seemed to be tearing away.

'Not if I have anything to do with it. Lay still, Kate. I'm going to get you into hospital.'

'No, not hospital. *Please*. I hate hospitals.' She started crying. 'Mum. Mum. Help me!'

Hilda knelt on the floor beside her daughter and stroked her hair. 'Hush, my petal. You won't go into hospital if you don't want to. *I'll* nurse you. Lie still to help the baby and stop that crying.'

Kate looked up into her mother's face in wonder. She had called her 'petal'.

'Yes, Mum,' she said quietly, the tears drying on her face.

An hour later, Kate was tucked up in bed after two young soldiers had carried her upstairs. Mary had asked them for help as they were walking past the house. Kate would not be going into hospital, Hilda had informed John and Mary. There was more infection in hospital than here and John was a doctor, so what did Kate need a hospital for? Fortunately, Kate's bleeding stopped once she was lying still and John knew that with bed rest and good nursing, her baby would be fine. Hilda's face beamed when he told her.

Every day, Hilda made Kate succulent soup to build up her strength so that the baby would be strong. They listened to the radio doctor who gave advice about the importance of drinking orange juice, milk and taking vitamins. Kate listened to him, while watching her mother knitting small garments.

'Were you ill with any of us, Mum?'

'No, right as rain,' Hilda said, then stopped knitting and frowned.

'What?' Kate was worried by the twisted expression on her mother's face, as if recalling some terrible anguish.

She stroked Kate's hair. '*Shhh,* petal. I was never ill when I was pregnant, only afterwards. I just thought it was tiredness with Colin, he was such a needy baby. Always wanting to be fed and pampered. Just like he was when he was older.'

Kate felt her mother's hand on her hair slowing down as she grieved again for Colin.

'What happened with *me*, Mum?' She wanted all her mother's attention for once in her life.

'You?' Hilda said, reluctantly casting her mind back to the worst time of her life. 'That's when I was first put in hospital, Kate. After you were born. It all seemed too much for me. Two babies to look after and living with your grandma. Always criticising me that woman was. Never a day went by unless she told me I was doing something wrong. Not changing your nappies properly; not cleaning the house enough; not feeding your father the way he was used to. In the end, I had a nervous breakdown and went into Hellingly. I was there for three months and when I came out you wouldn't go near me, only your grandma. Course, she loved it. Only Colin wanted me. He

266

opened out his arms to me the moment he saw me and said: "*My mummy.*" You ought to have seen the pickled look on your grandma's face. I thought my heart would burst. But you … you wouldn't go near me.'

'I'm sorry, Mum. I can't remember. I can't even remember Grandma.'

'Well, I'm glad about that. I had to stop myself dancing at the old bat's funeral.'

Kate smiled.

'Always thought your father could do no wrong and he believed her, of course.'

'How long was it before I went to you, not Grandma?'

'Three years,' Hilda said, heavily.

Kate gasped.

'She had to die first. You were four and our Colin five.' Hilda's hand fell from Kate's hair as she stared into the distance, lost in memories. 'You kept calling for her in the night for months after she'd gone.'

Kate had a sudden insight into what her mother's life must have been like living with her grandmother. She squeezed her hand.

'She made you love her more than me, you see, Kate. You never wanted me.'

'Oh, Mum, that's not true,' Kate cried. '*You* never wanted *me*. You were always saying terrible things to me when I was growing up. I thought you hated me.'

'*Shhh*,' Hilda said, stroking Kate's hair again. 'Don't get agitated. Remember the baby. You've got to stay calm. *Shhh*.'

Kate gradually relaxed under the hypnotic pressure of her mother's fingers. 'You don't hate me any more?'

Hilda flinched. 'I never hated you, petal. I just thought you didn't need me. I suppose I was jealous of you and your grandma. After she died you became so independent. You were so clever. So pretty. What would you need an old frump like me for?'

Kate's eyes widened. She had never heard her mother compliment her before in her life. 'You thought I was clever and pretty? Why didn't you tell me? I always thought I was ugly. You were always telling people how spotty and gawky I was.'

'Can you forgive me, petal? It was a wicked thing to do.'

Kate looked up into her mother's lined, tearful face: her salt-and-pepper hair and thought she had never seen anyone more beautiful. She took her mother's hand and kissed it.

'There's nothing to forgive, Mum. You love me, that's all I need to know.'

Hilda took out a large handkerchief and blew her nose. 'Well, they say God moves in mysterious ways, don't they? Today I know it's true. It's taken your baby to show me how bad I've been. How bad jealousy is.' Hilda took a deep breath. 'You see, you were everything I wasn't.'

Kate tried to sit up in bed, stunned. 'You were *jealous* of me? But you've got so many talents, Mum. You can't be jealous of me?'

'Lie down and keep still. I was. But that's the past, Kate. Now I've got a reason to carry on.' Hilda stood up suddenly and folded her arms across her ample breasts. 'So, from now on, young lady, I want you to do exactly what I tell you to. I want my grandchild to be a bonny baby.'

Kate smiled at her.

'All right? I'll leave you to have a sleep.' Hilda turned towards the door; then suddenly turned back, nervously, 'You said I had talents.'

Kate's eyes were drooping. She said, 'Yes ... one of them's being bossy, Mum. I'll tell you about the others tomorrow.'

Hilda smiled at her daughter before closing the door and walking downstairs.

Kate lay in bed each day, feeling comforted and loved. Exhilaration coursed through her body as she thought of her conversation with her mother. She now had the emotional strength to write the letter to Rob she'd been postponing for weeks. She was strong enough to use the expensive blue vellum notepaper Bridget had bought for her birthday. She had just got out her pen when there was a sudden commotion downstairs. She could hear laughter. Suddenly, the sound of eager footsteps running up the stairs and Charlie and Rose burst into the room: their young faces bright with drama.

'There was a raid on Berlin last night, Kate. The RAF bombed it for hours,' Charlie shouted.

'We've just heard it on the wireless,' Rose added. 'There are enormous fires everywhere –'

'Let me tell her,' Charlie interrupted, his arms whirling to illustrate his words. 'The Red Army's caught the Nazis in a pincer movement, north and south and the American Ninth and First Armies stormed across the Ruhr River into Cologne and the RAF's bombing Berlin! We've got the Hun on the run, Kate!'

Charlie and Rose hooted with laughter.

All at once her room was crowded with crying, laughing people; her mother and Mary came in to hug her and then each other.

'You mustn't get agitated, petal,' Hilda said tearfully to Kate. 'You lie back, but my giddyaunt, this is the best piece of news I've heard in years.'

'Apart from Kate's baby,' Mary said, laughing.

'Oh, that goes without saying, Mary.'

'But what does it mean?' Kate asked in bewilderment. How could they all be so excited about the bombing of one city?

'It means the end of Hitler, Kate,' Mary said. 'He's in a bunker in Berlin. He can't last out much longer.'

'It's the end of the war, petal,' Hilda said, smiling and crying simultaneously.

They all beamed at Kate who was bemused by the intense emotions swirling round the room. Her mother saw the strain on her face.

'Right, everybody out of here,' Hilda ordered. 'You're exhausting Kate. She's got to have peace and quiet.'

'Of course, she does,' Mary said. 'Come on, you two.' She motioned to Rose and Charlie to follow her out of the room.

'It's all right, Mum. I'm not an invalid,' Kate said when they'd gone.

'We're not having any mishaps with this baby, petal. I want you to rest until supper. You're going to have a feast tonight.' Hilda leaned over to kiss Kate, her face shining with joy. 'Oh Katie, what news ... your baby is going to be safe now the end of the war is so close. You get some rest.'

She walked out and closed the door behind her.

Kate calmed her breathing. She wanted to scream, to run around the room. Instead she picked up her pen and started to write.

29th February. 1945

My darling Rob,

I cannot begin to describe how happy I am at the moment, lying in bed. We've just had the most wonderful news about the Allied Forces closing in on Berlin. Do you think this is the end of the war, at last, my darling? I can't believe it after so many years, but everyone seems to think so.

But even more wonderful (for me) is the fact that my mother and I are united after years of separation. Truly united. She's actually told me she loves me! You can't imagine what that means to me. You've always felt loved I never have, until now. I feel I can conquer the world which is a wonderful state of mind to have when pregnant, your father tells me. Yes – I'm pregnant, darling! We are going to have a baby in less than five months' time. I haven't been able to tell you before because I was so mixed up in my mind. I sometimes thought I would go mad worrying about my commission in the WAAFs; worrying about having to tell you and our parents. I can hardly believe how supportive they've all been to me, Rob. Such a weight of worry has been removed from my mind. Oh, darling, I do hope you're as happy about the baby as I am.

I'm staying in your house with Rose and Mum; it's more peaceful since Dad is still drinking a lot. Your parents and Charlie have been wonderful to us. I don't know how we would have managed without them. As you know my mother went a little odd after Colin's death, but the news of our baby seems to have rejuvenated her. She started cooking the way she used to for Colin. Your father is ecstatic about her meals. I hope your mother doesn't mind too much. Charlie is very loyal to her and wouldn't eat my mother's food at first, but two days ago she put a home-made apple tart in front of him. He succumbed, I'm afraid. He and Rose are so grown up these days. I can't believe they're the same age I was when I fell in love with you!

Your mother is still busy with the Samaritan Centre, so perhaps she is glad to have some help in the house, although I'm sure her work will be easier soon, as the bombing on the town seems to have stopped. We haven't been hit by a flying bomb since last summer, so with Berlin captured, perhaps we won't have any more. What a wonderful thought.

Rose does all the shopping and I am cosseted for the first time in my life. It's a marvellous feeling. The only thing that worries me now is you. You have to keep safe for me because I want to see your face when you hold our baby for the first time. I want to see your joy. I know I sound sentimental, but I can't help it. My emotions sometimes get the better of me. One minute I am crying (with happiness) and the next laughing. Your father tells *me that it's perfectly normal, so I'm not worried about my strange state. My mother has already made about a hundred garments for the baby to wear, so I'll have to change it every half hour! I've just realised I called the baby 'it' but I don't know what else to call it. I wish I knew what gender it was, but Mum says that's part of the thrill of being pregnant – not knowing what you're going to get. I'd rather know.*

I know this news must be overwhelming for you, my darling, but I want to ask you what name you'd like to call him or her? I'd like to include everyone we love, but John Colin Charles Adams sounds stilted and Hilda Mary Rose sounds old-fashioned, doesn't it? What do you think of Jonathan James Adams for a boy and Bridget Victoria for a girl? I know we've got plenty of time to decide, but I want to think of our baby by the names we've chosen. Charlie and Rose have thought of hundreds of others from Ethelred to Gertrude. (I think they were joking.)

I'm looking out of the window at your beautiful beech trees and thinking of spring; buds bursting into foliage; the flowers blazing out of the ground. After an appalling winter these sights will be truly magnificent. Do babies turn women into poets, I wonder? Everything seems tinged with magic at the moment.

I know that you are still grieving for Colin, darling. So am I – and for Bridget, but we must look to the future now. To our son or daughter. Everything is going to be so much better after the war, especially after the Beveridge Report. I think about the future all the time now because of our baby. He or she will be born into a real Brave New World, not Aldous Huxley's. People will be helped by the state. Oh darling, I have such hopes for the future, so you mustn't get depressed. I discovered a poem in one

273

of the books your mother lent me. It's helped me a lot. I thought it might help you too.

DO NOT STAND

Do not stand at my grave and weep

am not there. I do not sleep

I am the thousand winds that blow

I am the diamond glints on snow.

I am the sun on ripened grain

I am the gentle autumn rain.

When you awake in morning's hush,

I am the swift uplifting rush

of quiet birds in circled flight.

I am the stars that shine at night.

Do not stand at my grave and cry,

I am not there; I did not die.

Didn't you tell me once that we come from stardust and eventually return to it? I feel Colin and Bridget all around me now. It's a good feeling.

We wait every day for a letter from you. <u>Please write</u>. We miss and love you so very much. Good night, my darling and take care of yourself. Come home to me soon.

Your loving wife to be,

Kate

Chapter 23

March was a crisis month for Germany after the Allied armies thrust deep into the Ruhr after their stunningly successful crossing of the Rhine and the capture of the cathedral city of Cologne. But people in south-east England couldn't believe it. Unremittingly, V1s and V2s flew over from rocket batteries in Holland as new ground launch ramps were built in The Hague. In spite of fierce coastal defences, enhanced by new techniques in radar, hundreds of these rockets reached their targets. The War Office desperately needed experienced Spitfire pilots to volunteer for a mission to knock out the V 2 rocket batteries.

It had only taken Rob one phone call to volunteer after Colin's funeral. He remembered what Oskar had told him 'confidentially' the day he and Kate had gone to his pub in Mayfair: Spitfires were being fitted out as bombers for special assignments and they were desperate for Spitfire pilots. A couple of weeks later, he was flying the new Spitfire XIV from West Malling in Kent. His hands were not deemed a matter of importance.

Rob had to undergo extensive training in precision flying and bombing. With a single-mindedness that the other pilots found daunting, he trained and studied reconnaissance photographs for hours after the others were relaxing in the Mess. He made no friends because he wanted no friends. He relaxed in his room doing his finger exercises or went for long solitary walks. Everyone left him alone, thinking him an odd fish. Relentlessly, he practised the new low-flying tactics and precision bombing which Fighter Command had introduced. They had learned much after the intensive bombing of rocket sites in Pas-de-Calais in Northern France and Peenemünde, a small island in the Baltic Sea. Rob studied the reconnaissance photographs of a new mobile firing-table the Germans had developed, the *Meillerwagen*: a network of steel supports from which the powerful rockets rose. They were barely visible from the sky. He studied photographs of the bomb itself: a forty-five foot long projectile, flying faster than the speed of sound, travelling in a parabolic path to a range of over 300 miles. It was a Wellesian nightmare, made reality. He had dedicated his first mission to Colin.

That day, the dispersal hut was a teeming mass of bodies studying flak maps, giving messages to ground crew and memorising meteorological details. Rob had already plotted and memorised the route and target they were going to bomb. He didn't go to the Mess for lunch; his stomach felt cauterised. He never saw the letter Kate had written to him, lying in his pigeonhole. Instead he went to his room to prepare for the mission. He took out his flying gear from his locker and checked all the pockets for the second time that day. All normal items had to be emptied from them in case he was captured. He swore as he found a screwed-up bus ticket in the bottom of one pocket and threw it into the waste-paper bin. It had a date and a destination which would help a German interrogator. He got out his special pack with escape aids: a compass, maps and money which he'd got from the intelligence section. Of course, he knew they would be confiscated if he was captured. But he'd also been given a small brass crested shoulder button which unscrewed to reveal a compass, and a collar stud from which the base paint could be scraped to show a magnetic needle. They gave him immense confidence. He took out his sheath knife from a drawer and put it down one of his flying boots as a precaution. Lastly, he took out his torch, covered with a filter of red paper, and placed it on the bed with his other things. Then he started to dress slowly.

An hour later, Rob was sitting in the cockpit of his new Spitfire. *SIRIUS* was painted in white letters on its port side. He only felt at peace in the plane. It didn't expect anything from him. He could rely on this model with its powerful Griffon engine and five-bladed Rotol airscrew that allowed him to climb to altitudes he had never reached before. He went through the usual checks: propeller in fine pitch, petrol tanks full, glycol temperature below 100° C, flaps up, gyro set. Then taxied to the end of the runway. He flashed the letter of the day to the tower and got a green light. Opening the throttle wide, he sped down the runway, increasing speed until he was off the deck. He reached 180 mph before throttling back. The squadron were getting into formation around him, but the security, the comradeship he had felt with his first Squadron had gone along with his unbelievable joy in flying: all gone with Colin's death.

'Transmit for fix, Red One.' He was roused him from his reverie by the Controller's voice in the R/T. He'd obviously been transmitting to the Squadron for several minutes.

'One, two, three, four, five; five, four, three, two, one,' replied Rob, smiling wryly as he remembered his eccentric course on 'Pip Squeak' on a disused football pitch.

The Controller gave the squadron a coded message concerning the latest weather report over Holland, then Rob heard the clipped tones of the S.L. addressing them:

'Okay, chaps. This is it. Vector 705°. You know what to do. Last one back buys the drinks. Good luck. Over and out.'

That was the last transmission they would have until after the mission. They had been instructed to maintain radio silence in case the Germans intercepted them.

Rob checked his *Gee* navigation system: a system which had increased the accuracy of bombing dramatically during the last few years. His folded *Gee* chart, strapped to his knee, was divided into grids, colour-coded and numbered. All he had to do was to identify and measure the time intervals of the pulses he received from his *Gee* radar receiver and then refer to his *Gee* chart. He would then know his position accurately to within two miles in 350.

He looked out of the cockpit to see the English coastline disappearing. Hastings was on his starboard side, with its two piers jutting out dramatically into the English Channel. His family lay beneath him. He imagined his mother preparing the evening meal; imagined Charlie and his father's faces as they ate it. He laughed briefly before a sudden, shocking need permeated his body. He clenched his fingers round the stick, suddenly remembering how powerful and painful love was. He groaned as he realised how appalling his neglect of them had been. He had never written to them after Colin's death; had never replied to the numerous letters they'd sent him. War and death had made him savage. And what must his Kate think of him? They were supposed to be engaged.

He remembered the night they had made love in that hotel bedroom during the Blitz; neither of them moving from the bed when they had heard the siren wail. He remembered her voice saying: 'if we're going to die at least we'll die together.' They had explored each other's bodies in wonder, while the searchlights highlighted anatomical details: 'like trying to piece a naked jigsawed man together,' Kate had said, laughing as one of his outstretched legs was exposed by an intense beam of light, while an abandoned arm was spot-lit by another. He hadn't recoiled even when the beams picked out his face; it hadn't mattered to him because it hadn't mattered to Kate. Then he had left her unprotected and exposed after Colin's death. He had read that people choose joys and sorrows long before they experience them. Why did he only choose sorrow? He made a sudden decision – to write everyone a long letter on his return. And Charlie. Perhaps Charlie needed him the most. He had written to tell Rob that everyone in school knew that his big brother was flying Spitfires again and would decimate the Luftwaffe. He hadn't given him anything he could boast about in school. But he could change that when he returned, couldn't he?

Rob instinctively checked his altitude. Five hundred feet. The squadron was flying low over the North Sea to avoid the German radar for as long as possible. They were heading for Egmond on the Dutch coast. Reconnaissance had discovered that there was a slight gap in the anti-aircraft and radar defences there. Almost there. Rob breathed deeply as the Squadron, in perfect echelon, descended even lower to a mere two hundred feet over the water. He briefly registered white capped waves over a grey sea and shivered, remembering the hours he had spent in the sea, fighting with the shroud of his parachute after he had been burnt. He concentrated on his flying. About seven miles from the coast, the Squadron ascended to 4,000 ft to avoid small arms fire. They came in over the coast in a shallow snaking dive down to 1,000 feet in case of attack. Fighter Command had adopted different tactics to Bomber Command after Guy Gibson had led the raid on the Ruhr Dam two years earlier and they had lost seven aircraft in their low-level sortie.

The ack-ack fire was sparse and didn't touch the fast, low flying Spitfires. There was a crackling in Rob's ears each time the German radar beam swept round towards the squadron, interfering with their R/T. The squadron descended further and the interference magically stopped. Suddenly Rob saw the targets in the distance: in the grounds of a large grey hotel were the tall, black Meillerwagens, the mobile firing tables. Rob's fingers twitched as he saw three monstrous V2 bombs waiting to be launched from them. Nearby was a housing estate and a Dutch hospital. The German High Command had built the rocket site in the grounds of the hotel and ran a V2 railway siding into a narrow gulley between the housing estate and hospital. Obviously they had chosen the location to act as a deterrent to enemy attack; any direct hit on the hospital would have been a disaster for Anglo-Dutch relations. But as C.O. Rawlins had said in briefing: 'That's why you Spitfire pilots are so important for precision bombing. The hospital must *not* be hit.'

Rob felt the adrenaline vortex through his body as he power-dived towards the target, his finger over the bomb release button. The Spitfire shuddered as he released his bombs. He heard the sound of an explosion as he shot over the target and veered hard to port, momentarily glimpsing the awesome sight of destruction. His bombs had destroyed a V2 and its Meillerwagen, creating an enormous crater in the ground. The surrounding buildings were untouched.

'Yes! Yes! Yes!' He screamed into space, *'That's for you, Col!'*

If there had been room in the cockpit, Rob would have got up and danced. Instead, he watched as each pilot jettisoned his bombs until the whole area was a massive cloud of smoke and fire. Then the squadron flew off at high speed. He looked out of the cockpit, expecting the full force of the Luftwaffe to descend on them. After all the dogfights he'd experienced in the past, it didn't seem possible: the sky was empty of enemy planes, yet this was the most dangerous mission he'd ever been on. It had been too easy.

The late afternoon air was unclouded either with cumulus or enemy. Rob scanned the skies, praying he wouldn't see any of the new planes the Germans had recently developed: the Focke-Wulf Fw 190 with its four 20mm cannon and two machine guns or the Messerschmitt Me 262. Nothing. The squadron continued its uneventful flight over the North Sea. Then, just as Rob was becoming numbed by the rocking motion of flying in formation, he heard the shocking sound of the C.O. screaming into his R/T.

'Bandits starboard. Break. Break. Break.'

Rob looked to his right and saw a tiny slanting black line which he couldn't identify. He broke out of formation, moving the gun button to *Fire* and slammed the canopy hood back, feeling stifled of air. The cold froze sections of his face. He now recognised the planes: flying towards them at frightening speed was a Squadron of the new formidable Messerschmitt Me 262s he'd seen in reconnaissance photographs. These planes had a devastating armament of four 30mm cannon and could easily out-run their Spitfires.

All at once, the sky became a weaving tapestry of confusion. Dimly, Rob registered the streaming glycol and white smoke coming from damaged planes.

'*Red One! Break!*' he heard someone shout over the R/T before the pilot was shot out of the sky.

Rob went into a vertical dive as the Me 262 following him shot yellow tracers into the space he'd just vacated. Another Spitfire fired at the Me and the German broke off his attack. A small part of Rob's brain acknowledged the intense pain in his hands as he went for a head-on attack with another Me. He saw his red tracers rake the fuselage of the plane, then hit the German petrol tank. The pilot parachuted out before his plane exploded in the air. Rob went into a half roll as another Me went into attack, then climbed steeply before diving. His vision momentarily blacked out with negative gee and he levelled the plane. When his vision cleared he looked around. The sky was empty. His hands shook with pain and tension as he swept the sky looking for the Messerschmitts. He was alone. Why? Suddenly all the pain he'd been suppressing pierced his brain. He screamed out into the twilight sky.

He flew low over the North Sea, not breaking radio contact, even though he was close to the coast. He was determined to reach base. He had survived, against all the odds. He started a letter to Kate in his head. *My darling Kate. I'm sorry I haven't written, but after Colin's death I felt dead myself. I was no use to you or myself then, but I've survived, Kate. I survived this mission and I know why. To come back to you. My beautiful, forgiving girl.*

The pain in Rob's hands forced him to abandon his thoughts of a letter. He looked at the altimeter setting. Safe to climb now, he thought. Nearly home. He pulled back gently on the stick to avoid increasing the pain in his fingers and automatically checked his rear mirror. His heart lurched against his ribs as he saw the unmistakable shape of a V1: a deadly black cross heading for the English coast on a parallel course. It shot past his starboard wing. Rob's shoulders shuddered with deep emotion.

No more. *Please.* No more. I don't want to be brave. I want to go home.

He could see the glow of its tail-jet in the darkening sky. Over 1,000 feet away. It might fall on empty fields, he told himself; might explode into a barrage balloon; might run out of fuel and dive into the sea. There was a shocking pain across his chest as he accelerated towards the V1. He knew he wouldn't have a chance unless he got within 300 yards of it, otherwise the tracers wouldn't reach it. But he was tired, very tired and his hands and eyes ached for rest. The evening star was bright in the sky as he fired his tracers. The V1 flew right through them. Rob gave a tortured moan. In the distance he could see the Sussex coastline; the bomb was heading towards it. There was only one tactic he could use now: the one that the Australian Flying Officer, Kenneth Collier, had used. He accelerated until he was parallel with 300 pounds of dynamite, forcing himself to breathe slowly to steady his hands. He was going to tip the bomb, by using his wing like a spoon to deflect its course. Hardly breathing, he tilted the Spitfire. An infinitesimal movement, forcing his hands to obey his brain.

The roar of the V1 was violent in his ears. He was inches away from death.

I *can* do it. I *can*, he commanded himself.

A slight judder, then suddenly the V1 toppled over, its gyrostabilizer out of control, and screamed into the sea.

At that moment, Rob was blinded by light. The coastal radar had picked up two curious converging blips on its screen and had ordered coastal defences to search the sky for enemy aircraft.

All they saw was a solitary Spitfire flying home.

The lights moved on and stars rocked on the surface of the sea.

AUTHOR'S NOTE

A number of brave pilots attempted the highly dangerous manoeuvre of 'tipping' V1s off course during WW11, and in doing so, saved many people's lives

In 1944, Mary Churchill, Winston Churchill's daughter, was part of an anti-aircraft battery stationed on the West Hill in Hastings.